# Finding Orion

# Finding Orion

Kristen R. Jaccodine

K Jacks Publishing

FINDING ORION
By Kristen R. Jaccodine
Copyright © 2024 K Jacks Publishing
All Rights Reserved



ISBN: 978-0-9978108-2-0 Trade Paperback
ISBN: 978-0-9978108-3-7 eBook

Book and Cover design by Glen M. Edelstein, Hudson Valley Book Design

In memory of my mom.
My biggest fan.

*Dedicated to*

Dennise J. Messier
Vince Mohan
Jerry verDorn

*I am thankful for your friendship and kindness.*

Somewhere between
the shadows of
life's brutal challenges
lies a warrior of
strength and hope,
your own Orion,
waiting for you to
discover and embrace.

-KRISTEN R. JACCODINE

Every awful thing that's happened in my life occurred on Tuesdays. At first, I chalked it up to a weird coincidence, but it's true when I really think about it. The second day of the work week is cursed. For me, anyway. I don't know what higher authority I pissed off to make this a factual part of my life story, but there it was.

Violent thunderstorms rolled through the area on that first fateful Tuesday night. I was five. My parents were on their way home from a dinner party. It was the kind of storm that rattled everything inside the house and woke you from a sound sleep. Unable to settle down, I wandered through the darkened rooms in search of my babysitter, Donna. I vaguely remember telling her it was too loud in my room. She pulled me onto our soft grey couch, tucked our plaid green flannel blanket around me, and then strummed soft, soothing music on her guitar to calm me. But, no matter how hard Donna tried, I couldn't fall back asleep.

Donna's concert was interrupted by knocking on our front door. In my hazy memories, Donna checked the peephole before she opened the door to two uniformed policewomen waiting outside. When the officers learned she was a minor unrelated to me, they instructed her to call one of her parents. I remember I curled into

Donna and hid my face from these strangers. As an adult, I knew they didn't mean to scare me, but through my young eyes, they did. I didn't understand why they were there or what they wanted. Once Donna's mom arrived, still dressed in her bright pink work scrubs (they only lived two doors down), we learned that my parents were killed in a freak car accident. They had been on their way home from the party when lightning struck a tree and split it in half. One part of the tree remained upright, but the other crushed the car's rooftop. Mom died instantly, and Dad a few minutes after the paramedics arrived. With no other family to care for me, I became a ward of the state. I lived with multiple foster families before I settled in with Steve and Ruth Thomas when I was seven. I don't know why the other families I stayed with returned me, but when the social worker brought me to the Thomas home, I didn't leave until I graduated high school.

The Thomases were an older couple. Mr. Thomas was an accountant, and Mrs. Thomas worked part-time at a local bakery. Mrs. Thomas liked to crochet and quilt. Mr. Thomas liked to read by the window. And when he wasn't reading, he tried to build little models. They were quiet, not overly affectionate people. Their house was neat and nice.

High School graduation was on a Tuesday night. Although I cannot say I enjoyed these four years of my life, I was excited to graduate. I wasn't the best student, but I worked hard. As happy as I was to reach this milestone in my life, I was sad that my parents were not there to see it. It was hard to hear my classmates be showered with hoots and airhorns while I only had my closest friend, Gray yell for me when I crossed the stage. Although I left them tickets, Ruth and Steve didn't attend the ceremony.

Earlier that morning, I gave them a basket full of gifts I thought they'd like. I had taught myself to crochet. I made hair bands for Ruth and bought model paint for Steve. They didn't open their present in front of me. I received a soft thanks from both. They were not home when I returned from graduation. The next day, when I brought out the garbage and recyclables to the garage, I noticed the gift basket with the pile of items deemed for donation. It was unopened. I remember feeling shocked at the sight. In the time I lived with them, I tried to do everything they asked me. I completed my chores, worked, and followed their house rules. I wasn't perfect and misbehaved at times as kids did, but I believed that I was an overall good child.

Throughout my time with them, Ruth and Steve were never outwardly affectionate towards me, but they were never truly cruel to me until that moment. Stunned, I numbly dropped the stuff in the appropriate bins. When I turned, I saw Ruth. In my memory, it was the only time I truly questioned why they took me in. I asked what I did that made them dislike me so much. They could've returned me like the other families did. By that time, I understood that foster parents received payment for caring for children who needed a home. The Thomases did not need money. Ruth failed to answer my question. She just stood there, still and silent. To this day, I do not know what came over me, but I felt such anger and hurt that the words spilled out of me.

*I'm sorry I could not replace whoever Travis was to you.*

When Travis's name exited my mouth, Ruth's resolve broke. It was the second time that I saw her cry. I felt bad and wanted to take the words back, but it was too late. I haven't seen or heard from them since the day I left. Before I moved into the Thomas home, I always seemed to move from one family to another on a Tuesday. While with the Thomases, I held my breath every Tuesday, worried it would be the day I had to leave. Yet, that day never came. When I finally did leave their home, it was a Thursday, and I was off to college.

Tuesdays. I hate this day. Not just because it reminded me of my parents but because my hardest exams for school, spilled coffee, worst work shifts, lost keys, and bad moments always seemed to fall on this day. Of course, not every Tuesday of my last thirty-five years has been plagued with misfortune. I've lived through plenty that passed without issue. Yet, whenever the day rolled around, I cannot help but feel off-balance and edgy. It's like waiting for the proverbial shoe to drop. And, just when I relaxed a bit, thinking the day would pass without incident, something happened when I least expected it.

The most recent event occurred one week ago when my co-workers and I were told our place of work was temporarily closing. I worked as the lead host at an elegant, pricey five-star bar and lounge on the Jersey side of the Hudson. Top Floor was a hot spot for top movie and television executives, CEOs, CFOs, and other high rollers. The space allowed all to comfortably mingle business and pleasure with clients, actors, significant others, and paramours. The place was exquisite, from the smooth maple molding that lined the mint green walls to the soft lighting that highlighted the cream-colored tablecloths. Diners imbibed expensive wines and spirits and nibbled on the fanciest hors d'oeuvres. On the outside, Top Floor was perfection. Internally? A raging inferno. If humans could simultaneously self-combust, the place would have fried to a crisp in seconds.

I loved it when I was first hired at Top Floor ten years ago. Granted, working my way up from server to lead host at a hoity-toity place like this did not fit my original life plan. I graduated from college with a degree in archeology and dreamt of digging up and discovering past worlds. However, college academically and personally exhausted me. The thought of more school did not appeal to me. I decided to take a break from the books and applied for jobs at some of the museums in New York City. When nothing panned out, I returned to what I knew. From my teenage years through college, I've always worked in a restaurant. The work was hard, but I liked it.

Growing up, I received monthly checks from the little my parents had earned through social security. These checks were deposited into an account. When I turned eighteen, I used this money and bought clothes and supplies for college. I did not have a car, although I did pass my driving test. I had money saved to buy one but opted to keep my finances simple.

Gray and I rode the big yellow bus to school together. We always sat together, usually in the first few rows of seats. For work, I hoofed it. Luckily, the house I lived in was within walking distance of a few places. I bummed rides from co-workers if the elements were bad. If I'm honest, I didn't mind not having a car. Walking allowed me to simultaneously keep the extra cushioning around my thighs and ass from expanding while decompressing after a shift. My core and legs were toned from pounding the blacktop. Why pay for that privilege when I could take in the fresh air and stay in shape.

Working at Top Floor afforded me the ability to buy my own place, pay my bills, and splurge when the mood struck. Living in Hoboken enabled me to enjoy small city living – nightclubs, restaurants, bakeries, the ease of moving from one place to another, and it was a straight shot into the city. Yet, as much as I enjoyed working at Top Floor and am thankful for what the job enabled me to do, I was ready for a change. I grew up in the country and attended college in the wilderness. I missed the peace and quiet of the woods and the slower pace at which life seemed to move.

This past week at home allowed me to think about my life. I do not know if Top Floor will re-open, and if it does, I may submit my resignation and look elsewhere. I could afford to stay out of work for a short time if it did remain closed. So, between binge-watching various shows and cleaning my place, I updated my resume and evaluated my options. I can frustratingly report that I have not come to any earth-shattering decisions. I finished writing the letter of resignation I started a few months back due to an infuriating day at work. That was also a Tuesday. I wasn't originally scheduled to work but covered at the last minute. Everything that could go wrong did, including unwanted advances towards me from a drunken guest. I've dealt with this kind of behavior at work before, and where it bothered me, I always let it slide. This time around, though, I couldn't. The poor handling of the situation by our ass of a manager made me start that letter. Gray convinced me not to act impulsively, so I tucked it away until now.

I met my co-workers, Amy and Karen, two days ago for coffee. They heard rumblings that Todd was on his way out. They asked me to contact Martin, our co-worker, who was buddies with Todd. I'm unsure why they thought I would get anything out of Martin. Sure, we worked closely, which forged a work bond, but we didn't hang out outside of work. They commented that I seemed to be the only person Martin talked to. I didn't know if that was true, but I texted him to see how he was and if he knew anything. When he responded, he shared that he was clueless.

Martin came to Top Floor a year ago with the highest recommendations and experience. He was hired as the lead waiter in charge of private parties. I thought it odd, as none of the staff at Top Floor started in this position, but after working with him for the first time, any suspicion I had faded. Martin was a pro. Respectful, mild-mannered, discreet, attentive – all the traits needed to run the private party rooms. I didn't care where he came from or that he was buddies with Todd. Working with Martin on the nights these rooms were occupied made everything run  more smoothly. While Martin may not be overly social with us, he wasn't rude either. The night I had to fend off the drunken customer, it was Martin who stepped in and helped me.

Not seeing him and my other co-workers nearly every day felt strange. Amy and Karen were work friends. I knew bits and pieces of personal information about them, as they did me, but that was it. That was the case with most of my friends. While in high school, I talked more to the people I worked with than the kids who were in my classes. Somehow, it seemed less complicated. And free of drama. We all worked for a common reason that superseded anything else. If Top Floor should close permanently, I more than likely would never see these people again.

My mind was spinning. I needed to relax and decided on a lavender-scented bath. I turned on classical music. I set my glass of bourbon on a little stool I kept in the bathroom and placed my cell phone next to it. I then stripped and climbed into the tub. As I slid into the silky, warm water, I closed my eyes, and willed the tension in my muscles to loosen. I sipped my drink and relished the burn of the golden liquor as it streamed down my throat. I slowly drifted away until the double beep of my phone signaled an incoming text woke me. I grabbed the dreadful device and read the message.

**Mandatory staff meeting at 10:15. Top Floor Dining Room.**

The separate party texts flew whenever we received a group message from work. Almost immediately after I read this one, Amy, Karen, and our other co-workers all messaged me and asked the same question. *What in the fuck was happening.*

*How the hell should I know?* I asked the walls of my small bathroom. They thought I knew more than them because of my role as hostess. I didn't. It was 9:30 p.m. Relaxation would need to wait. I flipped the switch to drain the water and remained in the tub until the last drop was sucked down. I then downed the rest of my drink before sending off a response.

**I'm in the dark, too.**

I then messaged Gray. Publicly, Gray was a professional actor and one of Hollywood's hottest stars. Privately, we were each other's lifelines. Our story started well before Gray's first professional acting role and did not play out in the public eye. Our friendship was solid, deep, and ours and ours alone. When we saw each other, it was in the comfort of our individual homes. Because of his job and the kind of patrons Top Floor attracts, Gray frequently has work and social meetings there but tried, when possible, to be there when I was not working.

On the nights when our professional lives did cross, we acted our parts and never tipped our hands that we knew each other's deepest secrets. Last week, he was scheduled to meet with a prominent casting director at Top Floor on one of my days off. The day after he had this meeting was when we learned that Top Floor would be temporarily closed. Other than a few text messages, I didn't know anything about the meeting. I haven't seen Gray in the time I've been off. This wasn't unusual. He was a busy guy between meetings, reviewing scripts, and whatever the hell else his manager, Sam, arranged for him. Still, he's unusually quiet right now.

**I just received a message from work.
I have a mandatory meeting at 10:15.**

Gray insisted I purchase this device. It was the most sophisticated form of technology that I owned. He could not fathom the notion that I was perfectly content with my old flip phone and had no need for all the whistles this one offered. Still, when I acquiesced, I couldn't help but smile at Gray's giddiness when he walked me through the phone. Mind you, I only used four functions: calling, texting, and the calendar. Occasionally, I surfed the web when I needed something, but other than that, the phone remained tucked in my pocket or crossbody. Of course, I kept that little bit to myself. Oh, and I texted in complete sentences. In part because that's me, and because it drove Gray crazy.

I hung up my towel, grabbed my empty glass and phone and then padded into my bedroom. There, I pulled on jeans and a t-shirt. I slid my feet into my worn out green checkered Vans. I grabbed my phone, wallet, and house key, and headed out.

It was a steamy spring night. Chatter from the different restaurants and bars filtered through the hazy air as I walked the familiar path to work. My chest tightened with each step I took. Sure, I could chalk it up to the unease of any staff meeting, but the burn in my stomach, the bile that slowly filled the back of my throat, made me think otherwise. No, with a dossier of bad Tuesdays, I couldn't help but feel that whatever I was about to learn, would be the newest addition to my list.

# CHAPTER TWO

If you asked me if I ever thought the manager and owner of Top Floor would be investigated and subsequently arrested for providing space for questionable activities, specifically a room for auditions that included adults having sex in front of an audience, I'd say you were delusional. Manager Todd was many things. Arrogant and useless prick were two descriptives that came to mind, but I never thought he was a sick creep. And Marjorie Shea, the quiet, uptight wife of Jed Shea, never struck me as someone who would support a sex room in her restaurant. Yet, that was the information we received from Mr. Shea and his attorney.

I sat with Karen and Amy. Everyone was there. All of us sat at tables together except Martin. He stood in the back of the room alone. Though I dropped my questions about how he landed his position, I knew other members of the staff did not. Now, learning that the guy who hired him was arrested made me question the truth about Martin all over again. When I glanced at him, he looked uncomfortable and out of place, but I could not place my finger on why.

"You'll hear it in the news…but Jeff Grafton…"

The mention of this name yanked me out of my headspace. I knew Grafton's name from Gray. Did Gray work for him? Did he want to? I couldn't remember. As I tried to pull these thought threads together, I heard my boss's voice in the background…Top Floor, permanently closing. Our final paychecks would include a bonus, health insurance would last another three months, and reference letters would be mailed to our home address…

"I realize this news is unpleasant…"

"Twisted is more like it," I heard Amy murmur.

"And upsetting, and for that, I am deeply sorry. I appreciate each of you and your constant professionalism while serving our patrons. I know it was not always easy, and for that, I thank you."

"But…" Karen mumbled.

"Before you leave this evening, you need to speak with members of the Hoboken PD. They agreed to question you here instead of at the station with the promise that none of what I shared with you this evening leaves this space. I trust all of you to respect that this is an active investigation, one of which involves my wife."

Just as Mr. Shea made this statement, we were joined by men and women in blue.

"Please be honest in your responses. Once you are finished, clean out your locker and exit the building. Be sure you have everything, as you will not be permitted to return."

Jed stepped away from his space and made room for one of the officers. I did not pay attention to the detective's name. I only heard that we were to remain seated. We could talk quietly among ourselves but could not text or make calls. We'd be called out three at a time to give a statement to officers stationed in different rooms.

"This is demented," I stated.

"It is," Karen agreed. "To think this disgusting business happened here and we, I don't even know what."

"This calls for a round of blowjobs," Amy proclaimed.

"I think I need to pass on any hard liquor right now," I stated. And I did. My stomach was in knots. Adding booze to the mix would not end pretty. When I learned of this meeting, I feared it would not be good news, but now, I'm also worried that losing my job was only the cherry on my cursed Tuesday sundae. My thoughts were of Gray.

Was this Grafton guy the person Gray was scheduled to meet? Did Gray know anything about him?

Would this Grafton business impact him? I wanted to give my statement or whatever the hell I needed to do and jet. I hoped I'd be called sooner rather than later so I could text Gray to meet me at my place.

But it was not yet Wednesday, so luck was not on my side. Amy and Karen left me in the first round. When my name was called, I was one of three employees left. I was led into one of the smaller party rooms by a male officer, where a female officer was already at a table. She had a notebook in front of her. She motioned for me to take a seat.

"Please state your name." the female officer started.

"Kenzie Mulroney."

"Your position at Top Floor?"

"Hostess."

"And how long have you been employed here?"

"Ten years."

The officer then looked up from her notes and stared me dead in the eye. It was unnerving, like she believed I had something to hide before she asked me a single question.

"Ten years? That makes you one of the oldest employees here," she commented.

"Next to our head chef, Marge, yes."

The next five questions all asked for information they could easily verify. As a crime show junkie, I guessed that after gathering this information, our answers would be checked. Our involvement in this situation may be minimal, but Jed was in this for a long haul. In the years I've known him, I've never seen him act so detached. I wondered if he had suspected something all along. After all, someone or something had to lead the cops here.

"What interactions did you have with Mr. Grafton?"

"As host, I greeted him and his party when they arrived and then showed them to their private room. After that, I did not see him until he left for the evening," I explained.

"Did you handle his reservations?"

"Never. Todd, our manager, did."

"Were you working when Mr. Grafton was last here?"

"It was my day off."

I felt my body tense, worried about where the line of questioning would go. Would they ask me about Gray? If I knew he had the meeting? If I knew if something happened? I knew the truth was on my side, but the nerves in my gut made me want to vomit.

"Did you know that Mr. Grafton had a reservation that evening?" The officer continued.

I explained that, even if I didn't record the reservation, part of my job was knowing the parties scheduled for the whole lounge. I made sure the tables and rooms were prepared for the guests.

The officer continued without missing a beat. "Do you recall how many members were in his party on that evening?"

"No."

"How many people were normally in his party?"

"Usually two to three, sometimes four," I answered.

"And did he always reserve one of the private rooms?"

"Yes."

"How often would you say he came here?"

"At least twice a month," I stated.

"What can you tell me about his guests?"

This question confused me. "I don't understand what you're asking."

"Did you recognize any of his party members? Were they females, males, a mix?"

This made me breathe a bit easier. Maybe the questions would not touch Gray. I searched my memory and tried to recall the times I greeted Grafton. Truthfully, over the course of a shift, I saw so many faces that they all blended. We were trained not to fawn over the rich and famous who entered our doors. That was easy for me since fame was not something I personally wanted. I preferred my quiet life in the shadows.

"From what I recall, Mr. Grafton usually had at least one female in his party. I never recognized them." I paused for a moment as a thought struck me, "They always seemed put together."

I spotted a flash of curiosity cross the officer's face. "What do you mean?"

I shrugged. "Most of the guests that come here are happy. Happy to drink, eat, be merry, and toss their bucks away without a second thought. These young girls, who came in with Grafton, though dressed the part, seemed passive, almost robotic. Like, they weren't present."

"Interesting observation," the male detective who brought me to the room responded.

I wasn't sure if I should respond, so I remained quiet. I watched the officer write all of that down. She then looked back at me. "Did you ever see or hear anything inappropriate when Mr. Grafton and his guests were here?"

"No."

"Did you ever serve him while he was here?"

"No. Once Mr. Grafton was situated, we were instructed not to disturb him. Martin, the head waiter, handled everything."

I internally flinched at throwing his name into the mix, but it was true. It wasn't up to me to decide who was involved in this mess and who wasn't. I just wanted to finish up and leave.

"Thank you. We have just a few more questions," the officer added.

I nodded.

The next set of questions involved Todd, Marjorie, and Jed. I candidly shared my opinion of Todd – a horrible, often verbally abusive manager. Complaints brought to Marjorie were ignored. Over the past year, Jed was not as involved in the lounge as he once was. It's one of the reasons why I wasn't happy here. Although a bit meek, Jed was a nice man and a good boss.

"Thank you, Ms. Mulroney. That's all we have for now. I do not believe we'll have any follow-up questions for you, but if we do, where can you be reached?"

"My cell phone."

I provided them with my number and then exited. I immediately went to the bathroom and splashed water on my face. After a few moments, I dried off and then exited. Once in the breakroom, I saw all the lockers were emptied. Quickly, I pulled the bag from my space and then filled it with the few items I kept there: a lightweight sweater, a small cosmetics kit, and extra heels.

Once my feet hit the pavement outside the building, I texted Gray and asked him to meet me at my place. I didn't care about the time. I held my phone in my hand and swung my bag over my shoulder. The humidity of the night was stronger now than it was before. I broke into a light sweat as I quickly walked towards my building. The usual early morning silence of the hall and stairwell welcomed me. I trudged up the three flights of stairs that led to my apartment. After I let myself in, I flicked on the lights, then shut and bolted my door. When I turned around, I spotted a physically disheveled Gray pouring himself whiskey. His light gray suit jacket was open, and his shirt tails were half in and out of his pants. I noted the top few buttons on his shirt were open and his tie hung loosely around his neck.

"You look like hell," I commented.

Gray entered my place through my back entrance. I realize this seemed sleuth-like, but when we were kids, he almost always entered my home through my bedroom window on the ground floor. It's a habit he just continued. It also kept our friendship hidden from my neighbors, not that they'd recognize him. Although right now, I don't think even his hard-core fans would.

"Gray," but my voice was cut off by the recognizable jingle of Gray's cell phone. For all his geekiness regarding technology, he rotated through the stock ringtones of his cell phone instead of downloading a favorite tune. "Do you need to get that?"

"Nope."

I stared at him as he poured himself another glass of whiskey. I decided to let that go. It was clear to me, that whatever happened to make Gray this unsettled, he needed time. I decided to fill him in on my night.

"I was just questioned by a local member of the police department about some Hollywood big shot named Jeff Grafton."

Gray's head shot up. His stare was so intense, I felt my face flush with the heat that radiated from them. I managed to continue. "It seems Grafton has a bit of a sick kink. He used one of the private party rooms at the Top Floor as an auditioning space. My shit manager Todd and Mrs. Shea allegedly helped him. Top Floor is officially closed, and I'm unemployed."

"Kenzie," Gray started. I ignored him and kept speaking.

"At the meeting tonight, when this Grafton guy was mentioned, I remembered you talking about him. I didn't realize auditions involved people having sex in front of an audience. I guess I'm more out of the loop than I realized."

I kicked my shoes off and then collapsed onto my couch. Gray shrugged off his jacket and let it drop to the floor in a heap. He then pulled the rest of his shirt out of his pants, yanked off his tie, balled it up and tossed it across the room. Gray then dropped next to me and rested his head on the back of the couch.

My eyes locked on his face. I tried to catch his deep brown eyes that looked everywhere but at me. "Grayson, look at me." When he finally did, my chest was pinned to the couch cushion. A frazzled, spooked haze replaced the everyday sparkle of his orbs.

He ran his hand through his hair and then over his face. "I… there may be trouble…"

My stomach dropped at the word. "Trouble," I repeated. I'm sure there was a better response, but no other word came to mind.

Gray crumbled forward. His elbows rested on his knees. He cradled his head in one palm, and his other arm was stretched across his leg. His fingers wrapped around his empty glass. He groaned as he leaned forward and placed the glass on my coffee table before he jumped to his feet. He crossed to my TV stand and pulled out the DVD of one of his movies.

"Do you remember when I filmed *My Truth*? It was written and directed by Dave Tilley?"

"Of course. You loved that role. It is my favorite film of yours."

Gray placed the case on the coffee table next to his glass. During my freshman year in college, Gray filmed this movie. He was cast in the starring role after he ended his time as the popular character of Sebastian Carver on the daytime drama *Justice*. I knew from Gray that Tilley was highly regarded for his edgy style and desire to produce thought-provoking films.

The Tilley film *My Truth* was centered on a man born into a mob family groomed to take over the family business. The twist? The FBI recruited Gray's character, Chenny Musto, unbeknownst to his family before he graduated from college. This role placed Grayson on the map as a solid, sought-after actor.

"So, why are we talking about it now?" I asked.

"Jeff Grafton is a casting director. He didn't do the casting for *My Truth*, but he works quite a bit with Dana Henry, who produced the film. Until then, I only knew Grafton by reputation- that if you were cast by him, you were solid. One day, Grafton was rumored to be on set to observe some actors for the next film he and Henry had in development."

"Okay…" I said unsure of where Gray was headed with this.

"The day he was there, I only filmed scenes in the morning. After I wrapped up, I headed to my co-star Greg Stone's space. We planned to grab a late lunch and then run lines."

Grayson took a break from his story and poured himself another drink. I did not understand where this story was headed, but I saw Gray's discomfort. I picked up the DVD. Gray's character was on the cover, framed inside the bars of justice. As I studied the case, it hit me.

My eyes shot up to him. "You called me. Hysterical. But you wouldn't say why you were so upset. I told you I'd come home to talk in person, but you were adamant that I stay at school. When I insisted it would be okay, you threatened our friendship would end if I did."

"I was out of my fucking mind when I said that. I never meant it." Gray's eyes softened at the admission.

"You scared the piss out of me! In all the time we've known each other, I've never heard you so distraught. And then to shut me out like that? Your tone, dismissal of me, threw me into a tailspin I almost didn't recover from."

"I'm sorry, Kenzie. I am forever grateful that it was at that time that the Coopers and Keating entered your life."

Dr. Ollie Cooper and Dr. Keating Finn were my archeology professors at Crestview College. Angie was Ollie's wife and the Kettle Cove chief of police. I would have been tossed out of college if it wasn't for them. These people were still an important part of my life.

"What happened next?"

"When I arrived at Greg's door, I heard muffled noises. At first, I couldn't tell what it was. Worried that something was wrong, I entered without knocking. What I saw…stopped me dead."

I guessed what the muffled noises were. "You walked in on Greg having sex?"

"He didn't know I was there. I left quickly and quietly. The next day, I heard…" Gray paused, "I heard rumors that Greg had sex in his trailer with someone Grafton brought and that he stayed to watch. It's how he auditions his actors."

Gray's revelation stunned me. I stared at him, silent, until my eyelids grew heavy with the weight of exhaustion. Finally, my mind registered what he told me. "So, it's true. What I heard about Grafton tonight, before Grafton considers someone for his films, he wants them to *knock boots* while he watches?"

Gray nodded yes.

I placed the DVD case down. I then looked at Gray. "The meeting you were supposed to have at Top Floor just before we closed, was that with Grafton? Is that why you think there could be trouble?"

Gray's silence launched my mind into overdrive. Where do I even begin to unwrap this? I wanted to yell *shit, Grayson,* but swallowed the words. Although a zillion questions raced through my mind, one look at Gray's demeanor numbed them all. I watched how the conflicted emotions of sadness, frustration, shame, and anger played across his face. It reminded me of the little boy I first met.

Gray was born in Hoboken. His mom had left him and his dad when Gray was three. He stayed here with his dad until he was eight. Then, one day, with Gray's toys and clothes packed, drove him to his grandparents' house in the farming community of Moose Creek in Northwest New Jersey.

The Kents lived two houses down from where I stayed with Steve and Ruth. I remembered seeing them every now and then at the house for coffee. In the Thomases' basement, there was a box of toys with the name Travis scrawled on the outside. I once asked who Travis was. Steve yelled at me to mind my business. I was too afraid to ask again. When Agnes and Harold left that night, Harold carried the box labeled Travis. Steve held Ruth as she cried while they watched them walk away. I remembered that day because it was one of the few times I saw them hug each other.

About a week after the box disappeared from the basement, I sat on the branch of my favorite tree in the Thomases' backyard. In the distance, I spotted a scrawny boy with shaggy black hair walking through the woods behind the Kent home. Until then, other than hearing about a grandson, I hadn't seen him. I was happy to know there was another kid my age on our end of the street. I thought it would give me someone to play with.

I jumped off the branch and headed into the woods to look for him. When I had found him, he had his back against the trunk of an oak tree, and his knees were pressed into his chest. His arms crossed over them. His head was hidden in the frame of his arms. When I tiptoed closer, I heard him crying. Without a word, I quietly sat beside him and did what I dreamt my mom did for me when I was sad. I wrapped my arm around his shoulders. When he had no more tears to shed, he pulled away and looked at me.

*Hi, I'm Kenzie.*

At first, he stared at me, not quite knowing what to do or say. Then, his high-pitched voice, shaky from crying, responded.

*Grayson.*

*I'll call you Gray. It's my favorite color.*

I had asked him why he was sad. It was on that day that I learned Gray's dad had died. Gray and I sat in the woods, under the shade of that oak tree, for the rest of that afternoon. I later asked Ruth if Gray could come over and play. She had called his grandmother, and before I knew it, Gray was at the house. Ruth made us lunch, and then we played in the backyard. We played games, climbed trees, and rode the bus to and from school together. We became best friends and trusted all our fears, nightmares, doubts, and everything with only each other. We were orphans. A club of two.

Now, even though we are older and have other people in our lives, we remain each other's lifeline.

# CHAPTER FOUR

Gray always told me the warmth of my kind green eyes, and the sight of my light brown hair pulled back in a sloppy ponytail comforted him. He'd tell me that people are relaxed around me because they knew they didn't need to pretend to be someone or something they were not. I never understood why people couldn't just be who they were. Just be real. While we were in high school, I used to think that I didn't have friends because I was seen as the "foster kid". I didn't attend the school dances because it made me sad. All I heard were the other girls talking about their moms taking them shopping for dresses when I didn't have a mom to do that with. I supposed I could have asked Ruth to take me, but I always assumed she'd say no, so, I never mentioned it. I kept myself hidden, guarded. I always encouraged Grayson to go to these things if he wanted to, but he chose to hang with me.

"Kenzie," Gray finally started.

Whatever he was about to say was again interrupted by the buzz of his cell phone. I stood up when I noticed he didn't respond to it.

"I'm going to change while you answer that."

"I don't need to," Gray insisted.

"You do. In the time you've been here, your phone has rung three times. If I had to guess, it's Sam. And if you don't answer, she will call me. So, deal with her." I stood up and walked away before he could answer.

Samantha Bailey was Gray's high school theatre teacher. My foster parents had a ping-pong table in their basement. Gray and I would play for hours at a clip.

A week into high school, we held a tournament for two. We agreed that the loser of this ten-game round had to do whatever the winner wanted. I beat Gray 10-5. I told him to audition for the school play. I knew that if Gray didn't find something of his own, something to buy into and see that he had a future beyond his life in our sleepy little town, he risked being strangled at the hand of his misery.

Gray auditioned and landed the role of George Gibbs in *Our Town*. He then performed in every show throughout high school. Over the summers, Sam hooked him up with local theatre groups and classes. She drove him to rehearsals when his grandparents couldn't. When he wasn't in theatre class or rehearsal, he worked out. Gray sucked at sports, but he was a pro at lifting. He liked that working out was a solitary action. Lifting strengthened his body and mind.

When we graduated, Sam retired to become Gray's manager. She had connections within the entertainment industry. At that time, Gray was a gorgeous, muscular young man with a haircut that magnified his curls and highlighted his golden brown eyes. He sported a meticulously kept unshaven beard that framed his perfectly squared face.

Gray's physique, coupled with his acting ability, landed him spots in commercials and minor television roles until he was contracted to play Sebastian on *Justice*. His film schedule permitted him to audition and perform in smaller stage roles. When Gray left the soap, he wanted to try his hand on Broadway, but the role for *My Truth* came through.

When I returned to the room, comfortably dressed in blue and green plaid boxers and a torn college t-shirt, I noticed Gray was in the same spot as I left him. I tried following the path of his eyes but could not determine what fleck on my carpet he was fixated on. I didn't ask if he'd answered his phone. Instead, I went with a different question.

"Did you tell anyone what you walked in on all those years ago?"

"Sam." he answered.

"Right. Let me guess, she told you to keep quiet." Gray did not need to respond for me to know the answer. "Did you actually want to meet with Grafton, knowing what you do about him?"

Finally, Gray turned to me. "I told Sam that I never wanted to be in a project that he was involved in."

"So, why did you take the meeting?" I didn't need Gray to answer the question. I put the pieces together. Sam misled him. His disheveled appearance, the distant, stunned look in his eyes. "What did you do?"

"I walked out. I exited the elevator and spotted him seated next to some dude. I left before he saw me." Gray explained, voice flat and resigned. "I then called his personal assistant to cancel. I apologized for the short notice, but claimed I was hit with a stomach bug."

This shocked me. "Does Sam know?"

"Probably. I split town for a couple of days after the meeting. I returned tonight for a fundraising event in the city when the news about Grafton broke."

"And you haven't talked to her?" I asked again.

"You said the cops talked to you?"

I let him dodge my question. "They questioned all of us. They wanted to know about my interactions with Grafton, what I noticed when he came in, the people he was with."

"Did my name come up?" Gray asked nervously.

"No. Have the police contacted you?"

Grayson's olive complexion was now a pasty white. His eyes were bloodshot. Worry lines filled every angle of his face.

"Did they?" I pressed.

"I've received messages but haven't returned calls."

"Earlier, you said there could be trouble. Ignoring the cops can buy you trouble, Grayson."

"I know, I just..."

"Just what? What are you worried about? You said, other than the other night, that you have not participated in any meetings with Grafton. When you walked in on your co-star, did you actually see Grafton there?"

Gray's inability to look at me once again was the only answer I needed. I desperately needed to reign in the disgust that bubbled inside me. I shot off the couch and carved a frenzied path on my carpet as I paced back and forth.

"I'm..." I circled my hand in the air. I wanted to punch something but knew that would not help matters. Instead, I stretched my arms and cracked my neck. "Okay. What matters now is what you do."

He cleared his throat. "Do?" Gray asked huskily.

"Yes, Grayson, do. Will you confront Sam? I'm assuming you're ghosting her because she left out the fact that your meeting was with Grafton. Will you tell the cops what you know about him?"

Up until now, Gray's explanation of Grafton was so still. Sure, he physically looked like hell, but his tone was calm. When I challenged him to make a move, it was like I knocked the wall down inside of him.

"You don't get it! You don't cross Grafton. If I say or do anything, everything I worked for will go to shit." Gray yelled.

My voice matched his. "And where is it now, Gray? The man's been arrested, for fuck's sake! It's time to wake the hell up and protect yourself!"

I ran my hand through my hair and took a deep breath. I picked up this habit as a child. It calmed me down. "Look, I know how much Sam's done for your career, but you don't owe her a damn thing. It's time to do what's right. Or does that not mean anything to you anymore?"

"Fuck, of course it does!" His raised voice forced him to stand and face me.

"Then?"

"How about this? I'll focus on my shit right now, and you figure out yours. Hell, get out of Hoboken and visit the Coopers and Keating. You told me they invited you up."

I stared at him. I was angry and felt like he was deliberately shutting me out. I could continue to argue with him, but it was pointless. He was right; we both had decisions to make. Some space and a change of scenery sounded good. Besides, even though I sensed that Top Floor would close, I needed to process it. I spent ten years of my life there. Regardless of whether I felt ready to move on, the place and the people there played an integral part in my life. I needed to grieve that loss and get my head straight. And Gray needed to deal with Sam and Grafton on his own.

"You're right. I'll call Ollie and Angie later this morning to see if it is okay to come up today."

"Today?" Gray asked. His tone was full of surprise.

"Why wait? There is nothing keeping me here right now. I'll lose my mind if I spend another second in this space. And you need to focus on you. Like you said. I can't help you here, so I'll leave and sort out my life."

"Kenzie…it's not that I don't want you here."

"It's fine, Gray. I get it. I'll book a rental car."

"No way. I'll arrange for someone to drive you."

"You don't need to do that," I insisted.

"When was the last time you were behind the wheel of a car?" Gray pointed out. I couldn't remember, but it had been a while. "Right. I'm not letting you drive five-plus hours to New Hampshire alone. Just text me after you talk to Ollie or Angie."

Too tired to argue, I gave in. "Fine. Thanks."

"Welcome."

Gray picked up his discarded jacket and pulled it on in silence. Without a second thought, instead of retracing his steps through the kitchen and back down the fire escape, he exited through my front door without another look or word. I followed him, pulled the door closed, and, once again, locked it. I then turned off all the lights and headed to bed. While on the way, I located Gray's discarded tie. When he tossed it, it landed just outside the doorway to my kitchen. I picked it up and placed it on top of the little cabinet I had in the hallway.

Once inside my bedroom, I peeked at the digital clock next to my bed. The glaring red numbers told me it was just past 2 a.m. I pulled back my covers and then crawled into bed. Even though it was a warm spring night, I felt chilled. I pulled all my blankets over me and created a solid burrow for me to hide in. Another terrible Tuesday was now behind me, and yet, I knew the effects of these events would follow me in the days to come.

# CHAPTER FIVE

After my parents died, sleep never came easy to me. As a kid, I remember I always felt antsy, but never understood why. Thoughts swirled through my mind in an endless loop. And when there was a thunderstorm? Sleep was impossible. Gray knew storms spooked me. As kids, we had a system. Whenever there was a storm, Gray would sneak out of his grandparents' home when he knew they were counting sheep and then would enter my room through the window. He would then slide into bed with me, assured me that I was safe and that the monsters that haunted my dreams could not hurt me.

Sometimes, Gray sang silly songs or told funny stories that helped me relax. And then, when he knew I was asleep, he'd return to his house. Once hormones entered the picture, we silently agreed not to share a bed. It's funny how two innocent kids became wacky and twisted when breasts grew, voices deepened, and pubic hair became a thing. Once our hormones settled, Gray held me at night. It was never sexual but comfortable and calm. To his fans, Gray was sex on a stick. To me, he is just Gray. Or at least he was. The man involved in this Grafton mess sounded, walked, looked, and smelled like my favorite color, but, last night, he felt like he was a bit of a stranger.

Bright sunshine crept through my blinds. I turned my head and squinted at my digital clock's glowing red lights. I groaned when I made out the time. It was 7:30 a.m.

*Ugh.*

Exhausted, I considered turning over to hide from the morning. But I couldn't move. It was like someone strapped bags of cement over my body and trapped me. So, I remained still and stared at my mauve-colored walls. At least, I think they are mauve. Right now, my retinas burned, like I swam in a vat of sand without goggles to which made my vision foggy. Of course, I didn't know anyone who would do such a thing, but, in a twisted way, I believe having sand in my eyes was better than the current cocktail of tears and lack of sleep.

Natural thunderstorms still rattle me, but I am better at managing them. The emotional shitstorm that drenched another one of my Tuesdays with pain also captured Gray in its grip. Depending on how this situation with Grafton unfolded, Gray could be impacted. I worried that however that story played out, the fallout would hurt Gray and in turn our relationship. I admit my fear may be irrational, but it's how I felt. Tuesday has again tossed me deep into the sea and left me to swim back to shore. Frankly, I'm sick of it. I'm tired of the dread that I felt every time this day comes 'round. I just want to feel normal and look at each day the same.

I pushed myself up and rubbed my eyes to clear them, I glanced around my room. With all the strength I could muster, I slid out of bed, pulled on comfy slipper socks and padded into the living room. The uncomfortable silence that seeped into the space in the early morning hours unsettled me. I spied my phone on the table where I left it earlier this morning. I held an internal debate as to whether I wanted to pick it up and check for messages.

*Get a grip Kenzie*

I finally picked it up and clicked one of the side buttons to wake it up.

Two messages, both from Gray.

The first:

**car set. Jessie is the driver.**

The second:

**safe travels mtg in Hartford 2day**

I stared at the screen; the texts seemed normal. Like our somewhat tense conversation never happened. This irritated me, as irrational as that may be, but still I replied.

**Thanks**

I then scrolled to Angie's number. I hit the call button and listened to the dial tone on the other end. I knew it was unlikely that Angie would answer. She was at work and was most likely caught up in a meeting about a case. I left a quick message and hung up. I then called Ollie.

I scrolled to his number and crashed on the couch while I waited for him to answer. Ollie picked up almost immediately. The sound of his cheerful voice brought a smile to my face.

"Hey Ollie."

He greeted me with a warm hello and asked what was up.

"I know it's short notice, but would you and Angie be alright if I came up for a visit?"

My smile widened when he warmly told me I was always welcome and asked when I planned on arriving.

"Today. There's some stuff going on. I can explain more in person, but I really need to see you both and get away from here."

Concerned, Ollie asked if I was hurt. I assured him I was fine and needed a change of scenery to clear my head. Ollie shared that their loft was mine for as long as I needed it.

"Thanks. I plan to leave here around 4. That will not get me to you until late."

Ollie assured me that was fine. He had late office hours and planned to check in with Keating at Comfort before he headed home. Comfort was a little restaurant located across from the entrance to campus. Keating and Ollie won it in a game of darts. They formally purchased the place for two dollars and placed ownership in both of their names. While a student at Crestview, I worked at Comfort as a waitress from my freshman through senior year.

Keating hired me. He was also my major advisor. I initially met with him during freshmen orientation and then again when I applied for the open job at Comfort. I worked as many hours as my class schedule allowed. Like high school, I preferred to be at work than in my dorm or on campus. It was through work that I talked to Keating. Eventually, I told him about my parents and that I was a foster child. We talked about the Thomases. In turn, Keating only shared that his parents and brother had passed away. He considered Ollie and Angie his family.

The more I worked at Comfort and talked to Keating, the more comfortable I felt around him. On the night that Gray called me upset but wouldn't tell me why, I tried to manage my emotions on my own, but when all my calls to Gray were not returned, my worry festered. I skipped my classes and retreated even more into myself. I tried to work but was so distracted and upset that I left in the middle of my shift one night.

There was a pond on campus. I liked to sit by the water. The slight waves gently brushed in and out, soothing my thoughts. The night I left work, that's where I went. I was so lost in my thoughts, in the glow of the moonlight that danced off the water, I didn't hear anyone come up behind me. Keating was not at Comfort that night. Neither was Ollie. Keating must have spotted me walking to the beach. I suspected he stood back for some time and allowed me privacy before he approached. I heard the warmth in his voice, which allowed me to see the sincerity in his eyes. I realized I needed to talk about Gray. If I didn't, I worried that I'd drown in the empty hole that threatened to consume me. I didn't have the tools to climb my way up and out. Gray, as much as he was a strong presence in my life, was a kid, too. With him, I was stronger. Without him, at that time, I felt alone.

Keating had been the first adult in my life to recognize something was wrong and cared enough to ask. It was then that I told him about my friendship with Gray. Keating never uttered a word until I was finished. And then, I feared that Keating would decide, like the Thomases, that there was something unlikeable about me. I worried he would turn his back on me, too, but he hadn't. Instead, he had gently placed his hand on my shoulder, squeezed it, and then, in the same even, warm voice, he spoke words that I remember to this day.

*Thank you for sharing with me. I understand you're worried about your friend. And that worry and fear has wrapped itself so tightly around you that you cannot see straight. But, if Gray is the one who encouraged you to apply and attend college and asked you to stay here because he believes in you, then trust his request. Your life here is your own, Kenzie. Live it. Be part of it. Find what it is you are seeking for yourself. And I suspect, if Grayson cares as much for you as you do him, he will call you when he's ready.*

I had listened to him that night, soaked in the meaning of his words, and trusted them. From that moment forward, Keating truly became more than an advisor and boss to me. He became a friend and later a father figure. But, as close as we were, we had rough patches. During my senior year, Keating encouraged me to remain in Kettle Cove. I had thought about it but decided to return to Hoboken.

The night I shared my history with Gray, Keating listened but never really understood our relationship. He believed I would be throwing my life away when I returned to Hoboken and Gray after graduation. He voiced his disappointment that I didn't want to go on to graduate school. Although Keating hid it, I sensed he had been disappointed that I still worked in a restaurant. Keating's judgment of Gray and me was hurtful. His actions and words had splintered our friendship. I once tried to address with him how he hurt me, but Keating dismissed it. Eventually, we worked through this, but our relationship changed.

When I visited Kettle Cove, there were times I saw Keating and times I did not. We spoke on the phone, emailed, and texted, but the ease with which I used to talk to him never returned. Thinking about it now, my last conversation with Keating had been about my frustrations with Top Floor. He was a straight shooter. At times, I still wanted and needed his take on situations like this.

Ollie asked if I let Keating know I was coming.

"No. I haven't talked to him in a few weeks," I answered honestly. "I'll let him know I'm coming," I promised Ollie.

And I would text him. I did want to see him, but I also knew I needed to be careful with what I shared with him about Gray. As much as Keating and I talked, I tended to leave Gray out of our conversation. But Ollie and Angie? They were different. Ollie was the playful uncle you see in movies or on TV. I loved talking to Ollie. He was charming, brilliant, and funny. Our conversations ranged in topics. He was a fantastic professor and, more importantly, an authentic human being. I came to know Angie by working at Comfort. She knew I was one of Ollie's and Keating's students. But we never talked about school. Angie was a slender, strong, and beautiful firecracker of a woman.

Angie had been the one who took me shopping and taught me how to do my hair, nails, and makeup. She served as a role model on how to be sexy without the boobs and booty hanging out. Angie nursed me through my first broken heart. She listened and counseled me after I lost my virginity. She always made time for a girls' day out. Angie was my mom, aunt, sister, and best girlfriend all wrapped into one.

While in college, they fully entered my life when I didn't know if Gray was about to exit it. My relationship with Ollie and Angie continued to grow once I graduated. They had visited me in Hoboken, and when I returned to Kettle Cove, it was with them that I always stayed. Unlike Keating, Ollie and Angie understood my friendship with Gray and what he meant to me. They never judged me for my decisions. Without Ollie and Angie, I'd be lost. That may sound melodramatic, but it's true. I would never have finished college if they hadn't entered my life at the moment they did.

I missed them. The more I thought about it, the more spending time in Kettle Cove made sense. Gray was a grown man who could make his own decisions. Whatever trouble this Grafton mess may cause him, he needed to deal with it. Keating told me to trust in Gray that night on the beach. I did then, and I need to know. What he decided to do with his knowledge of Grafton and with Sam was up to him.

Ollie asked if I needed to be picked up at the airport. I told him Gray hired a driver. He then asked if Gray would also be up for a visit.

"No… he's caught up in some stuff."

Ollie made me promise I'd extend the invitation.

"I'll tell him, Ollie. Now, I'll let you go. I need to pack, and I'm sure you have some classes to teach. "

We then hung up a few minutes later. I promised to text when I was on the road. It was incredible how a plan could renew your energy. After I hung up with Ollie, I texted Keating that I would be visiting. I then contacted one of my neighbors and asked if they would check my mail. With these details taken care of, I decided a shower was next on the agenda. My bath from the night before was interrupted when I learned of the employee meeting at Top Floor. When I entered the bathroom, I caught my reflection in the mirror.

"Girlfriend, you are a hot mess."

I turned on the water and stripped off my clothes. I then stepped into the warm, vanilla scented, steamy yumminess that was my shower. The steady pressure of the water pounded into my skin. I closed my eyes and forced myself to relax. I only opened them when I heard the rumbling of hunger pains in my tummy. Breakfast was next on the list.

# CHAPTER SIX

I put on clean, comfortable clothes and then had yogurt with strawberries and water for breakfast. After eating, I emptied my fridge of perishable food and started to pack. I didn't know how long I planned to stay in Kettle Cove, so I stuffed one large duffel bag with enough clothing for two weeks. I filled my backpack with books, my laptop, chargers, and toiletries. I also packed my good luck penny. It was a souvenir from my one vacation with my parents to Disney World. My mom got it from one of those machines that press pennies with your favorite character. Mine had Donald Duck. Once satisfied I had everything I needed, I triple-checked that all windows were closed and locked.

Jesse, the driver Gray had sent for me, arrived at 4 p.m. on the dot. He double-parked on the street. While Jesse brought my bags to the car, I looked around one last time before I closed and secured my front door. I stared at my unit in that stifling, windowless hallway for a few minutes. Then, without warning, gooseflesh covered my bare arms. I shook off whatever rattled me and headed outside. Jesse held the door open for me. I climbed in, kicked my shoes off, and then buckled up. Once we started moving, I never looked back. With images of Kettle Cove on my mind, I fell into a deep sleep.

The not fully flattened frost heaves of the road jerked me awake. I checked the time on my watch and noted we had been on the road for about five hours. I looked through the window. The Cooper's homestead was close. I looked around the car as I stretched. My neck and back popped as I did. It was then that I noticed a little gift basket on the floor next to me for the first time. Curious, I leaned closer with one outstretched arm. My hand pushed around the mix of snacks, only to stop at the sight of one specific goody. Ring Dings. They made me smile. I pulled them out of the basket and snorted at the fact that it was a solo package. Gray hated my eating habits. I didn't consider them poor, but they were not up to his health-nut standard. He frowned at the mention, never mind the sight of these packages of sin. What Gray didn't know was that while I ate them when in need of a sugar rush, I didn't have as big of a love affair with Ring Dings as he believed.

I kept a box in my kitchen because it reminded me of my parents. I remember we always had one white box with a red wave along the top, with block letters in red and white that spelled out Ring Dings on the kitchen counter. I didn't know which of my parents liked them, as I didn't remember either of them eating one. Gray knew this, but I let him think I kept them more because I liked them and not because of their sentimental value. Gray didn't hold attachments like that, and where I knew he wouldn't judge me, I didn't think he'd fully understand the importance.

Just as a teasing thought entered my mind, it vanished when the car stopped. I opened the door to Ollie. We immediately hugged. I felt the soft bristles of his beard rub the side of my face as he lowered his forehead to my shoulder. I glanced up and saw Angie at the door, arms crossed in front of her. Although it was dark, her posture seemed tense. The hold in which Ollie held me felt tight. Not in the, I haven't seen you in a while tight, but in the, something happened tight. But it was late and although I slept nearly the whole ride, I still felt tired. I imagined Ollie was too.

When we broke out of our hug, I backed up and glanced at his feet. I smiled before I looked back at him. "Do you ever wear shoes?"

Ollie rubbed his eyes. "Only when they make me love. How was your ride up?"

In the years since I graduated from Crestview, I've talked to Ollie as often as our schedules allowed. But it didn't hit me until now just how much I missed him. Ollie, aside from his warm smile and his beautiful accent, made you feel cherished. He paid attention and listened when you talked. He was like that as a professor and as a friend. He instinctively knew when and how to let things go and be. Ollie accepted that life is not perfect, but you could still find your way through to the light, even if you felt like you would be drowned by the darkness.

"I think Jesse needs to answer that. I slept for most of the ride."

Ollie and I both turned to Jesse, who placed the bags next to me.

"A little traffic in Connecticut, but other than that, it was a smooth ride," he said. "Where would you like me to put these?" Jesse asked as he pointed to my bags.

"I'll take care of them," Ollie told him.

I returned to the car to grab my shoes, backpack, and Gray's snack basket. I noticed Ollie carried my bags to the guest loft over their detached garage. The space below the loft was for Ollie's massive vinyl collection. The walls were lined with shelves of albums categorized by genre and year. In the middle were comfortable couches, a reading chair, a desk, and mini bar. Ollie often retreated to this space when grading papers.

Turning to Jesse, "Do you have someplace to stay tonight?" I asked.

"My brother."

"Cool. Thanks for the lift. I appreciate it."

Jesse nodded. "Call when you're ready to leave. I'll come back and get you."

"Thanks for the offer... I'll let you know."

Jesse climbed back into his car. I joined Angie at the bottom of their porch steps. I noted she looked like she just arrived home from work. That's not unusual given her job, yet something told me it was off. My thoughts of what it was were erased when Angie wrapped her arms around me. "Hi sweetheart! It is good to see you!"

"You too," I whispered.

"He's not driving back to Hoboken, is he?"

"No."

"Good." Angie said. She continued to hug me.

One of the many things I loved and admired about Angie was how warm and comforting her hugs were. I always wondered if the ease I always felt with Angie was what I would've felt with my mother. But like with Ollie, it almost felt like she did not want to let me go. Because if she did, I'd be able to see her whole face.

I pulled out of the hug and then grabbed her hands and held them in mine. I finally looked at her face. With the help of the deck lights, I noticed her eyes looked red.

"Angie, is everything okay?"

Before she could answer, Ollie returned.

"Kenzie…what in bloody hell did you pack?"

Angie turned away from me and looked at her husband. I followed her lead. I took in a somewhat out-of-breath, Ollie. He rubbed his biceps as he joined us by the steps.

"Well, if you got your out-of-shape ass back to the gym, you wouldn't be complaining, would you? Now, let's get inside. I have some of your favorite cookies, Kenzie."

"Out of shape? Have you felt these guns?" Ollie exclaimed.

He flexed his muscles as he gestured for me to follow Angie. I laughed at the warmth and familiarity of their teasing banter. It made me think that maybe everything was okay, and what I saw in Angie's eyes, felt in her and Ollie's hug, was just a figment of my imagination.

As a student, I visited their home several times. Sometimes, when Ollie and Keating attended a school function, Angie invited me for dinner and a movie. During the holiday breaks, when Gray was away filming, I stayed with the Coopers and continued to work at Comfort. During my junior and senior years, I lived in an on-campus apartment. I had received special permission to remain on campus during both the school year and summer breaks since I did not have a home of my own to return to. Over the summer months, I not only worked at Comfort, but I had also worked on campus in the library.

Every time I passed through the light maple door of the Cooper home and stepped foot into the cozy entryway, hung my coat up in their closet, and placed my shoes under the old oak wooden bench, I felt at home.

"Make yourself comfortable, sweetheart," Angie pointed to the family room while she headed to the kitchen.

"I'll help you," Ollie offered before he turned to me. "Still like your tea black?"

"Yes."

"Coming right up," Ollie said. He then followed Angie to the kitchen.

The warmth of this room was as I remembered. Two blue, green, and yellow plaid couches were perfectly placed in the center of the room, with a maple coffee table in between. One of the couches faced the brick fireplace, while the other faced the two front windows of the house. Tucked into the back corners of the room, on either side of the hearth, sat two light green wingback chairs. One for Ollie and Angie to settle in beside the fire, to read or write.

Their home felt lived in. It was neither neat nor messy but a perfect blend of both. Photographs of their son, Jack, were neatly placed throughout the room. Jack was currently stationed somewhere overseas as a Navy Seal. In the time I've known Angie and Ollie, I cannot say I knew their son well. While I was in college, he was in basic training. After he had graduated, he went away to training school. I knew how much Angie and Ollie missed him, so whenever he was home, I made myself scarce. They deserved to spend time with their son as a family. Although Ollie and Angie had always invited me to spend time with them, I almost always politely declined. From what I did know of Jack, he possessed a splash of both his parents' personalities.

I rubbed my eyes and collapsed onto the couch that faced their unlit fireplace. Although I slept on the ride up, I still felt exhausted. I remembered I needed to text Gray, but I had placed my phone in my backpack after we left Hoboken. I would text him as soon as I went upstairs.

"Your tea, milady," Ollie offered. I noticed Ollie held a mug of something warm for himself.

"Thanks." I took my first sip and then settled farther into the comfort of their soft cushions. "I'm pretty sure this isn't just black, Professor."

A mischievous smirk crept across Ollie's face. He took a drink from his own mug covered in musical notes and shrugged his shoulders. "My hand may have slipped a wee bit."

"Because the brandy bottle is normally next to the tea kettle?"

"Don't tell the chief," he added with a wink.

"You still think you can pull one over on her?"

"He can't, but he keeps trying," Angie answered. She then placed a dish of freshly baked chocolate caramel cookies on the table.

Ollie looked at Angie. "You never complain when I add a dash to your tea after a rough night."

"True," Angie admitted.

Angie sat next to Ollie on the couch across from me. He grabbed a cookie off the plate, "Did she just say that I am right?"

I noticed it again. Although Ollie's eyes showed a sense of pride, something was off. But what? I decided to wait a bit more before I asked if something was wrong.

"When did you start making this little concoction?"

"My mum gave me this drink after my football team lost the championship game."

"So, your mom thought it good to ply you with booze?" I questioned.

"Mum was a loving mother who liked her drink. She gave me the recipe when I was of legal drinking age."

"But?" Angie led.

"Unofficially? I already made a copy. I just added to it."

"Your mom never caught on to her liquor supply going low?" I asked.

"Oh, I'm sure she did, but with all this," Ollie pointed to himself, "She didn't have the heart to yell at me."

Whenever I heard stories of people's relationships with their parents, I wondered what mine would have been like. Would I have spent hours in the kitchen baking with Mom? What would Dad and I have done? Would it have been Mom or Dad who helped me practice driving? I think the more I wondered about the "would we," the more painful their deaths felt.

"What is it love?" Ollie asked warmly.

I knew I couldn't hide or mask the thoughts that whirled through my mind. "Sometimes I just wonder, if my parents hadn't died, what stories I'd have to share about them."

I stared at the liquid in my cup. Out of my periphery, I spotted Angie place her mug down, and then she moved to the space next to me. She then held my hands between her own. "I know that we're not your parents and would never try to be, but we love you as if you were our own."

"I know that. I love you both too."

With Angie next to me, I again studied her face and then looked at Ollie.

Angie squeezed my hands one last time and then let go. I took another sip of my tea. My eyes then settled on a candid picture of Ollie and Keating. It was one of them from a camping trip they once took. That reminded me that I never received a response from Keating.

"I texted Keating after we talked, Ollie, but I never heard back from him. Did you tell him I came up?"

My eyes darted between them. I caught the look they shared before Ollie placed his mug down on the table and stood up. Angie placed hers down, too. She then scooted back on the couch a bit so we could clearly see each other.

"What is it?" I asked. "Is Keating okay?"

Their continued silence caused the brandy Ollie spiked my tea with to burn in my stomach. I, too, placed my half-empty cup down on the table and waited for one of them to answer me. Ollie sniffled. When I looked at him, I saw him turn away from us. Ollie's fingers then wiped something away from his face. His posture and the fact that he didn't look at me told me something was very wrong.

My stomach dropped. I felt restless. I needed to know why they were upset.

"Please tell me what happened," I pleaded.

Angie took my hands again. She held them tighter this time. "Sweetheart, Keating's missing."

"What do you mean?" I asked. I looked at Ollie, who still had his back to us, and then returned my focus to Angie.

"We don't know where he is. Keating arrived at Comfort just after it closed last night. From what my officers were told, some of the staff last saw Keating in the parking lot. He told them he had a few items to take care of before he left for his conference. They took him at his word and left for the night. We learned that he was missing later this afternoon."

I looked towards Ollie. "Ollie, when we spoke, you told me to let him know I would be here."

Ollie finally faced me. He again wiped what I could now see were tears from his face. "Yes, love. I was at school when we talked. Keating did not have classes today but was normally in his office. After I finished teaching, I returned to my office. Keating's office was dark. Molly, our department secretary, shared that she had not seen him. I rang him, but my call went straight to voicemail. I texted and like you, had not received a response."

"Could he be somewhere that doesn't have good cell service?"

"It's possible, but we don't think so." Angie joined back in.

"Why not? Did you find his cell phone?" I asked.

"Not yet. But from what we can tell, he never entered Comfort last night. His car is gone. I sent one of my detectives and another officer to his house to check. Nothing appeared disturbed," Angie explained.

"So, maybe he is at a conference. In the last email I received from him, Keating told me he had one planned." I reasoned.

"I checked around, Keating was not registered for any," Angie gently stated. "Sweetheart, I know this is hard. Right now, we have a lot of questions without answers. But it's late, and we are all tired. So…"

Whatever Angie was about to say was interrupted by her cell phone. "Excuse me," she stated. She stood from the couch and answered the call in the other room.

Ollie then joined me on the couch. "I don't want to believe it either. All the questions you asked, I asked them too."

"He wouldn't just disappear, Ollie. There must be an explanation," I pressed.

"And maybe there is one. Angie and her squad are actively investigating. Right now, all we can do is try to remain calm and trust in them." Ollie did his best to reassure me, but I doubted he believed in his own words.

"If you think that, why were you crying?"

Ollie ran his hand through his hair. "I can't hide anything from you either, can I?"

"No." I stated.

"Keating's been off these last few weeks. He's canceled our plans and classes. When I asked him if everything was okay, he shrugged me off. My mate can be moody, so I left him alone. Now, I'm sorry that I didn't push."

"Don't go there, sweetheart," Angie directed as she returned to the room. "Keating is a grown man who made his own choices. We've always known that about him. My officers and Detective Deas are investigating as we speak. For now, we all need to get some sleep and will look at everything fresh in the morning."

I wondered how Angie thought I could sleep with what they just shared, but I also knew she was right. There is nothing I can do right now other than hope that this is some big misunderstanding.

"Do you promise to wake me if you learn something?" I asked.

"I will, honey."

I nodded to Angie. Ollie and I stood at the same time.

"I'll walk you over," Ollie offered.

"You don't need to do that," I told him, picking my shoes up while I headed for the door.

"Alright. Try and sleep, love. I canceled my classes tomorrow. So, I'll be here when you get up." Ollie shared.

"Okay."

"We're happy you are here," Ollie told me.

I exited the front door and walked the short distance between the deck and the steps up to the loft. The feel of the grass, then gravel beneath my bare feet, was familiar and peculiar all at the same time. Once at the top of the steps, I opened the door and turned to see Ollie wave before he disappeared into their house. I then shut and locked my own door. I quickly located my cell phone and called Gray. Straight to voicemail.

"Gray, please call me. It's important. I'm at the Coopers'."

I paced around the space, phone in hand. I stared at the screen and willed it to ring. But it didn't. I scrolled through my texts and located the one I sent to Keating earlier that morning. I wondered if maybe the message didn't go through, only to be disappointed when I saw that it did. I decided to call him.

Straight to voicemail. The deep sound of Keating's perfectly recorded message sent shivers down my spine. When the beep signaled to leave a message, I breathed and spoke.

"Ollie and Angie told me they don't know where you are. Please let us know if you are okay. I'm at the Coopers. Please call us. We love you, Keating."

I ended the call. Even though I should be tired, I couldn't settle my nerves or stop my mind from imagining the worst. I decided to unpack my clothes as a distraction. I picked up my duffel bag and carried it to the bedroom. I played music on my phone while I put my clothes away. I tossed my shoes into the bottom of the closet. I pulled out a pair of light sweats and an old t-shirt of Gray's to change into. I returned to the living area and retrieved my backpack. I located my toiletry bag and placed the items inside it in the bathroom.

With these tasks completed, I checked my phone. No missed calls or texts. I shut off my music and tried Gray once more. My call again went directly to his voicemail. I pushed my worry down and spoke with as calm a voice as I could.

"It's me again. I hope you are okay. I didn't want to say this over voicemail, but Ollie and Angie told me that Keating's missing. He, well, he went to Comfort late last night, but failed to go home last night or to campus today. He's not answering his phone, and his car is missing. I don't know what to do. I'm gonna try and sleep. Please call me when you can."

* * *

After I ended the message, I wandered around the space for a few minutes. After my fifth loop of the living room / small kitchen area, I traipsed back to the bedroom. I dropped my phone on the end table and crashed on the bed. I pulled the throw blanket over me and turned on my side. Eventually my body caved to exhaustion.

The morning greeted me with fresh sunlight and birds chirping their morning hellos. Their gleeful calls filtered through my open window and filled the air with happy vibes. I burrowed farther into the soft, cushioned abyss of my covers. I took a deep breath and allowed the fresh air to fill my lungs. Then, I crinkled my brow, confused at the sounds. Any noise I heard inside my apartment was generally muted through the glass of closed windows. Alarmed at the thought, my eyes sprung open. Disoriented, I looked around. Crisp blue walls, photographs of mountains and woods, and the fresh smell of the country. It took me a minute to remember where I was.

I flopped back on the bed and stared at the ceiling.

"You're in the guest loft at the Coopers house in Kettle Cove. They told you Keating was missing," I whispered to myself.

Keating! I quickly picked up my phone and checked for any messages. My heart sank at the absence of any new texts or voicemails. I debated whether I should try to contact Gray again but decided against it. He had enough to deal with. I didn't want to add to the pile, especially when there was nothing he could do. I didn't think there was anything any of us could do other than wait and hope we'd find some clue as to what happened.

I checked the time and saw it was just past ten. I dropped my phone back on the table and then pushed myself up. I didn't remember it, but at one point during the night, I slid under the other blankets. I pushed them off and pulled myself out of bed. I decided to shower first.

A half-hour later, I felt more awake and refreshed. Barefoot, I picked up my phone and headed to the main house for breakfast.

"Morning."

Ollie, dressed in an ash gray t-shirt, sat at the table on their back deck. He spotted me through the open screen door.

"Morning," I smiled.

Ollie pointed to the coffee pot on the counter. "Pour yourself a cup and join me. The muffins are already out here."

The oversized mug set out for me made me giggle. In black, block letters, the phrase, "Get Lost with Desmond" was printed on one side and a picture of the island man himself, Desmond Hume on the other. Desmond was a character from the television show *Lost*. Desmond was Angie's and my favorite character from the show. We also love Desmond's portrayer, Henry Ian Cusick, and followed his work post-*Lost*. I had bought Angie this mug for her birthday one year, yet I always seemed to be the one who used it.

After I fixed my cup, I joined Ollie outside. On the small table were Angie's blueberry muffins. I placed my mug down and sat in the seat opposite Ollie. I sipped my coffee and looked around their yard. I absorbed the beauty and wonder of this magical place. I knew people absolutely loved city life, but how could anyone pass up the chance to see sunlight dance on the tree leaves, smile at the birds and hear the water rush over the rocks and breathe the fresh air into your heart and lungs?

"Did you get any sleep?" Ollie asked.

I pulled one cotton covered knee up to my chest and folded the other leg underneath it and took another sip of coffee. "Some. I forgot where I was, how quiet it is."

"Miss the sounds of the city?"

"I missed the silence."

"We missed you."

I nodded, "I'm sorry it took so long for me to return this time."

Ollie waved me off. "No apologies needed love." He pointed to the tray of muffins. "Let's eat."

I dropped my legs to the floor and pulled my chair closer. I then grabbed a muffin and buttered both halves while Ollie went for the half-and-half mixture of butter and jelly. For a while, we ate in silence. Although I suspected this was more about Ollie giving me the space and time to gather my thoughts. There was so much to talk about before I learned about Keating, and now, it seemed like he was the only thing we should talk about. The rest could wait.

"I don't understand, Ollie. Where is Keating?" I started.

I watched him take a bite of his muffin and then wash it down with some coffee. "I don't know. I am as lost as you are."

"Is he really missing? I mean, how does that happen? Is it possible that someone took him?"

"It's possible. Hopefully we'll know more soon. Angie received a call earlier this morning that Keating's car was found."

"Just his car?"

"From what Angie said, there was no sign of Keating," Ollie relayed.

"So, what does that mean? What do we do now?"

"All we can do. Wait. I thought we would go to campus today. Angie asked me to check around his office one more time. See if I see something strange or out of place that the cops missed."

"Can I come with you?" I asked. I didn't really know if I wanted to be on campus right now, but I also didn't want to stay here by myself.

"If you want."

"What about Comfort?" I asked.

"We closed for the rest of the week. I'll talk to the staff over the weekend," Ollie shared.

"And Keating's classes?"

"They were canceled for at least today. My supervisor did not want to make any decisions until we had more information."

"I've heard that if a person is not found within forty-eight hours…," my voice trailed off.

"I know, love. Hopefully something more comes from his car."

All I could do was nod. Words failed me. I didn't know what to feel beyond fear and worry. What did you do when someone was just missing? Do you assume that if not found, something bad happened to them? Or did you hold out hope that, maybe the missing person just needed a time-out from their life? That they will come back and explain. Neither of these thoughts appealed to me, yet they seemed better than the alternative. Which was no answers. I knew this was a reality too. I wanted to think otherwise, but if Keating disappeared on Tuesday, my personal experience told me the outcome would not be favorable.

"I'm thinking about retiring," Ollie threw out.

His statement pulled me back from reliving the ugly events from my Tuesday's passed. I wasn't sure I heard him right. I knew Keating had talked of retirement in one of our last conversations, but Ollie had never mentioned it.

"I swear Kenzie, the students don't listen, they don't read, and are so caught up in their snaps and chats, they forget about the real world," Ollie complained. "It's driving me bloody mad."

In the times I had spent in Keating's and Ollie's company, I often wondered how Ollie, the carefree spirit, and Keating, who only went barefoot in the shower, were such amazing friends. Yet, when it came to their profession, they were clones of each other.

"So, what you're saying is they are not me," I sassed. My comment made Ollie laugh. That's what I had hoped for when I said it.

"You, love, are one in a million," he softly stated. The amusement that flashed in his eyes was short-lived. Instead of the humorous glint I was accustomed to seeing, he looked worn out.

Ollie's compliment both warmed and embarrassed me. As a student, I was not the best. I enjoyed learning, had been a decent test taker, and remembered most of what I heard. But, when I was in high school especially, my focus was work. I wanted and needed to earn and save money for the time before I was no longer a foster kid.

Then, during my senior year, with Gray's encouragement, I attended the college fair hosted by our high school. That's where I discovered Crestview and thought earning a college degree could be in my future. After I talked to the admissions rep, I picked my grades up, applied, and was surprisingly accepted. For the first time, I felt wanted and believed in by someone other than Gray.

Lost in my head, I failed to realize Ollie was studying me. "You still don't believe it, do you?"

"What?" I asked.

"How amazing you are."

"I almost landed on academic probation my freshman year." I pointed out.

"And then graduated with honors."

"I was lucky to have you, Angie, and Keating in my corner. If it wasn't for the three of you, I don't think that I would have made it."

My freshman year had been challenging. It had been the first time in ten years that I had been away from Gray. It had been strange, not seeing him every day. As much as I wanted to be independent, living and attending school in a different place had been odd. I supposed most college freshmen felt this way until they adjusted to this new life and then the loneliness faded away.

My first roommate and I didn't fight, but we hadn't meshed either. I remember she attended classes and then hibernated in our room the other part of the time. At that time, I only used my room to sleep and change. Once I had started working at Comfort, I went there. I'd complete my homework before or after my shift ended. And if I didn't go to Comfort, I studied in the building that housed the president's office.

My life as a college student was unfamiliar and strange. I grew up in a small town where almost everyone knew I was an orphan. I hated the pitiful looks I received. My peers had judged me without bothering to talk to me. Some had spread rumors about how my parents had died. I had asked my social worker if I could have a copy of the police report or talk to someone so I could see for myself what happened. Once I had the confirmation that their death was accidental, I was able to ignore the pot stirrers. I knew the truth and that's all that mattered to me. Other than Gray and my job, my high school life had been miserable.

The moment I became a Crestview Blue Jay, a member of this community in the shadow of the mountain, my past was as hidden as the spirits who haunted the older buildings on campus. People said hello and invited me to join their table at dinner. My classmates had invited me to study groups. I went, made small, casual talk, but still mostly kept to myself.

When Gray called during the early morning of my freshman year, freaked out but refused to tell me why, I was terrified. I had been friendly with people, but nobody knew about my connection to the then former soap stud Grayson Kent. Maddie, who lived on my floor and was in a couple of my classes, had reached out when I missed a few times. But I hadn't known if I could trust her. She had posters of Gray in her dorm room and had shared that he was her favorite actor. I worried about confiding that my best friend was the object of her obsession. If she knew that Gray was in my life, would she be my friend because of me or because of Gray? One of the points Keating had made to me the night he had found me on the beach was to give people a chance.

*Kenzie, I'm grateful that you are my student. You are bright and capable, and from what I've seen so far, you are liked and respected by your classmates. So, why don't you give us a chance? You may find out we're not all bad.*

I didn't have a lot of choices, so I took a chance and trusted Keating's advice. With his and Ollie's help, I caught up in all my classes. My midterms exams that semester were abysmal, but I plugged along and pulled myself out of the swamp of bad grades. And I finally let Maddie in. I had told her about my parents and my bad high school experiences. I had confided that I had recently received an upsetting call from my only friend at home that I hadn't known how to manage. I never shared his name. And Maddie never asked. Instead, she took me out to a party with the plan to get me drunk. That didn't happen, but she helped me find my own place on campus.

"We supported you, but we didn't do the work for you," Ollie began, "In the end, you listened, accepted our help, and made a life for yourself."

"That time for me in college was hard. It was the first time I was away from Moose Creek and from Gray. And then, when he had called distraught but didn't tell me why, I didn't know what to do. Keating had encouraged me to give the people here a chance. And I did."

"Keating's been known to motivate a student or two in his years."

"He was there for me when I feared I was about to lose Gray. And now…," I trailed off. An image of Gray flashed through my mind. "Now, in a weird cosmic replay, I'm again worried about Gray, only this time, Keating isn't here. Although, if he was, I don't know that I could tell him what's happening."

Ollie leaned forward. He folded his hands and rested them on the table. "What's going on with Gray?"

I wanted to spill everything. I knew I could tell Ollie about Top Floor closing due to legal issues, but Gray's involvement with Grafton, both in the past and now, was not my business to share.

"I just learned the reason why Gray was so distraught back then. It involved this casting director…"

"Jeff Grafton?"

I looked at Ollie with surprise. "How do you know about him?"

"It's all over the news. How is Gray involved?"

I took a deep breath and then finished my coffee. "On Tuesday night, I learned Top Floor closed its doors. I don't know all the details, but from what I was told, one of the owners and the lounge manager allegedly allowed Grafton to use one of the private rooms for his *business meetings.* When I told Gray about it, he finally admitted to me that Grafton was the reason he called me so distraught when I was in college. Now, all of these years later, he was scheduled to meet with him."

"Did he?" Ollie asked.

"Gray told me he walked out as soon as he saw him."

"You believe him?"

"Yes, but I feel like he's keeping something from me. When I saw him, he was distraught, angry. He was open one minute, closed off the next. I wanted to help him, but he insisted I come for a visit and figure out my next step."

"And then you learned about Keating. I'm sorry, love."

I appreciated Ollie's empathy. I squeezed away the tears that welled in my eyes. "Tuesday strikes again."

# CHAPTER EIGHT

After we cleaned up breakfast, we returned to our seats on the back deck. So far, Ollie had refrained from asking any questions about Gray and Grafton. I'm not surprised, but I am grateful. Being married to a cop, I'd guess that Ollie was used to not being able to ask questions about cases. But I also knew that he was perceptive and knew I would never betray Gray's confidence.

"Are you worried Grayson is in trouble?"

"I'm scared that he will not stand up for what he knows is right because he's worried about the consequences to his career. And if he doesn't share with the cops what he knows, he'll lose part of himself that he'll never be able to get back. I was so frustrated with him the other night that I wanted to deck him. I thought a good slap upside the head would knock sense into that stubborn brain of his."

"If you want to punch him, love, then the lad is swimming without a net. Where's he now?" Ollie asked.

"At a meeting in Connecticut. A friend of his is a playwright. Gray wants to return to the stage. I called him last night and told him about Keating, but I haven't heard back."

"I'm sure he'll call."

"I hope so," I whispered.

"Did you have any idea that Top Floor would close?"

I slouched farther down on the chair so I could rest my head against the back of the seat. I stretched my legs out in front of me. "A week ago, Tuesday, I received word that we were temporarily closed. At the time, we weren't given a reason. I now know it is due to the Grafton investigation."

"What happened?" Ollie probed.

"The staff was called in by one of the owners – Jed. He shared that his wife and the manager were arrested for allegedly helping Grafton. As a thank you for our service, we get a bonus in our last paycheck and a letter of recommendation."

"Were you asked to give a statement?"

"We were all kept for questioning. I was asked about my inter-action, if any, with Grafton and my observations of him and his guests."

"I know I joked about the weight of your bags…I take it you packed for more than just a few days?"

I ran my hair through my now dried hair. My eyes fluttered over the treetops and caught sight of a few birds gliding through the air, seemingly without a care in the world.

"Is that okay?"

"You are welcome to stay as long as you need."

"Thanks," I took a deep breath, "Truthfully, I had thought about resigning from Top Floor for a while. I'm disappointed and disturbed at what may have happened while I was working there, but I'm also ready to move on."

"I can only imagine how difficult it is to learn that your place of work served as the setting for shady business. Angie and I will help you in whatever way that we can," Ollie promised. "And trust that you'll figure out what comes next for you. Gray will too."

I wished I could bottle his optimism. "I want to believe that, but…"

"But, what?" Ollie prompted.

"If he talks to Sam, listens to her, I don't…I don't know."

"The woman between you," he mused.

"What does that mean?"

"Nothing, love. I just know you're not a fan."

"The feeling is mutual," I mumbled. I realized I sounded like a petulant child but didn't care. As much as I appreciated all Sam did for Grayson, she would not have put him in this position if she genuinely cared about him.

"In the times I've seen you together, I see how fiercely protective Gray is of you."

"Sam doesn't like it. She hates that I see through her and am not subtle when I've warned Gray about her true intentions."

"And what does she say now?"

I straightened up and faced Ollie. "This time? I don't know. She called when Gray was at my place, but he ignored it." I laughed. "The one time I insist he takes her call, and the ass let it go." I shook my head incredulously. "I can't help him with this, Ollie. I can listen and encourage him to follow his heart, but I don't understand his world. I've always feared that the ugliness of his profession would swallow the very best of him. Now, it might, and that terrifies me."

Overwhelmed, tears poured out of me without warning. Ollie pulled me up and into a hug. I cried into Ollie's shirt. Silent, Ollie allowed me the time to empty the tears from the tank. And then, with a calmer breath and drier eyes, I released my hold on his shirt.

"I'm sorry, I didn't mean to lose it like that."

He placed his hands on my shoulders, "There is nothing to apologize for, love. This situation is an eerie repetition of your lives. You are both at a crossroads. For now, just give each other space. We'll deal with the fallout when we know what that is, all right?"

"Okay."

"Good. Now, we need to head to campus. If you no longer want to come, it's okay. I can swing back and pick you up after I've finished," Ollie offered.

"No, I want to come. I know I won't be of much help, but I can at least be there for you."

Ollie wiped away the tears that now gathered in his eyes. "Let's meet by the jeep in ten."

I returned to the loft and brushed my teeth. I rubbed some mousse into my hair and then ran a pick through it. I checked my phone and made sure I didn't somehow miss the object vibrating against my ass. No messages. Frustrated, I shoved the object back into my pocket, grabbed the loft keys, and exited. I locked the door behind me and then descended the steps at the same time Ollie backed his royal blue Jeep Wrangler out of the garage. After I climbed into the passenger seat, I caught Ollie's questioning look.

"What?"

"Did you want to grab your shoes?"

I looked at my bare feet and shrugged. "Do I need them?"

Ollie rewarded me with one of his brightest smiles, "You're a lass after my own heart, Kenzie Mulroney."

"I guess we are true *soul*mates."

He laughed. "We are."

# CHAPTER NINE

We left the driveway and headed in the direction of campus. I looked out my window and noted both the familiar and unfamiliar scenery along the route from the Coopers' house to campus. As we neared the entrance to school, I thought of Ollie's spontaneous admission about retirement. That sparked a question.

"Do your students take advantage of office hours like my class did?"

"Yes, but they are both needier and more brazen."

I noticed some tension creep into Ollie's voice. I noticed his paled knuckles as they gripped the wheel. I refocused my attention out the window and continued to watch the road. "What's wrong?"

Glancing in my direction, "Last semester, uh, I had one male student, not in the major, develop a fascination? Crush? I don't know what to call it, on me. He worked as an assistant in the English department. We talked a few times here and there, but other than that, nothing."

"Okay…"

"Then, Keating pointed out that the student continued to visit, even when he was not working. I believed he was a harmless lonely kid who needed someone to talk to. Then he started showing up at

Comfort, sticking around when I was there, taking off when I wasn't."

"What happened?"

"He was let go from his job and the Humanities Department chair addressed his behavior. It worked for a bit, then picked up again a few weeks later."

"Did the student do anything overt?"

"Nothing physical - I mean, nothing I saw or heard. Eventually, I stopped interacting with him. One night, Angie and I were at Comfort together. The student came in – I don't know, I guess he saw me kissing her and lost it."

"What did he do?"

"He flipped a table and threw a glass against the wall. A few customers restrained him, but he shook them off and left. Angie radioed it in to one of her patrol units to be on alert for him and they picked him up."

"Is he still on campus?"

Ollie shook his head. "No. Although Keating disagreed, I opted to not press charges against the lad. His parents paid for the damage and that was it. I have not heard from or seen him since."

Ollie always looked for the best in people and in his students. I didn't know if Ollie knew it, but many of my classmates were infatuated with him. I'd be lying if I said I wasn't one of those students whose heart fluttered every time his warm, chocolate eyes focused on me in class while his beautifully accented voice made our sometimes dry course material come alive. Angie once called me out on it. Her observation terrified me and made me think I shouldn't spend time with them. But she laughed it off. *I'm not blind, Kenzie. He's one of a very hot kind.*"

I can't imagine this was the first time a student of his took their interest in Ollie a step too far. Yet, something about this situation clearly rattled him. I wondered if it was part of the reason why he wanted to retire. I let my thoughts go when we turned onto Blue Jay Way. I scanned the familiar sights before me – Campus Security was on the right, and Apple Pond was on the left. The grand white house stood a little farther up on the hill. Of all the buildings on campus, I never stepped foot inside that one. I turned to ask Ollie what the building was now used for, only to have my question die upon hearing his.

"Kenzie, when you were my student, did I ever make you think there was or could be something more between us?"

Of all the things Ollie could have asked me, this question was not one of them. It took a few minutes to pull my words together.

"Did I?" he asked, alarmed.

"Ollie, of course not! I'm sorry. No, I never mistook your kindness and attention for something more. And from what I remember, my drooling classmates understood the same."

"Okay," he stated while physically releasing his breath.

"What did this kid do that made you doubt yourself?"

Ollie pulled into a space behind his office building and cut the ignition before he turned to me.

"It was Keating…he…"

But whatever Ollie was about to say was cut short by an older, redheaded woman who approached the car. "Ollie, who's that?"

"Molly, our department secretary."

"She looks serious."

"She always does." Ollie rolled down the window and leaned out. "Molly, is everything okay?"

"Beth needs to see you," she answered.

"Okay. Now? I have a meeting scheduled with her later this morning."

"Yes. She's free now. It is about Keating," Molly answered in the flattest voice I'd ever heard.

"Did Beth hear something?" Ollie asked. I heard the urgency in his voice.

"She's in her office." Before Ollie could respond, the redhead retreated to her car.

Ollie turned to me quickly and then looked back at the office building. "There's a pair of, uh, Angie's Birks in the back. Would you be okay on your own for a bit?"

Of course, I wanted to go in with him, but I understood that whatever Ollie's supervisor needed to tell him, it more than likely had nothing to do with Keating's whereabouts. "I'll be fine," I assured him. "Go, talk to your boss."

Ollie nodded silently and then stepped out of the Wrangler. I followed him to the back trunk. After Ollie opened the door, I peeked inside and spotted several pairs of Ollie's shoes. I eyed him knowingly and kept my lips sealed.

"Just because I don't wear them doesn't mean I don't have them."

"Have shoes will travel?"

"Something like that." He handed me the keys. "I'll see you in a few." I watched Ollie walk towards the entrance of the building where his office was. After he disappeared inside, I wondered what information his boss had about Keating.

I then returned my attention to Ollie's pile of shoes. "Do you have any left in your closet?" I whispered to the air. After a few minutes, I located Angie's size 32's.

I dropped the shoes to the ground and then slid my feet in. I then closed and locked up the Wrangler. I stuffed Ollie's keys into my pocket and then leaned on the driver's side door. My body instinctively turned towards the sparkling pond. That area, the tiny beach, the boathouse, and the dock all held so many memories for me. Moments of my life that helped shape who I am. I felt the pull, the desire to breathe in the air, sound, and comfort I always found there. I was not ready to face that space yet.

I turned away and faced Angelo Hall. This classroom building took the space of a farmhouse. When I was a student, the offices of the performing arts professors and one classroom were located there. The house was built on the property in 1765. The history of this house is interesting. According to the stories I heard, an alleged murderer who fled to Kettle Cove from a different state was captured here. Other rumors stated a different homeowner was involved in the Underground Railroad. I didn't know if either story was true.

There also used to be a barn across the street. That was used for theatre and musical performances. And then behind the barn was Apple Pond. Before I walked anywhere on campus, I decided to first use the restroom. On my visits back after graduation, I came to campus with Ollie and Keating and saw that Angelo Hall was constructed, but I never had reason to enter it.

After I washed up, I exited the bathroom and looked around the lobby. Ollie and Keating's offices were on the third floor. Keating had told me that when the house was demolished, they salvaged the original windows and doorframes and that a child's shoe was found between the wall and floor on the second level of the home. He explained that New England families placed a child's shoe inside a wall of their home for luck. As I walked through the lobby, I located the white shoe that was now on display. It was encased in a special box in the corner of the room with a plaque that simply stated, "For Luck."

As an archeology major, history fascinated me. I loved to learn about old cemeteries, buildings, and space. With old buildings came ghost stories. The old White House had its share of reported paranormal activity. One story involved the spirit of a little boy who allegedly died after he had tumbled down a flight of stairs. His spirit was reported to be seen in the room where my freshmen year college writing class was held. I never spotted a ghost. But I didn't know what I would've done if I had. Honestly, what did anyone do if they saw a ghost? Did they say "Hey"? Pass out? Vomit? What?

Although a difficult decision, it was eventually decided to knock the farmhouse down. I had heard the structure was sound, but the rest of the space was no longer safe. I knew Ollie and Keating, with some other professors on campus fought to have the house placed on the historical registry. They argued the house played a significant role in the history of the area. Unfortunately, that battle was lost. Ollie and Keating had warned me that the buildings were gone. Even though I knew this, nothing had prepared me for the fifty-ton weight that crushed my chest when I saw the vacant space. Intellectually, I understood the demolition's rationale, but it saddened me emotionally.

Over my four years at Crestview, I only had one class in the White House. In that room, with floorboards that creaked and windows that got stuck when opened, I had my first and only class with Maddie. Although we had recognized each other from our hall, we had not really talked until we were paired up as partners for an assignment. It was through this conversation that I learned Gray was her favorite actor.

When Gray gained popularity from the soap, we agreed to keep our relationship private. And then, with the accolades from his performance in *My Truth*, students and teachers we had attended high school with were interviewed for an article that was written about him. My name had been mentioned as his closest friend, but when

I moved away from the Thomas home, I didn't leave a forwarding address. I only returned to the area to visit the cemetery where my parents were buried. When I had talked to Gray about Maddie, he had greenlighted my sharing the truth of our friendship. I never did.

*　*　*

My on-campus work-study job was building sets. I came to enjoy theatre because of Gray. My high school work schedule didn't allow me to work behind the scenes, but it did in college. My job was to build and paint the flats for each performance. This experience enabled me to understand a bit of Gray's professional world. I also attended nearly every performance as a student. These buildings, especially the barn, played a role in my time at Crestview. Whenever I returned to campus after the break, the White House and barn welcomed me home.

Thoughts of my time here as a student told me I had to follow where my mind, body, and soul wanted and needed to go. Fear be damned. I exited Angelo Hall, crossed the road, walked down the hill, and then turned into the entryway of the pond. While a student, I walked to the pond every night that I could. I almost always came on my own. On the clearest of nights, the stars could be seen for miles. At the time, there was a small boathouse with a short dock. I sat on the wooden planks with my back to the wall of the building and watched the water. There's something mystical and freeing about the water at night. It drained all the stress of the day away with the gently lapping water. I felt more connected to the earth and my surroundings when I came here. Even though I had normally been alone, I never felt lonely.

Over the years, the dock and small boathouse were replaced by a classroom building. I kicked off Angie's Birks, picked them up in one hand, and then stepped onto the beach. I liked the gentle feel of the sand as it sifted through my toes while I walked towards the water's edge. I dipped one toe into the cool water and then located a rock to settle on. With Angie's shoes next to me, I stared at the water and replayed different clips of my time spent here. I once saw Halley's Comet pass overhead and tested my knowledge of the constellations.

Sometimes, other students would be here too, but, usually, I seemed to be alone. I had asked Maddie to join me a couple of times, but she always declined. Maddie was an extrovert. We had clicked, and she helped me shed some of my shell. She convinced me to attend some school dances and encouraged me to talk to others. Maddie showed me that there was more to life than work and that I was permitted to relax and enjoy myself.

As a Crestview Student, I wasn't known as the girl whose parents died but as Kenzie, the chick who hung out with Maddie.

It was through one of the dances during our sophomore year that I met Shane. For the first time, I was honestly interested in someone. We hung out a lot and eventually hooked up. We had had sex for a few weeks until, one day, he broke it off. I was heartbroken. He had been my first. I had believed him when he told me how much he had liked me. Of course, I eventually figured out his intentions toward me had never been honest. He had just wanted to score.

When all this happened, I had first called Gray, but he had been filming and could not talk. I wanted to talk to Maddie about it, but by that time, she had found a different group of kids that didn't include me. That had hurt more than being dumped by Shane. One night, I felt so down that I went to the beach. Except, it had been one of the nights when several people were there. So, I kept walking and eventually landed at Comfort.

It was a Tuesday night. I remember once telling Keating that they were bad luck days for me. I hadn't wanted to tempt fate that something would go horribly wrong if I had worked on this day. If Keating thought I was out of my mind, he had never let on. He and Ollie just silently agreed to never schedule me for this day. I had always appreciated that about them.

Comfort had a small deck off the back. It overlooked the river that ran behind the restaurant. To access this space, you had to go inside. I had not paid any attention to who was there when I entered and crossed through to the door that accessed the deck. Even though it was November, we had not yet put the chairs away. A few minutes after I had settled in, I was joined by Angie and two mugs of white hot chocolate.

"Did you see Orion? He's brighter tonight," Angie had commented.

I knew she was referring to the constellation. I had confided in Angie that I studied the stars and tried to learn the different ones. I'm embarrassed to admit it, but I can only identify the Big and Little Dippers and Orion.

"I did," I admitted.

"When I was younger, I used to tell my mother he was the only man I could depend on." She then looked at me as if she could read everything on my mind and stated something I had never forgotten. "You'll find your own Orion one day, sweetheart."

We continued to drink our hot chocolate while I shared with Angie what had happened with Shane and Maddie. After we had finished our drinks, she invited me to stay at the house. Ollie and Keating were away, and she had wanted company. Angie shared with me that it had been the anniversary of her brother's death. Although always difficult for her, that day was harder because she had just dealt with a situation that mirrored her brother's. That night, although it had not been the first time Angie and I had chilled together, it was a moment that shifted my friendship with her.

Throughout the rest of my time as a student at Crestview, I kept mostly to myself. I lived in a single, worked at Comfort and the theatre. I talked to Ollie and Keating in their offices and spent time with Angie. My friends were my co-workers. Most of them were older than me. I saw Maddie here and there, but whatever connected us as freshmen faded away. After that night with Angie, I purposefully looked for Orion every fall. I hadn't found him in Shane or Maddie, but I learned that didn't mean I should ever stop looking.

A sudden breeze ripped off the pond and chilled my exposed skin. The sensation brought me back to the present. I wrapped my arms around myself for warmth and thought about the events from the last few days. Top Floor's closure, Gray and Grafton, and then Keating's disappearance. Keating...

I shivered again, although it wasn't because of nature but the imminent upheaval of my breakfast. I stumbled off the rock toward a small grassy spot and puked. Once satisfied that my tank was empty, I crossed to the pond and splashed water across my mouth. I straightened up and searched for the calm and direction I always found as a college student. Yet, regardless of how hard I tried, I couldn't find it. Though settled, my stomach ached with a cocktail of emotions I hadn't felt in a very long time. The last time I did, the person who stopped and helped me through it was part of the reason I felt this way again.

# CHAPTER ELEVEN

Lost. The last time I felt like this, I was on this beach alone. Sometimes, I came here to escape the dorm's noise, to think and feel connected to something more than just me. I sat on the beach or the dock and stared at the water for hours. Those silent conversations I held with the sand, water, moon, and stars often proved more cathartic than getting lost in the bottom of cheap beer or wine. It was this spot all those years ago where Keating found me. That one conversation altered my path as a student at Crestview and as a person.

What twisted irony. On this beach, I was homesick and upset about Gray and felt out of place. Several years later, I'm again worried about Gray, and as much as I want it, Keating won't find me here. I didn't know what to think, only what I feared. I wish I was built differently. I am afraid to learn about Keating and learn that a damned Tuesday took yet another person whom I loved from me. But I cannot bury my head in the sand and pretend that this isn't happening. It was. I needed to accept the fact that Keating wasn't just away at a conference or on vacation. I also knew that I wasn't alone in my feelings. Angie, Ollie, and I had each other. As for Gray, I knew Ollie was right. I needed to trust that Gray could take care of himself and would be in touch with me when he was ready.

And I needed to trust myself. I'm not the same girl I was all those years ago. I'm no longer a powerless kid. Keating may not be here to take my hand to pull me up and out of the sand, but all the lessons he taught me were. I cannot sit here and hope the answers will just come to me. I needed to believe in my abilities and be proactive. And, where I did not have Keating, I did have Angie and Ollie. And, I had the strength of this place.

I checked the time on my phone. I'd been on the beach for over an hour. I didn't know how long Ollie's appointment with his supervisor would last, but I could check in with him. If Ollie was still in his meeting, I could wait for him. I grabbed Angie's shoes, and left the beach. Once my feet hit the pavement, I brushed the sand off, slid Angie's Birks back on, and retraced my steps up the hill.

This time, after I entered Angelo, I headed right up the steps. The first two flights I took quickly and then slowed on the third. It was not that I was out of shape, but a bit wobbly from tossing up the contents of my breakfast. After I exited the stairwell, I turned towards Ollie's office. Earlier, by the pond, I thought of Keating. I didn't, however, consider the onslaught of emotions that would slam me when I walked towards his office. Although this was not the same space, I visited Keating and Ollie, it was nostalgic. All the times I visited them in Franklin Hall busted through my memory banks like a broken pipe and knocked me off balance.

I braced my hand on the wall and used it as a guide. I noticed Ollie's door was firmly closed, but Keating's was open. Could he be? I found a splash of adrenaline and closed the distance between me and the open office door. I imagined launching myself into Keating's arms. Then, I would give the professor an earful for the scare he put in us. But, as quickly as that spark of hope had flooded my system, it drained when I spied Ollie behind Keating's desk. The floor lamp lightly illuminated the otherwise darkened room.

I leaned against the door frame, folded my arms across my body, and warded off the chill that once again found me. I studied Ollie. He appeared to be searching for something.

"Ollie?"

"Keating resigned," Ollie flatly stated without looking up.

His response shocked me. Uncertain if I had heard Ollie correctly, I asked him to repeat himself. "Did you just say he resigned?"

"His letter was received this morning."

I could count on one hand how many times I've seen Ollie angry or annoyed. That's not to say he never was. It's just, well, I never witnessed it until now.

"Ollie..."

Finally, he looked at me. "We planned to retire together. It was us, our system." Without warning, Ollie picked up a file from the desk and pitched it across the room. "Why the fuck would he not tell me? He just up and left all his responsibilities behind without giving the rest of us a second thought. That selfish bastard!" Ollie then leaned back in Keating's chair and stared at some unknown spot on the ceiling. Molly came over to me in response to Ollie's rare outburst.

"Is he alright," she whispered.

I shook my head no. I looked back to Ollie, who now covered his eyes with his hands.

"I'll be right back, Ollie." I didn't wait for him to recognize whether my words registered with him. Molly followed and directed me to the privacy of her office.

"Ollie just told me Keating mailed in a letter of resignation."

Molly stared at me blankly. I didn't know if it was because she was surprised by what I just said or if she knew but could not comment. Either way, the air between us was awkward. I needed to break free of that.

"I need to call Angie."

"I believe Beth already did," Molly responded.

That was good. I figured Angie and her officers would want the letter for evidence. They needed to dust for prints and verify it was signed by Keating. Maybe they could then track where it was mailed from. At least, that's what the cops on the crime dramas I binged did.

"You're Kenzie, right?"

"I am."

"I recognize you from your picture in Keating's office," Molly explained.

She saw the confusion on my face, as I didn't know which picture she meant.

"Keating kept your senior portrait on his desk. People who didn't know you as a student always asked who you were. The pretty girl with a bright smile. Keating told them you were the daughter he never had."

This revelation surprised me. I thought of Keating as a dad, but it didn't occur to me that Keating viewed me as a daughter. I didn't know what to say or feel about that. But I was saved from a response when Molly and I jumped at what sounded like a book slamming against the wall in Keating's office.

"I need to check on him," I told Molly.

"Is there anything I can do?"

"Thanks, but I don't think so."

Molly turned back to her work after I exited her office. I briefly thought about messaging Angie, then quickly dismissed it. If Ollie's supervisor already contacted her, she'd know the frame of mind he'd be in. Until she arrived, I needed to be there for him.

This time, I didn't linger at the door but forced myself to walk in and around Keating's desk. Ollie remained seated, his elbows on the desk with his head cradled in the palms of his hands. I placed one hand on his shoulder and gently squeezed it. "We'll figure this out, Ollie."

Ollie then straightened up and covered my hand. "I'm sorry about my outburst, lass."

"No worries."

"Did I scare the daylights out of Molly?"

"She's a bit shocked. Who knew you'd kept that talent for profanity hidden under all that charm," I gently teased.

"I'll need to apologize," Ollie softly stated, ashamed of his actions. He let go of my hand and then closed his eyes. "This doesn't make sense."

"Would he *really* do that to you? Is he capable of being so selfish?"

I looked around the office and smiled at how neatly organized everything was. Not a book out of order or a paper out of line. Everything was orderly and efficient, just like Keating. I never knew him to make rash decisions or do anything spontaneous. On the other hand, though never reckless, Ollie was a spur-of-the-moment guy.

Their personalities were so opposite, and yet their bond was beyond description. They shared their work life and knew each other's struggles with the inner hoopla on campus. They supported each other when faced with disgruntled students and defended their classroom policies. Keating dressed impeccably. His jeans, pants, shirts, and tees were all neatly pressed. He never showed up in class without a freshly trimmed beard or shoes. Whereas Ollie did as he felt. He shaved when the mood struck. Eventually, he just let his beard grow but kept it neat. Ollie was free-spirited, and Keating, well, wasn't.

Ollie pushed himself away from Keating's desk and stood. He then moved around the office while my eyes wandered to the objects on the desk. With Molly's comments about my picture fresh in my mind, I looked for it. My eyes stopped at one singular spot.

"What is it, Kenzie?"

"My picture is missing."

"What?" Ollie asked. He moved back towards me and the desk.

"Molly told me before that Keating kept my picture on his desk. It was my college graduation picture. I don't see it."

Ollie placed his hands on his hips. "We didn't touch anything here. I don't remember if that was here after he disappeared." Ollie stopped while he spun his body around in a circle, eying all the objects in the office.

"Is there something else?"

"It's what I don't see."

I looked closer and searched for what Ollie discovered. My eyes traveled over the walls, bookshelves, and desk, but I wasn't sure what Ollie meant.

"The painting of Mt. Monadnock that I gave him is also missing."

# CHAPTER TWELVE

An eerie silence settled over the room. I watched as Ollie mentally cataloged everything else in the office. His eyes scanned the walls, bookshelves, and the tops of the filing cabinets. To my eyes, nothing else was out of place. Photographs he took from different trips, his mug full of used staples that he oddly collected, and his spare set of reading glasses were still, I assumed, in the spot they were supposed to be. The books Keating inherited from his predecessor, an extra sweater, pens, and little props one would expect to see in a college professor's office all seemingly sat undisturbed.

"Was the photograph there?" I asked. "When the cops searched the office after Keating disappeared?"

Ollie closed his eyes as if it helped him travel back in time. When he opened them again, he stared at the open space on the wall. "I believe it was there, but one of Angie's officers took pictures of the office. She can look at them to be sure."

I rubbed my bare arms with my hands to warm them. Unable to shake, the cold feeling, I grabbed Keating's brown marled sweater off the coat rack and pulled it on. The slight trace of Keating's cologne drifted into my nostrils. The sensation both warmed and unsettled me. A peak at Ollie told me he, too, was stunned. What did this mean? One day, Keating was present, and the next, he was just gone. No word. No dust trail was left behind. Just nothing. And now this? A retirement letter and missing items from his office? I mean, what in the actual hell?

Suddenly, I felt unsteady on my feet. My head was fuzzy, and my vision blurred. My chest felt like an elephant landed on top of me and crushed me to the ground. I needed air. I stumbled to the door and tripped over my feet. But two strong arms prevented my face from greeting the floor.

"Whoa…steady there, lass. Let's step out of here." Ollie led me to the hall and then to an open conference room. Gently, Ollie helped me settle into a chair. "Take slow, even breaths, in and out."

Ollie sat in a seat across from me. He leaned forward enough to let me know he was here yet back enough, so I didn't feel crowded. "You are safe. We both are. It's going to be okay."

His assurances calmed me. Slowly, the weight on my chest lifted, and my breathing returned to normal. When I no longer heard my pulse in my ear, I finally looked at Ollie. "I'm okay."

He ran his hand through his messy hair and then collapsed back into his seat. He focused on something off in the distance.

"What the hell happened, Ollie? Where is he? Why does this feel so…," I started. I refused to finish that thought.

"Planned?" Ollie's eyes connected with mine.

I took a noticeable breath. "Yes."

"I don't know, love. We need to talk to Angie."

"Molly told me Beth called her after she read the letter," I remembered.

Ollie sat up quickly. It was like a thought that just occurred to him and it made him straighten up. "Will you be alright if I check in with her?"

"I'm okay. Go, call her," I assured him.

Ollie stood and pulled his phone from his pocket. Just as he did, his phone rang with the familiar ringtone of Janis Joplin's *Bobby McGee*. It was Angie. Both fans of the late singer, Ollie, believed it was his fate that he worked at the college she once had performed at.

"Hi, sweetheart. I was about to call you…" I heard Ollie start, and then he trailed off. I guessed Angie must have interrupted him. Whatever she said caused his body to go rigid. It was like he was shocked by some unknown entity. When he turned to me, I noticed something strange in his eyes. It was a look that both troubled and angered him.

Ollie disconnected the call. He studied the screen for a long time before he stuffed the device back into his pocket. Eyes cast downward; Ollie's face paled…

"Ollie?" I worriedly asked.

After some time passed without a response, I jumped out of the chair, "Ollie? What is it?" I crossed to him in two steps and firmly grabbed his hand to get his attention. "Ollie!"

My raised voice snapped him out of the daze he was in. He gently squeezed my hand. "I'm sorry, love; I didn't mean to frighten you. That was Angie. One of her officers will be by to pick up the letter."

"We need to tell them about my picture and the photograph," I reminded him.

"Yes, we will."

He still, however, seemed distracted by whatever Angie shared with him. When Ollie started to move, I remained glued to my spot. When Ollie noticed our hands were no longer connected, he stopped and turned to me.

"Kenzie?"

My thoughts raced; I couldn't keep up with them. Keating disappeared without a word. A mailed retirement letter arrived at the office, and two personal items were missing. Are these pieces to the puzzle? Will they, especially the letter, lead us to something important? Or will we still be in the dark? It wasn't until I caught the shadow of Ollie's figure before me that shook me out of my daze.

"Love?"

I searched for the strength to voice an idea that proved challenging to unwrap. "Could he be closer than we think? That maybe he didn't run off and, instead, found some local place to hide?"

"What would he be hiding from?"

"Life." Softer, I added, "Us."

Ollie dropped his head. Fear, anger, and many other emotions flashed across his handsome features. "The Keating I thought I knew would never do something purposefully cruel to the people he loved. Now, I don't know what all this means. But let's get out of here. We'll talk everything through with Angie and figure out where to go from here."

I heard Ollie tell Molly and Beth that an officer would be there to pick up the letter.

After we said our goodbyes to them, we descended the stairs of his office building and returned to the jeep. While in the stairwell, a few students greeted both of us with a hello. For the first time since I'd been on campus, it struck me that it seemed awfully quiet for a school day.

We walked the short distance to the jeep in silence. I remembered Ollie gave me the keys, so I unlocked the doors, and we climbed in. Once inside the vehicle, I handed the keys to Ollie. I put my seatbelt on. When I didn't hear the engine turn over, I turned to Ollie. He sat still, keys still in hand.

"Ollie?"

"Angie will send the letter to the lab to be examined. Hopefully, that will provide us with some answers," Ollie answered as if he hadn't just been somewhere else in his mind.

By the time Ollie put the key in the ignition and fastened his own seat belt, more students exited Angelo Hall. I studied their faces. I naively wished that Keating's tightly trimmed, gray beard would appear among the crowd. He'd come to the jeep and tell us to meet him at Comfort. There, he would explain. But, the outline of his angular face, with warm brown eyes and wavy, graying black hair, never showed.

After the students had all cleared, Ollie shifted the gear to drive. No matter how odd and unsettling all of this was, I didn't believe Keating was close. I know I said it, but that was fear talking. In my heart, I knew better. When my parents died, although I didn't understand it as a kid, I immediately felt this emptiness that couldn't be filled. I came to believe that was why the thunder truly woke me up that night. Somewhere, deep inside me, I had sensed they were gone. With Keating, I felt numb. I didn't know how or what to feel or think. I feared if I let myself travel down any of the roads, I'd hit a dead end, and that made my insides churn with sickening bile.

"Can we go to Comfort?"

Ollie turned to me.

"Sure. I'll ask Angie to meet us there."

I nodded yes. Ollie pushed the appropriate buttons to connect with Angie via Bluetooth. After the second ring, her voice filled the jeep.

"Ollie?"

"Darling, can you meet us at Comfort?"

"Of course," Angie agreed.

"I didn't tell you before, but when we were in Keating's office, we noticed Kenzie's graduation picture and the photograph of Mt. Monadnock that I gave him were missing."

I was honestly touched after Molly told me Keating had my senior portrait on his desk. Not because I thought Keating insensitive, but, because even after our falling out, he still thought enough of me to keep my picture. And to now know he had introduced me as his daughter hurt my heart.

"They were there when his office was initially searched. I will have Deas and Garrett dust for more prints and follow up with security. I'll see you in a bit."

Angie's voice drew me back into their conversation.

"We're on our way there now. See you soon," Ollie responded.

Instead of driving down Maple Road, we turned left onto Luce. We drove past the now vacant property where Pax Hill sat. Although the old house was already demolished when I started college, I once saw a picture of it with a wraparound porch. It was housing for students who were in recovery from substance use.

When I asked Keating why Pax was closed and eventually leveled by a controlled burn, he said it was deemed too old and expensive to maintain. He was angry with the decision to destroy this safe space for students on campus.

"Do you know why Keating never drank?" I asked.

"What makes you ask?"

"We just passed the lot where Pax was. It reminded me of how pissed Keating was when he told me about it. I know he always wanted what was best for students, but I don't know, something about Pax seemed personal."

Ollie's silence again spoke to me. I knew he was already upset by whatever Angie shared with him at the office, and I didn't want to add to that. I jumped in before he could answer. "It's not important. I just always wondered."

"Keating didn't care for the taste of alcohol of any kind. It didn't bother him when others drank around him unless it became excessive."

"Is that why he never wanted to serve liquor at Comfort?"

"He believed there were healthier ways of coping after a long or stressful day. He wanted to provide a place for students not interested in drinking, a place to go. We let the liquor license go after we took ownership."

"So, what aren't you telling me?"

Ollie smiled. "Nothing gets past you, does it? Keating's parents had been fond of the bent elbow. Their drinking landed them in trouble when he was a young lad."

"So, he swore off the stuff?"

"He feared the risk of developing a problem if he drank. Especially since he was obsessive about things, to begin with."

That made sense to me. I knew very little about Keating's parents. I continued to study the scenery outside, surprised when Ollie spoke again.

"Did Keating ever mention Evan to you?"

"Evan? No. Who is he?"

"Keating's ex. They saw each other before you were a student."

"Was he a drinker?"

Ollie paused again. I didn't know if he was purposefully tiptoeing around the subject or if he honestly didn't know how to phrase his thoughts.

"When they met, Keating believed Evan didn't drink. That they were the same."

"Teetotalers," I said.

"Right."

"And this dude never corrected him?"

"No. I never questioned it, but my perceptive wife thought there was more to Evan's abstinence than dislike. But neither of us believed it was our business to say anything. Keating was happy, and that's all that mattered."

"Until he wasn't?"

Ollie simply nodded.

I put some of the dots together. "Was their breakup over Evan's drinking?"

"Not the drinking itself, but that contributed to it. Evan broke Keating's heart and, I think, a bit of his soul."

"And they haven't talked since?"

"Not that I'm aware." Ollie stated.

I sense Ollie was holding back. I understood there were parts of their lives I didn't know anything about. And that's okay. It's like kids not wanting to or needing to know how often their parents had sex. Still, I felt like a larger part of the story was missing.

"I'm sorry, Kenzie, I don't mean to stonewall you; it's just, there's a lot of unpleasant history with this part of Keating's life."

"It's okay."

"I promise I will share the whole story with you," Ollie assured me.

I let the conversation of Evan go for the rest of the short ride to Comfort. Whomever he was and whatever role he had played in

Keating's life, it clearly had hurt Ollie and made him uncomfortable. I also wondered, why Ollie would mention Evan now? Was it because I asked why Keating never drank or for a different reason? I thought back to the look on Ollie's face when he spoke to Angie at campus. She told him something that made him turn ashen. Was this Evan guy back? Did he have something to do with Keating? So many questions. I had to push them all from my mind until Ollie filled me in. As we pulled into the parking lot of Comfort, I realized I had to prepare myself for entering another space that was full of memories with Keating.

# CHAPTER THIRTEEN

We were the only car in the lot. When Ollie and Angie told me that Keating was last seen in this parking lot before he vanished into the night, I realized I only thought about how I felt about the man who was missing, but not how I felt about the places he was connected to.

"How are the employees handling all this?" I asked as we walked toward the front door.

"From what Doug told me, they were all rattled. He met with them this morning. Angie told me her officers were done with their investigation and cleared us to reopen, but Doug and I thought it best to give everyone some time."

I nodded in agreement. I thought of all the cops at Top Floor the night my co-workers and I were told it was closing for good. It was scary and uncomfortable. Ollie and Doug, Comfort's long time manager and someone I worked under, made the right call.

After Ollie unlocked the front door, I followed him inside and closed the door behind us. He crossed through the space to the far wall and switched the lights on. I moved inside and looked around. The place hadn't changed one bit. All the warmth exuded from the walls, tables, flooring, and large fireplace with comfortable leather couches around it. The space, although quiet, felt alive and comforting. In fact, if I hadn't known I last worked here fourteen years ago, I'd think time had stood still.

Keating designed Comfort to be a safe haven for all. It was a place you came to relax after a long day in class or at work. It was where students studied for exams and celebrated their success. Comfort gave people just that, comfort from the brutal winters, from the stressors of life, and a place where everyone welcomed you. It was like Cheers sans the alcohol.

Keating was the businessman. He paid the bills, made the food orders, hired and fired the staff, and handled payroll. Ollie's optimistic and calm demeanor created the warm and peaceful atmosphere. He handled the wall art and music. Ollie also worked with Tia, the chef, on the menu. Doug handled all the scheduling and was there when Ollie and Keating could not be. They made Comfort a happening place. Or at least, as happening as you could be in sleepy Kettle Cove.

"There's some blueberry lemonade in the fridge behind the bar. The glasses are in the same place. I'll rustle up some grub for lunch," Ollie shared. "You'll be alright? Angie will be here shortly."

"I'm good," I assured him.

Ollie smiled before he disappeared behind the kitchen doors. I pulled out three glasses behind the bar before grabbing the blueberry lemonade from the little fridge underneath the counter. Keating kept the area looking like a bar, complete with shakers, mixers, stemmed and unstemmed glasses, and beer mugs, yet there wasn't a lick of liquor. To him, comfort was about being surrounded by friendly faces, good food, and fun. And healthy, non-alcoholic drinks that still put a smile on your face and didn't leave you with a hangover. Of course, you could BYOB. But, in my time working here, I don't t recall anyone pulling out their own alcohol. Angie believed Comfort helped decrease the number of DUIs her force issued throughout the year.

After I poured the drinks, I walked around the bar and ran my hand over the names of the patrons who frequented Comfort since Keating and Ollie owned it. While vacationing in Alaska, Keating had learned the people of Ketchikan had a custom. Family and neighbors gathering for a meal showed the heart of a home. Everyone who ate at a table that was not their own signed the tablecloth and became part of the home's history. Keating loved this idea and implemented it at Comfort.

The bar top was carved from wood from an oak tree that fell on Keating's property during a harsh winter storm. People carved their names into the wood. Some added little designs and short messages. The wooden stools that circled the u-shaped bar had backs, and lower pegs to rest your feet on, came from restored barn wood. One of Keating's friends made both the bar top and stools.

I sipped my drink and scanned the names. I trailed my fingers over the ridges, the different signatures from the artists to the non. I stopped at Maddie's name. She had carved her name one night when I was at work and she was studying. When Maddie distanced herself from me, she stopped coming to Comfort. She preferred the bar down the road that served alcohol. As I looked at her name, I briefly wondered where she was these days. I never went to our class reunions, but I knew through the pictures emailed to me, that Maddie had.

I had carved my name next to Ollie, Angie, and Keating. We finally carved our names in the week I graduated. Keating and Ollie encouraged all the employees to carve our names in after we completed our first month of work. I purposefully decided to wait until I graduated. I saw it as a gift to myself, that, I made it through those four years and that earned me the right to sign the bar top. Jack's name was there too. He was home when I graduated and joined us for dinner.

I thought of that night. Keating and Ollie bantered about the purpose of horror movies while Angie, Jack, and I laughed at the points each had made. Keating was a closet horror movie fan, while Ollie thought them disturbing. Now I can't recall everything they said, but I did remember that as relaxed and happy as I was, I also feared that that night would be the last time I would laugh with them. I worried that after I graduated and returned to Hoboken, that my relationships with them would fade. Ollie and Keating would have different students and Angie would make popcorn and drinks with her friends. I would become just another former student. Of course, that didn't happen. Now, I don't know if I'll ever hear Keating's laugh again.

"Kenzie? You, okay?"

I turned to the sound of Angie's voice. So lost in my thoughts, I never heard her enter, never mind approach me at the bar. Chief Cooper was never known to pull punches. Many people were put off when someone was direct, but not me. Angie was both blunt and gentle. And had a built-in bullshit detector. If I even thought about feeding her a line about being fine, she'd see right through it. She taught me, along with Ollie, that honesty was always best.

"I'm, I'm not sure how to describe it. I mean, it is surreal being here, in this place." I scanned the whole restaurant before I looked back at all the names etched into the wood. "Looking at these names, of the people I thought would be in my life for, well, longer than they were. And Keating..."

Angie grabbed a glass of blueberry lemonade and sat on the barstool beside mine. "I know, honey. I feel it too. Keating and Ollie created something special here. That magic, I feel it every time I enter that door."

I rubbed my hand across the bar. "How many places do you know have a bar, barstools, drinkware, and no liquor? Keating teased Ollie for his free-spirited mind, but I think Keating sometimes rivaled him."

Angie laughed. "My Scot and the professor were quite a duo. They agreed on more than either of them let on but loved ribbing each other. They were in many ways like you and Grayson."

"Yeah..." I answered half-heartedly. I never compared my relationship with Gray with Ollie and Keating. But Gray and I also teased each other.

"I know you're upset about him, sweetheart. And, as much as I crush on him, I'm your number one fan."

The look on my face must have reflected my worry over Gray. Being close to someone who was perceptive, who was trained to look beyond the obvious, was intimidating. Angie's skill set in this area was annoyingly extraordinary.

"But, before we talk about the sexy Mr. Kent, you should know that just as I was about to leave the station for here, I received a visitor looking for you."

"Someone looking for me? Who?" I asked confused.

"An investigator named Martin Benson."

My jaw dropped in surprise. Then confusion. Martin? Martin who worked with me at Top Floor? Wait, Martin was a waiter. Right? Unless, but wait, none of this made sense. The inner conversation in my head filled with questions. Why would he be here? Unless…was it about Gray? Did something happen to him? I pulled my phone out and quickly checked it for messages. My hands shook with fear. Gray still hadn't responded. I fought with my fingers. Willed them to steady so I could send Gray a text.

**Plse tll me your ar k.**

I hit send before I corrected my errors. How did Martin know I was here? Did he talk to Gray? My thoughts continued to churn away in my mind and threatened to run away from me. My pulse quickened as the weight of this situation smacked me square in the face. My chest felt heavy, my skin clammy, my breathing…

"Sweetheart…look at me. Kenzie. Honey. Look at me."

I heard Angie calling me and felt her take hold of my hands. She squeezed them to capture my attention. Damn Gray and this mess. His life, the world he lived in. I never wanted to know the inner workings of it. Gray respected that. Now, I felt like a door I never opened had threatened the person most valuable to me.

"Kenzie," Angie called.

She squeezed my hands again. This time, it worked. I forced myself to look up and catch her eyes. I focused on the warmth I saw in her brown orbs. That enabled me to slow my breath and match it to hers.

"That's it, sweetheart, simple breaths in and out. Like that," Angie continued to prompt.

As my breathing evened out, I felt myself vacate the space in my head and return to the room. Once able to focus, I looked around and saw that both Ollie and Martin were with us. Both men kept their distance and gave me space.

Once I felt settled, I let go of her hands and picked up my glass of lemonade. I drained it. It was then that Ollie crossed to me.

"Have some crackers too, love, it will help."

Ollie took the stool behind me and rubbed my shoulders. I did as he directed. I learned, almost immediately, that he was right. The swirling nausea that had churned my insides faded with the crackers I ate. I sensed Ollie's eyes on Angie's, secretly asking what happened. But I knew. For the second time today, I had a panic attack. I hoped to all the Gods this didn't mean that my Thursdays were also now cursed. But, before I could venture too far into that territory, I heard Martin.

"Kenzie, everything is okay, I promise." Martin calmly stated.

I turned to him. My face felt clammy, but my vision cleared. It was indeed Martin, his trademark black dress shirt and pants traded in for blue jeans and a yellow t-shirt. He watched me cautiously. Many questions ran through my mind, but the one I desperately needed an answer to tumbled out first.

"Is Gray okay?" I shakily asked.

Martin stared at me like he was confused about my question. Did he not know who I was talking about? That's why he was here, right? To tell me something happened to Gray? That's part of what the cops did. They came to the door and delivered bad news. I mean, why else would he be here?

"Honey, why do you think something happened to Grayson?"

I looked at Angie and then back to Martin. "I haven't heard from him, Angie."

"Grayson is not hurt, Kenzie. I promise," Martin shared.

I let out a breath. Gray was safe. With that knowledge, I felt my strength return. And with my strength, my fury. I stood up, grateful my legs, which felt like marshmallows moments ago, not only held me but enabled me to move closer to his space with vigor.

"You're a cop? Is that why you always kept to yourself and acted like you were above everyone else?" I accused.

He took a step back from me and then shoved his hands in his pockets.

"Well?" I waited.

"Can we sit?" Martin pointed to a table. I nodded and followed him to the table.

"Angie and Ollie stay." I directed.

"That's fine," Martin stated. He took a seat on one end of the table, and I sat across from him. "Can we start again?"

"As what exactly?" I firmly asked.

"Why I am here."

I sat back and crossed my arms. "Fine. Explain to me what the hell is happening."

"I will tell you as much as I can."

For a moment, we just watched each other. My eyes scanned his face. I looked for any clue that signaled his presence was for something other than what he claimed. But, as carefully as I studied him, I saw nothing other than the kindness he had always shown me as a colleague.

"I'm listening."

"I'm not a cop. I work as a private investigator with a firm in New York City," Martin started. "I was assigned to work undercover at Top Floor."

"To investigate Grafton?" I asked.

But Martin shook his head no. "Not at first. My firm was hired to investigate some internal dealings. My assignment expanded when I witnessed Grafton's activities and the parties involved. It was then that the local PD were brought in. I can't say more than that."

"The detective I spoke to at Top Floor never said I couldn't leave town." I defended.

"The police know that you did not have any involvement with Marjorie, Jed, or Grafton." Martin confirmed. "I cleared you and your co-workers of that."

"So, what are you doing here?" I asked. "How did you even know where I was?"

"I ran into Amy," Martin answered honestly.

"So, you just followed me here?"

"My mom lives in the area. I'm visiting her."

"I thought when you worked undercover, you weren't supposed to reveal your true identity to people?" I asked.

"We're not." Martin conceded.

"So, what, you're just breaking that rule?"

"I'm here to talk with you unofficially," Martin answered.

"Unofficially. So, nobody knows you are here?" I was nervous. If Martin knew who Grayson was, he more than likely knew that we were friends. When the detective at Top Floor didn't ask me any questions about Gray, I thought I dodged that bullet. Now, a PI was asking about him. Why? Was it possible that Gray knew more about Grafton than what he shared with me?

"My part of the investigation is over, but the detective in charge of the case is a friend. I know from him that he hasn't heard from Grayson. I know you and Grayson Kent are tight. I told my friend, unofficially, that while I was here to see my mom, I'd talk to you."

"And how do you know about me and Gray?" I asked. I knew it was a stupid question, but I wanted to delay answering any questions about Gray for as long as I could. Besides, if Martin was not a cop, I didn't need to talk to him.

"I'm an undercover private investigator, Kenzie. Part of my job is vetting who I'm interacting with."

"So, you know everything about me?" I asked him. I hated that my voice was tinged with discomfort. I hated that my privacy was violated.

"I, yes, I know everything. And that's how I discovered your connection with Grayson." Martin admitted. "Look, Kenzie, I'm not here to cause you pain or to announce your relationship with Grayson to the world."

"If that's true, then I'll ask again, why are you here? Why didn't the detectives ask me about Gray when I met with them?" I questioned. Then I turned to Angie. "Do I need to answer these questions?"

Angie turned to Martin. "Are you unofficially trying to help Grayson? And if that is the case, you told your friend that you knew Kenzie and thought that could, in turn, help them and Grayson?"

Martin kept his eyes on me. "I understand you want to protect him, but this business with Grafton is serious, Kenzie. I know Gray never worked with Grafton, but had a meeting scheduled with him recently. A meeting set up by his manager, Samantha Bailey."

"Tell me why you care so much about helping a man you don't know," I stated. "Because in all honesty, Martin, I'm not sure that I can trust you or why you are here, officially or unofficially."

The mystery of how Martin landed his job as head waiter at Top Floor now made sense. Jed hired him, so he must have known who Martin really was. He must have suspected that his wife and Todd were into some questionable business. But what doesn't jive with me, was why he was so interested in helping Grayson. Was there an ulterior motive? I wasn't sure if Martin would respond.

"I've been an undercover investigator for fifteen years. I've seen good people get caught up in bad things. From what I can see, Grayson is a good guy. I don't want to see that happen to him," Martin started. "I understand you feel betrayed, violated even. And for that, I'm sorry. I truly am. I genuinely like you Kenzie. You are smart, sassy, kind, and giving. The staff at Top Floor depended on you and you never let them down. I get that you don't trust me, but I'm being honest when I honestly want to help. Please let me."

I looked at Ollie and Angie. I wanted their take, their approval. If they sensed that Martin was on the up and up, then I would answer.

Even though they knew Gray, they were more removed from this situation and could see everything with clearer eyes.

As if she could sense my hesitation, Angie stepped in. "If Kenzie answers your questions, are you okay if my husband and I stay? And if your questioning is out of line, I'll put a stop to it."

"Of course," Martin replied.

Angie looked at me. "Go ahead, sweetheart."

I returned my attention to Martin. "Ask what you need." I acquiesced. What else could I do? I just hoped that my decision to trust Martin would not backfire.

artin straightened up, folded his hands, and placed them on the table. He steadied his breath. "Kenzie..." only to stop when glasses were placed before him and me. My eyes trailed up the fingers, forearm, and bicep of Ollie.

"I thought you could both use this," he said. Ollie winked at me and then backed away. He then sat next to Angie, who, when I caught her eyes, rolled them in exasperation.

Martin, who caught the exchange, looked back at me. "What am I missing?"

"Comfort is dry. I suspect my friend over there just spiked our blueberry lemonade with something a little stronger," I explained.

Martin picked up his glass, took a sip, and then smiled before he put it down. He then looked at Ollie. "Thanks, man." Martin then returned his attention to me. "What I said before, I meant, Kenzie, you are not in any trouble. And from what I know, neither is Gray."

"Jed hired your firm to investigate Marjorie and Todd, and then Grafton entered the mix. At the meeting, Jed already knew that Marjorie and Todd were involved with providing Grafton a venue to conduct his peep show." I summarized.

Martin did not confirm or deny what I said. It didn't matter.

"Kenzie, I said it before and promise you again now, your relationship with Grayson is your own. I respect that," Martin began, "I saw Gray exit the elevator of Top Floor. Grafton was already there with other members of his party. I then saw Grayson leave the moment he spotted Grafton."

"You worked that night. You know what happened," I countered. I caught Angie's look. Although empathetic, her expression was clear; do not become defensive. I then backed off a bit.

"Gray told me he was scheduled to meet with someone to discuss a possible role in a new rom-com. The meeting was scheduled before we closed and was on what would have been my day off."

"Did Gray know who he was meeting with?"

"No. He told me he had a meeting, but never said whom it was with. I was under the impression he didn't know."

"Isn't that unusual?"

I shrugged. "Gray and I do not talk a lot about the inner workings of his career."

Martin studied me. I didn't know if he believed me, but it didn't matter. It was true. Gray and I didn't talk about the business end of his job. It was weird, though, as I would think Gray would have known who he was scheduled to meet with. Although, I wouldn't put it past Sam to lie.

"Have you talked to and seen him since that meeting?" Martin asked. I noticed a change in his voice. The previous questions he asked with confidence. Now, he seemed uncomfortable.

"Somehow, I think you already know the answer to that question." I calmly stated. "But, yes, I saw him at my place after our meeting at Top Floor."

"What did you tell him?"

I closed my eyes and fought against the tears that threatened to fall as I replayed my conversation with Gray. His admission of once witnessing Grafton's behavior, that that was the reason he shut me out all those years ago. And that when he had confided in Sam, he had listened to her and kept quiet. It was career suicide otherwise.

The boy I knew wouldn't stand for this, regardless of the cost to him. I couldn't wrap my head around where that person disappeared.

"When I told him about Grafton, Marjorie, and Todd - "I started. Martin then interrupted me.

"Prick that he is," Martin interjected, "Sorry, continue."

"Allowing Grafton to use Top Floor to get his jollies off, I asked Gray if his meeting was with Grafton. And if it was, what did he do. He told me just what you said, that when he spotted Grafton, he turned around and left. Gray then told me he had contacted one of Grafton's people, feigned illness and then he split town for a few days."

"Then what?" Martin followed up.

"Then nothing. He left the meeting without looking back."

Martin stretched one arm out onto the table after he rubbed his temple. "If he left his meeting upon seeing Grafton, would it be safe to say that he knew something about him?"

"You'll need to ask Gray that question." I didn't want to share any more with Martin. He wasn't a cop, and as much as I wanted to believe he only wanted to help Gray, I still felt uneasy about his angle. If Martin sensed I was holding back, he didn't say. Instead, he moved to Sam.

"What can you tell me about Gray's manager, Samantha Bailey?"

As much as I disliked Sam, I struggled with the idea that she would have knowingly placed Gray in that situation. I wondered if when Sam scheduled the meeting, she made it clear that all that would happen was a conversation about a role. But, if that were true, why would she have kept Grafton's name from Gray? She had to have known he would not react well to seeing the man there.

"She was Gray's high school theatre teacher. She saw his talent, had some connections, and was instrumental in helping him break into the business." I answered truthfully.

"But?" Martin prompted.

"I am grateful for how she supported Gray, but that's about it."

"Why is that?"

"I think she's a selfish, greedy bitch." I simply stated.

Until now, although I felt their presence, Ollie and Angie remained at the bar as silent observers. After I expressed my opinion of Sam, I thought about the conversation Gray, and I had about her. If Sam was somehow caught up in this situation with Grafton, maybe more than she let on to Gray, then I would no longer hold back. I wondered what Angie was thinking. I suspected that as much as she may have wanted to, she could not shut down her cop mind.

"That's direct," Martin mused.

I shrugged my shoulders. "Gray is aware of my feelings in regard to his manager."

"Did if he spoke with Sam?"

"I only know, until that point, he hadn't," I shared. I thanked whatever lucky stars were out there for me that she had not contacted me either.

"Okay," Martin stated.

"Anything else?" I asked.

Martin tapped his fingers gently on the table, as he considered his next question. "The detective you met with, she shared the observation you made about the women who had accompanied Grafton to Top Floor, with me."

"What about them?"

"Do you remember if you ever saw the same person twice?" Martin asked.

His question stumped me. Being the host, I greeted a lot of people throughout one shift, but Grafton was the kind of patron you didn't forget. His big personality fit with his flashy colorful suits and slicked back silver hair.

"I don't think so. I do remember, he came in with two guys and was later joined by a third. His reservations always worked that way. Grafton showed up with his party members and was later joined by usually another male."

"Do you remember when that was?" Martin asked.

"A couple of months back. I remember because one of his guests hit on me and a couple of the other waitresses when Grafton wasn't looking."

"Huh. That's interesting. I don't remember anyone leaving the room until Grafton did. The party room he used had its own bathroom, so nobody needed to."

"Well, this guy snuck out. Now that I think of it, I think we had to toss him out for harassing some of the guests, too. Maybe that was a night you had off? I don't know. But that was the only time I remember Grafton with men."

"Is there a way to check?" Martin asked.

"Our system was designed to store reservations in a backup server. Jed should be able to provide you with a history dating back at least two if not three years. It will give you the dates, times, and number of party members under each reservation. Grafton's reservations are easily spotted because they are listed as a party room only."

"Thank you. I'll pass that on to the police detectives," Martin answered.

It struck me that Martin didn't seem to know that. Then again, maybe he wouldn't. In his role, where he knew of the reservations, he did not make them, nor did he have access to how the system operated. As someone undercover, I would have thought that was something he would have made it his business to know.

"Grafton's guests…there is concern about who the party members truly are. Am I reading that right?" Angie piped in.

"Yes," Martin responded.

The nausea that had burned my insides earlier returned. It was sickening enough to know that this Grafton guy auditioned actors by watching them have sex. If the women or men were somehow forced to play this role, it made the whole situation even more disgusting.

Martin slumped down in his chair. He ran his hands through his shaggy light brown hair. He looked exhausted. "You look like hell, Marty," I commented.

He snorted. "Thanks."

"Will Gray really be, okay?" I shakily asked.

"He needs to share whatever he knows. The longer he holds out, the more he looks like he's hiding something."

"Why didn't the detective ask me about him?"

"They didn't know to ask," Martin answered honestly.

The look I gave him left no room for interpretation. I wanted an explanation for that response. Martin's returned silence told me he wouldn't respond to that question.

"Okay." Martin checked his watch. "I need to head back. When you talk to Mr. Kent, please tell him the longer he ignores the detective's calls, the more suspicions arise. You can also tell him the cops know that Grayson did not meet with Grafton at Top Floor. I told them he walked out. If he has nothing to hide, then he should be willing to talk."

Martin finished his drink and then stood up and turned to Ollie and Angie. "Thanks for the drink and for giving me the time to talk with Kenzie." He then turned back to me. "Are you staying in Kettle Cove for a while?"

"Yes."

Martin looked around the room and took everything in. "I can see why you like it here. It's warm, comfortable, inviting."

"It is."

"It's a little like where you grew up."

Taken aback by Martin's observation, I second-guessed my cooperation with his questions. Did he go to Moose Creek to check up on Gray and me, too? "You visited Moose Creek?"

Martin must have seen the suspicious look on my face because he immediately backtracked. "No, I'm sorry. I didn't mean…My mom's grandparents lived there. She visited them every summer. When I came along, I visited them too. It's a nice area."

"It is," I agreed, surprised to hear a tinge of sadness in my voice. Moose Creek was a beautiful place. Like Kettle Cove, as different from city life as one could get. I didn't miss the people who lived there, but my tree in the Thomas family backyard? The apple orchards? The rolling hills and farmland? I did.

Martin nodded goodbye to Angie and Ollie and then headed towards the door. I jumped up and followed him to the door. "Why did you really come?"

"When working undercover, we are trained, warned, not to get close to people." He paused. "I follow that rule. But you, like I said earlier, I liked you from the moment we met. I don't come across many people like you in my job. But you, you're a refreshing change. I wanted to be honest with you and see if maybe when this case is cleared, we could be friends," Martin admitted bashfully.

I thought about his candid admission and filed it away for a later time. "I appreciate your honesty," I stated. "And that you stuck yourself out there for me to help Gray."

"I understand a thing or two about friendship and loyalty. But I meant what I said; he needs to speak with the detective."

Martin then turned to leave, only to look back. "If you happen to see or hear from anyone at work, please don't blow my cover. It's bad for business."

I nodded. "Not a word."

I watched Martin until he entered his car. After I closed the door, I turned to see that Ollie and Angie were now seated at the table, Martin and I had just vacated. There was food in front of them. Before Martin came in, Ollie was putting something together for us. I forgot all about it until now.

"Come eat something, sweetheart," Angie called to me. "It will help take the edge off."

I knew Angie was right. But before I joined them, I needed to contact Gray. I put my finger up, "One minute," I stated. I then pulled my phone out and called Gray.

Voicemail. I disconnected without leaving a message. I returned my phone to my pocket and then joined Ollie and Angie at the table.

# CHAPTER FIFTEEN

Gray and I went to the movies as often as we could as kids. Sometimes, we scrounged up some bills and loose change to pay for our tickets. When we didn't have the funds, well, let's just say we *found* our way in. At that time, movies were still on film, with somebody sitting in the projector booth running the machine. The projector had different speeds. Sometimes, the film became jumbled, scrambling the voices and speeding up the images on the screen. That's how I felt right now, in Comfort's warmth and familiar space. Images of the times I spent with Keating mixed with memories of Gray flashed before my eyes like that broken projector.

The rush of images made my head spin and my heart ache. I was totally spent. Like I didn't have any energy to move the fork that was in my hand to my mouth. I'm just so tired of feeling like I'm constantly on the cusp of losing someone or something important to me. I'm sick of my fuckin' cursed Tuesdays, of dreading this seemingly ordinary day for everyone else but me. When will it end? When can I just have boring, normalcy?

"Kenzie?"

"Love?"

I heard Angie and Ollie call me but felt like I couldn't move my eyes in their direction. I dropped my fork and sat back in the chair.

From the corner of my eye, I saw Angie get up and move so she could sit next to me. She wrapped her arm around me and pulled me towards her. I let her comfort me and drew from her strength until my thoughts settled.

After a few moments, I caught Ollie's eyes and soft smile. I allowed myself to feel the love and concern they both had for me. Every once and a while, I needed these little gestures. I imagined everyone did. To know you were not alone made every challenging situation feel like it was manageable.

"I'm sorry for zoning out on you. I'm just, I'm so tired of feeling scared that another person I love is hurt or is gone."

"Sweetheart," Angie started, "Look at me."

I rubbed my eyes and turned to her. "You have nothing to apologize for. A lot's happened to you in the past few days. You take the time you need to process it and know that Ollie and I are here for you. Grayson too."

Grayson. I wished he would return my messages. I needed some sign of life so that I wouldn't worry. Ollie and Angie didn't know what Gray shared with me about Grafton. Just as I felt it wasn't my story to tell Martin, it wasn't mine to share with them. I was upset with Gray for not telling me or anyone what happened. And now, that one choice may come back and haunt him. Where I believed I needed to protect Gray, I was also upset that he placed me in this position.

"I hate this. I hate that I'm hiding something from you, but – " I started.

"You talked with Gray after learning disturbing information about someone you know and worked for, for ten years. Emotions were already high. And whatever Gray shared with you, that you kept from Martin and cannot share with us? it's a lot to hold in love," Ollie shared.

I looked at Ollie and saw the truth behind his words. I felt like I owed them more of an explanation. I was about to say something when Angie cut me off.

"You do not owe us anything. We understand. But what Martin advised?" Angie said as if reading my mind. "Grayson needs to speak with the cops and be completely honest with what he knows. It's the only way to begin to move through this."

"What Gray told me, what I kept from Martin. Will that come back to bite me or Gray?" I asked. "I mean, I just learned what Gray knew of Grafton. I didn't feel it was my story to share, and, honestly, I don't know if it is the same as what is happening now. And the cops never asked me about Gray."

"I know you will always protect Grayson. You have since you were kids. But, in this situation, you also need to look out for yourself. This Benson guys? He didn't strike me as wanting to hurt you or Gray. My suggestion is you call Martin and tell him whatever story Gray shared with you. You make it clear that you only just heard about it," Angie advised.

"But…" I started.

"Sweetheart, you purposefully kept yourself out of Gray's life for a reason. An ugly part of his professional life dropped into your life without notice. It's okay to feel upset about it, to react. Your human. And your relationship with Gray is strong. You'll get through this," Angie affirmed.

"I need to try him one more time."

I pulled my phone from my pocket and clicked on his number only to be greeted by his voicemail. "Hey, it's me. A strange thing just happened, please call me so I can explain."

I looked at Ollie and Angie.

"Straight to voicemail."

Not sure what to do with myself, I got up, walked behind the bar, grabbed the Swedish towels and cleaner, and started spraying down the bar. Spray, rub, and repeat over all the names and designs carved in. This time, I didn't pause in front of those I knew; I just kept going until I reached the other side. I looked at the wipe and crinkled my eyes. "Who's been cleaning this joint?"

Ollie chuckled and joined me by the bar. He took the cleaner and towel from my hands and placed them back where they belonged. "We've had some struggles with that recently."

I looked at them both. "What if I returned to work? Here?" I blurted out. "I mean, I am unemployed. And Ollie, you're finishing up the year; Angie, you're working, and I'm not good at having nothing to do."

"I think it's a wonderful idea!" Angie exclaimed. "But I don't want you to feel like you have to. I mean, you can take time off, read, relax, adventure with this one," Angie said, pointing to Ollie. "Keep him out of trouble."

"Hey…" Ollie playfully slapped her across the arm. "I am perfectly able to keep myself out of…" Ollie's voice trailed off as he caught both of our arched brows. "All right, I like a little mischief but I think it's a great idea. But Angie's right, love, you don't need to work here. Doug and I can figure it out."

"I've had so much time off I'm going out of my mind. I need something to keep me occupied instead of worrying about every-thing. And I'd think that I don't know, maybe Keating would want me here. To help keep this place going when he cannot be."

"I think he'd like that," Ollie answered.

All the talk about Gray and Grafton made me momentarily forget to ask Angie about Keating's car.

"Angie," I started, "Ollie said you found Keating's car?" I didn't want to get my hopes up, and yet, I did.

"Yeah, uh, we found it abandoned just on the New Hampshire / Massachusetts line. There was no sign of him. The car's being dusted for prints, but I'm not confident we'll find any other others besides his," Angie explained. "I'm sorry, honey."

"It's a good sign though, that there didn't seem to be any kind of struggle, right? Like, he's not hurt or anything?" I asked, hoping to find something optimistic about this find.

"Yes, that is a good sign," Angie conceded.

But it also suggested that if Keating wasn't injured or hurt by someone else, he more than likely left voluntarily.

"Did you know this, Ollie?" I asked.

"I'm sorry, love. Angie told me earlier over the phone. I just needed some time to process it, and I didn't want to worry you more than you already are." Ollie explained.

"It's okay Ollie, I understand." And I did.

"Good. And, if you want to return to work at Comfort, well, it would be more comfortable with you here." Ollie shared seriously before smirking. "You see what I did there?"

Unable to help myself, I laughed. "You are…."

"Clever, charming, witty, what?"

"A dork. But those things, too." I teased.

"What do you say we clean this up and find some adventure?"

"Sounds good to me," Ollie answered.

"Angie?" I asked.

"I need to return to the station, but you two, go ahead. I'll see you at home for dinner."

Angie said her goodbyes and left Ollie and me to pack the food into a small cooler Keating kept in his office. I cleaned our glasses and returned them to their space behind the bar.

"Ready?"

"Yes," I answered. I dimmed the lights and exited the front door ahead of him. Ollie closed the door and ensured that it was locked. Once inside the jeep, Ollie turned to me.

"What are you thinking?"

"Just that Martin was right. This place is warm and comfortable."

My first day back at Comfort was a Tuesday. It was a bit surreal that on the week anniversary of becoming unemployed and learning my best friend was mixed up with the same crazy shit that connected with the closing of Top Floor, I was back to work. I traded my black dresses and heels for t's, jeans, and sneakers. I was returning to a familiar place, even though the last time I worked at Comfort was during my senior year of college. But, that last time, Keating was there. Returning to Comfort as an employee after all these years without him on my cursed day made the tension knots in my body set my stomach on fire.

Admittedly, when I had told Ollie and Angie I would work at and help Ollie run Comfort, I blurted it out without thinking. The time off from Top Floor taught me that I needed to feel useful. Hanging around the Coopers' home for one or two days was one thing, but long-term? No. Besides, my instincts told me this was the right choice for me to make. It wasn't often that I trusted my gut for positive things, but, this time, it seemed right.

That morning, I woke up nervous. It dawned on me that while I had many years working in restaurants, I didn't have any experience running them. When I confided my fears to Ollie and Angie that first morning, they both had assured me I would be okay.

"You think that traditionalist changed a damn thing? Everything is the same as when you graduated. Honestly, Kenzie, the place is frozen in time. It needs your spunk and your charm," Ollie assured me.

With hugs for luck and keys, I stepped out of Ollie's jeep and headed to the entrance. Ollie and I talked with Doug. We agreed to keep Comfort closed on weekdays for another week. When we did reopen, it would only be for Crestview students craving sustenance while they prepped for final exams. We would fully reopen to everyone over the summer.

That first day was thankfully quiet. I still had not yet heard back from Grayson, even though I left additional messages for him to call me. In my last message, I had told him about Martin. Martin has not contacted me since his surprise visit. I'm both okay and bothered by this. He revealed his identity and claimed he wanted to help Gray and that he wanted to be friends. Yet no follow-up calls? Was he waiting for me to make the next move? Yet, how would I know if the cell number I had for him even worked?

I needed to put all thoughts of Gray, Martin, and Grafton out of my head. I decided to dive into work at Comfort and didn't let myself come up for air. Doug and I completed an overall inventory of food and supplies so that we could place an order in time for reopening. I then evaluated every part of Comfort from floor to corner to ceiling.

Over the next few days, I vacuumed, scrubbed, and dusted. I noted that the artwork was old and could benefit from a change. The menus needed to be reprinted and replaced. And where the mugs, glassware, plates, and utensils were all fine, they too could benefit from an upgrade. Doug and I agreed that these aesthetic changes could wait until the summer.

Although I just started back, Ollie, Angie, and I had already developed a routine. One of them dropped me off in the morning, and Ollie always picked me up in the late afternoon. This system worked for now. I didn't need a car in Hoboken. But, if I planned to stay in Kettle Cove, I would need one. Admittedly, internally

I considered remaining in Kettle Cove but hadn't voiced these thoughts. I wasn't sure I was ready to hear myself admit out loud that I was ready for this change. That being here felt right. It took time, but I connected with the land when I was a student. In some ways, it was my friend. In a way, the tree behind the Thomas home was my confidant. If I said this out loud, that also meant I planned to leave Hoboken and Gray.

I wasn't ready to go there yet. First, Ollie and I planned to check on Keating's house later this afternoon. Ollie offered to take me home if I didn't want to go, but I assured him I wanted to go with him. Being at Comfort without Keating, knowing he was not about to enter the door or exit his office, was strange. At the same time, when I worked here as a college student, there were plenty of times that Keating was not in. The thought of entering his home, his personal sanctum, without him, felt wrong. Yet, I felt like I needed to do it. His disappearance from his life at Kettle Cove, from our lives, still didn't feel real. I needed confirmation that he wasn't just home because he was unwell or away on vacation.

Other than the discovery of Keating's car, the mailed retirement letter, and two pictures missing from his office, nothing else has turned up. Angie has not yet received the analysis of Keating's retirement letter. She told Ollie and me last night that she would follow up with the lab today.

When Keating was first reported as missing, his house was searched. Nothing was found disturbed. Ollie only noted that Keating's hiking backpack was missing from the hook in his hall closet. Angie confirmed that during the first sweep of his office, my graduation picture and the photograph Ollie took of Mt. Monadnock were present. That meant someone had been in there after Keating disappeared. Angie planned to meet us at Keating's so we could not only pick up the mail and water the plants but verify that nothing else was touched.

Angie received some information about Keating's office. Detective Deas and other Kettle Cove officers re-interviewed students and staff members. It seemed that a yet-to-be-named male entered the office space sometime after the cops left Wednesday. Since none of the locks were disturbed, the intruder must have had access to the building and Keating's office.

When Molly was re-interviewed, she recalled seeing a strange male around the building a few weeks prior to Keating's disappearance. Molly also noted that the keys to Keating's office were where she kept them, locked in her desk drawer. If a key was used to enter the office, it more than likely did not come from Molly. Still, Angie had the items bagged and ordered that the office spaces be re-printed. Angie stressed that even if the mystery man was discovered, he may not have anything to do with Keating, and where it was possible something could come from the prints, we shouldn't get our hopes up that it would lead to something more tangible regarding Keating's whereabouts.

I recalled the look on Ollie's face after discovering Keating's retirement letter. Ollie talked to Angie on the phone; something spooked him, something he didn't want to share with me. At least not then. I didn't press. Later they shared that Angie filled Ollie in on the news about Keating's car. I believed them, but the darkness in Ollie's eyes after the call told me there was something more. What that more was, I didn't know.

After my parent's death, I only returned to my house once. My case manager took me there to pick out some of the toys I wanted while she packed up my clothes. The images of my home were fuzzy, but I remembered how it felt. The house had been quiet. Still. Like it was frozen in time. My toys were still scattered about the family room. My bed was how I left it when the thunder and lightning woke me. A person could see a family had lived there, yet there was nothing but emptiness. The love and laughter that once filled those rooms were all dried up. Other than a couple of pictures of my parents, I had none of my mom's jewelry or dad's favorite shirt. If he had one. I don't even know what happened to any of their stuff.

I tried to take the box of Ring Dings, but when my social worker discovered the box was empty, she discarded it. The pictures I have help me remember what they looked like and what we looked like as a family. I appreciated these, and yet, it had hurt to look at them because, while I'm older, they aren't. I didn't have years of pictures tucked into a frame that documented our years as a family.

I anticipated feeling a similar silence when I entered Keating's place. A home that was once lived in was now a vacant space. The difference between Keating and my parents was I knew my parents couldn't return. Their items could be donated. Our house could be sold. Mom didn't need her makeup and Dad didn't need his shaving kit. What do we do with Keating's things? How long would the silence live in his home?

Ollie wasn't due to be at Comfort for another hour or so. I poured myself a large glass of freshly made iced chai with maple syrup. I then parked myself on one of the comfortable leather couches and pulled the coffee table closer to me. After I placed my glass down, I turned to the hill of paperwork. On my left were the bills recently paid, order forms were on the right, and, most importantly, the to-do list I developed over the last few days.

As hard as I tried, it was difficult to stop my mind from wandering to Keating. When my parents died, I felt a hole carved inside of me. They were gone before I had the chance to really know them. Most of the time, I'm unsure if my faint memories of their voices, laughter, and smiles could be trusted. Had I made up my mom's bubbly giggle and my dad's deep voice? Or did my brain record their sounds, which enabled me to replay them whenever needed?

Although I was too young to understand it, I learned how to live without my parents. As an adult, I accepted that death was part of life. Yet, when it came to Keating, I couldn't apply any wisdom. My parents didn't have a choice in how their life story ended. With Keating, how did we move forward without answers? How did we grieve?

Keating showed up at Comfort one night and then drove off without ever entering the building. When Angie, Detective Deas, and other officers interviewed staff and students, nothing unusual was reported. I knew his cell phone was still active since I messaged him first to say I was coming up for a visit and then that night, when Ollie and Angie told me he was missing. I assumed the detectives in charge also checked his phone records and bank accounts. Based on everything we knew, nothing nefarious happened.

It is not illegal to walk away from your life. Yet, this felt like a crime. Even though our relationship changed after I graduated, I have a hard time reconciling that the man I knew would knowingly vanish from his life with a big fuck you to everyone he left behind. Or maybe time changed him.

I heard through Ollie that some of Comfort's employees and his campus colleagues did not believe Keating purposefully dropped off the grid, but that something tragic had happened. Whether by accident, his own hand, or someone or something else's, was a detail we may never know. I didn't know how long a person had to be missing before they could legally be declared dead. Fuck, this whole situation pissed me the hell off. Damn Tuesdays and damn Dr. Keating Finn for adding to the misery of this awful day.

# CHAPTER SEVENTEEN

I f you continue to stare at this mound of paperwork, you'll fall in love."

I smiled at the sound of the Scot's voice. I looked up in time to see his bright, crooked smile cross his face. "I'm not that desperate."

He sat on the edge of the couch across from me. Ollie rested his forearms on his legs and folded his hands together. "You're doing fantastic, lass. Angie and I are so proud of you."

My eyes moistened as I looked at Ollie. "How is it possible to simultaneously miss and be furious with him?"

Ollied reached across the table. His fingers wrapped around the bend of my elbow. He encouraged me to stand with him and then pulled me into a hug. I rested my head directly against his chest and closed my eyes as tears silently cascaded down my cheeks. After a few moments, I felt the soft pressure of Ollie's lips on the top of my head before he loosened his hold on me.

"I feel it too, love."

I stepped out of his embrace and began to pick up the papers. "I keep replaying everything in my head. Did I miss something in our last conversation? Was there something I should have said differently? Should I have accepted his offer to visit sooner?"

"You know, if I ever tried to speak for Keating, he'd rip every beautiful lock out of my head."

I smiled when Ollie shook his head, which caused his grey-speckled hair to fly around. "Truth."

"But now, I think he'd be okay if I spoke for both of us. Keating loved you. He loved having you as an employee here, as an advisee, and later as a special person in his life."

"Did he? I mean, he was furious that I didn't remain in Kettle Cove after I graduated. He blamed Gray and told him so at my graduation party."

"I'm sorry he did that."

"It changed us, Ollie. I was so angry at Keating for how he treated Gray, for believing that I was incapable of making my own decisions about my life. Gray is my oldest friend. He's my family. For a long time, he was all I had. Yes, he really hurt me one time, but other than that, he's always been there. I never doubted that Gray would always be in my life."

"You didn't know if you could trust that we would remain part of your life after you graduated. At that time, you had thirteen years of history with Grayson compared to our four. You weren't ready to let go. I know, love. So did Angie, and so did my stubborn mate. Keating couldn't admit that he would miss you, Kenzie. We can replay all our conversations as many times as we want, but that will only lead to madness."

"You're right."

Ollie shrugged. "It happens, even though the Chief rarely admits it. Let's get out of here. Angie's meeting us at Keating's. We'll check the house and then plan dinner."

Ollie helped me return all the paperwork to the office. We then locked Comfort up and loaded it into his jeep. The drive to Keating's place was quiet, save for the soft hum of the Eagles that drifted through the speakers. The drive from Comfort to Keating's house was about twenty minutes. As we moved closer, as if he sensed my hesitation, Ollie quietly grabbed my hand and held it until he needed to make the final turn into the rocky dirt driveway that led to the post and beam home.

As much as I loved his place, the view of the mountain, and the serene environment, the setting was spooky! It's like a scene from *The X-Files* or a Stephen King novel. A person was alone in their car, driving down the road. The pavement switched to gravel. Thick, towering trees lined both sides of the road and blocked the natural light. It's dark and eerily quiet. The driver wanted to speed up but didn't want to blow a tire and risk being stranded, prey for anyone or anything jumping out at them. I shivered at the thought and focused on Ollie.

"Is this the first time you've been back?"

"Second. I came after the police finished their initial investigation of the house. I walked around with one of the officers to see if I noticed anything missing," Ollie answered. He shifted the car into the park and then turned off the engine. "Angie asked the Inicio Chief if he could have some of his guys occasionally pass by at different times of the day to check on things. Keating's neighbors watch the property, too."

"As much as I love it here, I always wondered how he could stay here alone and not be freaked out by how desolate it is."

"He liked the solitude. Trusted the elements. It's how he was raised."

"I guess. I know Keating put off the vibe that he was a happy single man, but now knowing he was once in love, I can't believe he'd just given up on finding it again. Do you believe he truly wanted to live the rest of his life alone? As much as my heart's been broken, I still hope to find..."

"Your Orion?"

"There has to be a close second to you out there," I shared jokingly.

"Well, it's hard to find perfect." Ollie smiled wildly.

"Seriously, he never wanted to find someone else to share his life with?"

"I don't know. He never talked about it. After Evan, he filled his life with his books, hiking, fishing, and helping his students."

"It's not the same."

"Your presence in his life filled some of the darkness that Evan left behind. You brought him happiness and gave this place," Ollie pointed to the cabin, "some much-needed light."

I turned my attention to the familiar dwelling in front of us. The sight of Keating's home both warmed and pained me. My eyes traveled over the weather worn lines and edges of the weathered brown house and wide front porch. I wanted to come with Ollie so I could directly face that Keating really wasn't here. But now that I was here, I felt my resolve fade. I couldn't face it. I didn't want to step inside and feel the still silence.

For the second time that day, Ollie again wrapped me up in a hug. It didn't matter that the gearshift jabbed into our abs. My head tucked into the corner of his neck and shoulder. I allowed myself this moment of grief before I squeezed my eyes shut and forced the water-works upstream. I fought to control my feelings and summoned the strength to go inside. I counted backward to ten and pulled myself together and out of Ollie's arms.

"You don't have to come in love. I can go in and check things out alone."

"No, I want to come. I only returned to my house once after my parents died to pack up some of my toys, clothes, and family photos. I wasn't allowed to wander around the rooms and find whatever closure I could find at five. As hard as it is, I feel like I need this."

"Okay."

While Ollie climbed out of the jeep, I pulled the window visor down and checked myself in the mirror. The site horrified me — bloodshot eyes, red-tipped nose, and whisps of hair fell out of my ponytail.

"I'm a hot mess," I whispered.

"You're beautiful."

Ollie exited the vehicle, which gave me time to gather myself. I grabbed a tissue from the door pocket and blew my nose. Using the mirror behind the window visor to fix my hair, one thought played through my mind.

*This is wrong. I shouldn't be here without you greeting me. Without the smell of beef and veggie burgers on the grill. You would mock Ollie for his influence on my lack of shoes and wardrobe. And Ollie would playfully reply that he couldn't help being the cooler guy. Then, you would wrap your arm around my shoulder and welcome me into your home. Into a home that you made me feel could also be mine after I graduated. This really fucking sucks, Keating.*

Once my feet hit the ground, I felt Ollie's warm hand squeeze my shoulder. As we approached the house, an unfamiliar vehicle carelessly parked off the side of the driveway caught my attention. It was slightly hidden behind Keating's shed.

I stopped. "Ollie, whose car is that?" I asked. I pointed out the candy red BMW.

Ollied followed my finger. "I don't know...." But something in his eyes told me he suspected.

"Ollie?"

"Wait here and call Angie."

I sensed Ollie planned to enter the house alone; I grabbed his hand and pulled him back. "No, Ollie, we wait for Angie."

Before Ollie could argue, a Kettle Cove police car pulled into the driveway and parked next to his jeep. Ollie pulled me to the safety of Angie and the officer with her.

"Ollie?" Angie questioned. "Something wrong?"

"We think someone's here."

"Who, sweetheart?" Angie prompted.

"I don't know. We walked toward the house when Kenzie spotted a red BMW. It's behind the shed over there."

Angie turned to the officer with her. "Radio the Inicio police for backup. I'm going to check things out."

"Angie…" Ollie called after her.

Ollie grabbed her hand. "I'll be fine, honey. Stay here with Kenzie."

From the corner of my eye, I saw Ollie nod. Angie glanced in my direction and reassured me with a smile before she followed her detective, who was now by the vacant BMW. After the officer recorded the license plate number in a notebook, he jogged back to the squad car. I assumed he called for backup and called the plates in.

"She'll be okay, Ollie," I whispered. I placed my hand on his forearm and gave it a gentle squeeze.

Ollie turned his attention back to the eerily silent house. Angie hadn't entered but opted to walk around the perimeter. The detective quietly climbed the front stairway. At first, he jiggled the front door handle. He then backed away and turned right. Along the way, the detective peeked in the windows around the porch that wound along the front and side of the house.

A chill crept under my skin. I rubbed my arms to warm them. I worriedly looked around and watched for someone or something to reveal itself. Yet, all that met me was unsettled silence. I needed to shake this feeling, so I focused on Ollie. I saw the worry for his wife etched in every feature of his face.

I envied their relationship and wanted what they had. When I watched them together, I thought of my relationship with Grayson. In high school, most believed we were together. We found the rumor comforting and let it stand. We once discussed taking our relationship to a different place. We even kissed to see how it felt. But it was over as quickly as it started when we realized that we weren't romantically attracted to each other.

Yet, if you believed in such things, fate brought us together. Gray, as cynical as he was about some things, believed that we shouldn't dwell on or question what happened in our lives and accepted that they did and moved on. I struggled with this. I cursed every God I could for taking my parents from me. How could any kindhearted, genuine being believe that making a child an orphan was a good thing?

Although Gray agreed that losing our parents dealt us a devastating hand, it was because of our loss that our paths crossed. If my parents raised me, where would I be now? Would I know how to look for my own Orion? Or was my life always meant to intersect with Gray, the Coopers, and Keating? Maybe Gray's right in that I shouldn't question it and just fully accept that they were.

As I looked at Keating's empty home, I realized I was at a crossroads. I had claimed a place of my own in Kettle Cove when I was a student. After I graduated, I didn't trust what I discovered here. So, I returned to Hoboken and to Gray. I didn't regret this choice. As I stood there, barefoot among the trees and the mountains, I was still connected to this place.

Keating didn't understand that I didn't feel obligated to return to Hoboken and Gray. Gray has only ever wanted me to be happy. My decision to leave Kettle Cove was about my personal insecurities. I didn't believe that I'd still have a place in the Coopers' and Keating's world once I graduated college. My life history to that point taught me that I could only trust what I knew. At the time, that was Gray. I returned to what was familiar and comfortable to me. I didn't think Keating had ever attempted to understand that. The fact that he never accepted Gray's role in my life hurt me.

Gray and I shared a deep friendship. We accepted and loved each other as equals. We couldn't give each other parental support and guidance because our life experiences had happened at the same time. Ollie and Angie taught me about the unconditional love and safety a child felt from parents. In the deepest fringes of my mind, this soft and beautiful feeling was familiar. I believed that when my parents passed they requested that I would meet people who would become my guardians. I had to believe that. If I didn't, the chilly silence of life would eat me alive.

So lost in my thoughts, I barely registered a shift in Ollie's demeanor. When I did, it was to move out of his way as he sprinted towards a man who had just jumped down Keating's front deck steps. The man nearly took a digger upon landing. While the stranger prevented himself from falling, he was clearly unprepared for Ollie. With the strength and agility of a linebacker, Ollie knocked the guy flat on his ass. When the man attempted to stand, Ollie pushed him down with his foot.

"Oof. Fuck. Get your foot off of me."

Shocked over what happened before me, I searched for words that would not come. Instead, I witnessed Ollie lower his frame, foot still firmly pressed onto the stranger's back. He then growled. "You, stay on the ground like the slug you are." Satisfied the man wasn't going anywhere, Ollie lifted his foot just as Angie appeared on the scene.

"Let him up, Ollie."

Ollie kept his eyes on the person but did as he was directed. I shifted my eyes from Ollie and watched the mystery man slowly push himself up, first to all fours and then to his feet. After he dusted the dirt from his khaki pants and hands, he stood fully and allowed me to take in his entire appearance.

With a stocky build, the man was about an inch shorter than Ollie's 5'9". His hair, a mixture of silver and brown, was cut short and neat. Dull grey eyes peered through his silver, thin, wire-rimmed glasses that were perched perfectly on his slender nose. His mint green polo was now partially untucked from his pressed khaki pants. He was sockless, feet adorned with dark brown loafers. This man did not strike me as someone who liked getting dirty.

Now surrounded by two police officers and me, the guy seemed to ignore us and focused solely on Ollie.

"Oliver, I wish I could say it's a pleasure to see you again, but I'd be lying." He then turned to Angie. "And the wife is here too. Chief Cooper, you look lovely, as always. I still cannot fathom the idea that you are married to this animal. In fact, I'd like to press charges for brutality."

Ollie snickered and then looked away. He clenched and unclenched his fist as he did. "For what? You were the one snooping around a house that doesn't belong to you," Ollie challenged.

"You tackled me and then trapped me on the ground like a dirty insect," the man rounded.

"That's an insult to bugs." Ollie retorted.

The man fully turned to Angie. "Chief Cooper, would you please do something about your husband before he attacks me again?"

"And what would you like us to do, sir?" The man next to Angie responded. "I observed a civilian stopping a potential thief from leaving the scene. But, if you want to file a report, I'm more than happy to have the Inicio officers, who are on their way, take your statement at their station."

"Who are you calling a thief, officer? I came by to visit a friend. When I saw he wasn't home, I turned and left," the man explained.

"You ran away when you spotted two police officers," Ollie yelled.

"Enough!" Angie's firm and controlled voice filled the woods and silenced all living creatures. In a matter of minutes, Angie took charge and demonstrated why she was the boss. She then pointed and waved to something or someone behind me. When I turned, I spotted two additional uniformed officers walking in our direction.

"Chief Cooper?"

"This man is Evan Chenk. He was spotted running down the front steps," Angie explained. "Could you please check the doors and windows on the house for any evidence of breaking in and entering? Detective Deas and I will wait here with Mr. Chenk," Angie instructed. She then handed one of the officers a set of keys. "These open the front door of the house. Please clear the inside as well."

The Inicio patrolman followed Angie's orders and approached the house. The man who was with Angie, I now know was Detective Deas. Ollie and Angie mentioned that he was the officer leading the search for Keating. He directed Mr. Chenk to the Inicio squad car, while Angie stayed with us.

"Please stay here. Once the house is cleared, we'll go inside with the officers and check everything." Angie softly stated.

"Why is Evan here?" Ollie grumbled.

I turned to the man now trapped between the squad car and Detective Deas. "That's Keating's ex?" I asked, but my question was lost in the building stand-off between Ollie and Angie.

"I don't know, sweetheart, but please, do not antagonize him."

"Antagonize him? We caught him running away." Ollie exclaimed.

"I know you have questions, Ollie, but we must remain calm and smart."

"You don't seem surprised to see him," Ollie leveled.

"Honey…"

The tone of this exchange was tense. To diffuse it, I spun toward Ollie. "Maybe Evan knows something. You told me he liked to taunt his closeness with Keating to you. Maybe that arrogance can help us."

I stood next to Ollie. I felt him back off slightly, though his eyes remained connected to Angie's. I pushed myself on my tippy toes and whispered in his ear. "For Keating. The rest you can deal with later."

Without a word, Ollie turned away and walked towards the edge of the property. Angie nodded at me with silent thanks before she joined her detective and Evan beside the squad car. I remained rooted to my spot between Ollie's jeep and the front steps of Keating's place. Ollie needed to cool off, and Angie made it clear to keep back. So, I waited and stared at the house in front of me.

My thoughts raced. In the time I've known Ollie, I've never seen him show such disgust for another person. And Angie didn't seem surprised to see Evan. It felt like Ollie believed that too. It seemed odd to me that Ollie had only just told me about Evan and Keating, and now, he's here. Was it out of the blue? When I told Ollie that maybe Evan knew something about Keating, I said it to calm him down. But maybe he did. When he ran down the steps, it didn't appear to be just a man who discovered nobody was home, but someone who didn't want to get caught.

A thick tension filled the air as we waited for the officers to be cleared. Behind me, I heard Evan's voice. He continued to insist that he didn't do anything wrong and couldn't be kept against his will.

But Angie and Detective Deas ignored him. I shut his voice out and hoped that we'd be given the clear to move soon.

A few tense moments later, the Inicio officers signaled to Angie. I watched as she joined the officers at the bottom of the steps. Ollie reappeared by my side. We remained silent as we watched the exchange in front of us. Angie then waved us over.

"Ollie, please go in with one of the officers and look around. They stated nothing appeared disturbed, but it would be helpful for you to double-check."

Ollie nodded and followed an officer inside.

"May I go in too?" I asked.

"Go ahead, sweetheart. I'll join you in a few minutes."

I followed the path of Ollie and one of the Inicio officers. Before I crossed through the door, I steeled myself for the noticeable silence.

A person's home revealed their thoughts, dreams, interests, hobbies, and their past. Here, I listened to Keating as he played acoustic guitar and learned the history behind the artifacts he purchased from the different places he had traveled to. He kept these treasures in his great room, which took up one-half of the space on the first floor. Off this room was his personal library. I had only entered that room once, but I remembered wood shelves lined two of the walls in that office. They housed Keating's neatly arranged collection of both fiction and non fiction books. On the third wall, he had a collage of family photos. The library was the most personalized room in the whole house.

All I knew about Keating's parents and brother was that they were deceased. He never talked about them or the rest of his family. I thought that odd, given the historical snapshots of the time they had spent together that covered this one wall. These photographs painted the picture of people who had laughed, smiled, and loved each other. Yet, Keating's silence on his family made me wonder if these photos were only the surface of his story. I once asked Ollie about them, but all he had shared was that he had only met Keating's brother, Jasper, once. Ollie thought that Keating and Jasper were close, but they drifted apart prior to Jasper's death. Keating had never disclosed the reason for his distance from his family and Ollie shared that he never asked.

I wondered if Keating had any extended family. If so, where were they? Did they know Keating was missing? When Ollie told me about Evan, I realized that I knew very little about Keating's personal life. As an advisor, he listened, encouraged, and helped his students discover the best of themselves. As a boss, he expected each employee to be reliable and to follow through on our delegated responsibilities. On a personal level, I knew Keating loved to hike, fish, cross-country ski, read, and travel. He preferred to explore the hidden treasures of the world.

Keating's beautiful home was nestled in the woods. He had hosted parties for his advisees here both in the fall and spring semesters. Keating hosted my graduation party here. It was a small gathering that included my co-workers from Comfort, Angie, Ollie, and some of my other professors at Crestview. When all the prying eyes had left, Gray joined the celebration. Memories filled me with joy, laughter, and love were created here. When Keating asked me to stay in Kettle Cove after I graduated, he offered me a room to stay in.

The room was located on the first floor, next to the library. I believe it was always a spare bedroom, but I had no idea if it was furnished. At the party, Keating brought me to the room and showed me the bed and dressers he purchased. I had already told him and the Coopers I planned to return to Hoboken, but he insisted I see it. I assumed he thought it would change my mind about leaving. When it didn't, while he hid his disappointment from me, he had taken it out on Gray. The party was supposed to be a happy occasion and it was. Until it wasn't. I'm sure that whatever passed through Keating's mind when he first opened that door to me, he hadn't thought that would be the last time I saw this room.

Now, as I approached the room, I wondered what was on the other side. Curious, I pushed the door open and flicked on the light. The site shocked me. It was spotless. The maple bed and matching furniture appeared to be free of dust. Everything was the same as when I last saw it, yet the smell was fresh. It was like the space was waiting for a guest. Maybe it still waited for me.

I stepped inside and ran my hand over the plaid quilt I once commented to Keating that I liked. Sometimes, quilts told a story – of places, family history, and interests. This one comforted me with its splash of blues, greens, grays, and yellows. The color pattern, seemingly random in design, made me feel safe, warm, and protected. If I said this to a shrink, I may be told that these feelings may have surfaced because of some deep-seated memory of my parents and our home. That may be true, but this quilt spoke to me.

The bed was on the back wall, centered, with two end tables positioned on each side. A picture frame on one of the tables caught my eye. Upon closer study, it was a photograph of Gray I had never seen before. I could tell by the cut of his hair that it was recent. Confused, I flipped the frame over, opened the fasteners, and pulled the picture out. I checked for a date and location on the back, but there were none. I flipped it over and studied the photo for other details but didn't recognize any of it. It looked like the inside of a restaurant, but not one that I knew.

The longer I stared at the photo, the more anxious I was to talk to Grayson. Gray's smile told me it was a posed picture. His natural smile formed on his face whenever he was truly happy and excited about something. In those moments, Gray didn't have his hair done and dressed the way he wanted to. This picture was clearly designed to attract an audience.

I tried to recall whether Gray ever mentioned seeing Keating in recent months. But I came up empty. Gray always told me when he encountered someone we knew. I'd think if it was Keating, he wouldn't keep that from me.

So, if Gray saw Keating…

"Kenzie?"

I looked up to see Ollie at the door.

"What do you have there?"

"It's a recent picture of Gray. I'm not sure where it was taken, but it was recent based on how Gray looks."

"Is there a date on the back?"

"No."

I put the frame back together sans the picture and placed it on the table's flat surface. I then stood, crossed to Ollie, and showed him the picture.

"Why would there be a recent picture of Gray here?" Ollie asked.

"I don't know. Gray traveled a lot these last few months. Their paths must have crossed at one point. But neither of them mentioned it to me," I answered. With one last look at the photo, I slid it into my back pocket. "Where's Angie?"

"I believe she went back outside."

"That guy, Evan, why would he be here? Could he know something about Keating?"

"I don't know. To my knowledge, Keating was not in touch with him. Or at least, that is what he led me to believe."

After we exited the bedroom, we heard voices coming from the direction of the kitchen. The kitchen was down the hall from this bedroom. As we walked toward the sounds, we were greeted by Angie.

"Evan is in the kitchen with Detective Deas and one of the Inicio cops. They are questioning him."

"Here and not the station?" Ollie asked.

"It appears that Evan never tried to enter the house. He doesn't have keys on him or any kind of device to break in. He ran when he heard Hunter and me on the porch. We are informally questioning him now and will then take him to the station."

"Did you know Evan's been slinking around again?" Ollie's voice hardened.

"Ollie…"

"Did you?"

I knew then that whatever Ollie was upset about earlier was still brewing.

"Can Ollie and I be present when you question him?" I asked Angie.

After the words left my mouth, I worried that I again overstepped. Although I did not know the whole story, Evan's reappearance stirred something in the usually chill Ollie I didn't recognize. I hoped that if we could be present when Evan was questioned, it would answer the questions Ollie had. And it gave me a chance to learn for myself, who had such a hold on Keating that it splintered his friendship with Ollie at one point.

"You can join us, but please let the officers conduct the questioning," Angie agreed. "Understood?"

I placed my hand on Ollie's shoulder and nodded. Without another word, he entered the kitchen ahead of Angie and me. Once I crossed through the door, my eyes immediately settled on Evan. He didn't move from his space when he saw us enter. I couldn't place my finger on it, but there was something in Evan's eyes and demeanor that made my skin crawl.

The last time I felt an immediate dislike and distrust of another human was when Todd started at Top Floor.

"And you, you're Kenzie, right? One of Keating's former students. You were one of his favorites." Evan answered, his eyes fixated on me.

His stare felt cold and analytical. I swallowed the throw-up burp that just filled my mouth and didn't respond.

"I've seen your graduation photo. I thought you were beautiful then, but now I know you you're even prettier in person," Evan continued.

The comment struck me as odd. My graduation photo? I glanced in Angie's direction and caught the look on her face. Her subtle nod told me we had the same thought. We both turned our attention back to Evan. His fake smile was all I needed to know. My work life, especially the last ten years at Top Floor, taught me how to read people. Maybe it was a harsh judgment, but the way he sat comfortably behind Keating's solid oak kitchen table, I wondered why Keating became involved with this slickster who wasn't so slick.

Angie then took over. She formally introduced Detective Deas and the other officers in the room. Det. Deas stood behind Evan when Ollie and I first entered the kitchen, now crossed to me, and graciously pulled out a chair for me to sit. He then returned to his spot by the counter. Angie sat to my left while Ollie stood behind me. I didn't need to look at him to know that his posture was more than likely rigid, arms crossed in front of his chest.

I needed a distraction from the discomfort, so I looked around the room. In the last few conversations Keating and I had, he talked about redecorating the kitchen. Despite all his plans, it was clear that Keating never got around to that project. The same smooth maple cabinets lined two of the four walls. His neat woodblock countertop sat between the top and bottom rows, completely clear of clutter. The only adornments on the counter were a butcher block full of knives and the blown glass utensil holder that I made him. Full glass doors along the upper cabinets revealed a colorful array of beverage glasses, coffee mugs, and dishware. The table and chairs we made from recycled barn wood. Truthfully, I didn't know why Keating wanted to update the kitchen. It was beautiful.

My eyes returned to Evan. As much as I hoped that he might know where Keating was, I also hoped that Keating was far away from this man. I wondered if I should join Ollie at the counter and show my solidarity with him. Ultimately, I stayed put. Evan continued to study me. He made me so uncomfortable that I couldn't keep my mouth shut.

"Why are you here?" I asked.

"Direct. No wonder Keating liked you," Evan answered.

"Yet, I cannot figure out why he liked you."

Evan's fake smile widened even more. "Tough, too. I like that."

Angie then stepped in. "That's enough. Evan, we opted to question you here instead of the Inicio station in good faith. I'll ask you to address me and the officers here only. Or we will move this conversation elsewhere."

The arrogance painted on Evan's face faded when he detected Angie's tone. She was not one to mess around with. He seemed to recognize that.

"Mr. Chenk," Det. Deas started, "Why don't you tell us why you were snooping around the property?"

"Snooping?" Evan answered, his voice tinged with surprise. "I wasn't."

Ollie jumped in, "Don't start with the bullshit games."

Ollie's voice dropped to an octave that was laced with anger and distrust. All eyes shifted to Evan, who also appeared rattled by Ollie's tone.

A silent standoff took root between Ollie and Evan. Neither man moved nor showed a willingness to break first. My eyes shifted to Detective Deas and Angie. Would one step in before a fistfight erupted?

"Ollie!" Angie shouted. "We'll handle the questions."

Evan smiled at the firm scolding Ollie had just received from his wife. Evan then looked at Det. Deas. "Like I told you before, I knocked on the door, and when Keating didn't respond, I wandered to the back."

"And you automatically thought to try the windows to see if they were unlocked?" One of the Inicio officers stated. "Sounds like attempted break and entering to me."

"Breaking and entering? Are you crazy? I would never..." Evan defended. Only to stop when Angie again took control of the conversation.

"Mr. Chenk, let me put it plainly to you. You can either explain what you are doing on private property here or at the Inicio police station." Angie began. She then looked at the Inicio officer, "Are you in agreement, Trooper Richie?"

"You got it, Chief. Let's go, sir." Trooper Richie said. He then motioned for Evan to stand, only to stop when Evan spoke.

"No, wait a minute, Chief Cooper, officers, we don't need to make an official case out of this," he said. Evan's voice was calm and collected.

Angie nodded at both officers. "We're waiting."

"I was in the area and thought I'd stop by to say hello. Keating and I met for lunch recently. I was just following up." Evan started.

"Where did you meet?" Angie asked.

"At Chappy's Brew."

"When was this?" Angie asked.

"On Wednesday. In fact, it was the third or fourth time we met up," he stated, as his eyes shifted from Angie to Ollie. Clearly, he wanted a reaction. He got one. Ollie exited the room through the back door without a word. I desperately wanted to knock the smirk off of Evan's face. Although I planned to follow Ollie out, I had a feeling Angie was about to deliver the blow that did just that.

"I see your husband is still a bit sour about my presence in Keating's life," Evan chided.

"Actually, I think it's a mixture of relief and disappointment," Angie countered. "Keating went missing Tuesday night, so either you're lying, or maybe you had something to do with his disappearance. Which is it?" Angie stated. Her strength of posture demonstrated that she wasn't to be messed with.

Like a snake, Evan slithered farther into his seat. "I…"

Angie put her hand up and stopped Evan from continuing. "Before you answer that question, you can also explain why your fingerprints were on a letter mailed to the college that was allegedly typed by Keating? Why you've been around campus, and why were your fingerprints found inside his office?"

This revelation startled me. Shocked, I snapped my eyes to Angie's, but she lasered in on a clearly rattled Evan. How would he have a letter Keating wrote? Unless Keating was with him? Or did Evan really know about his whereabouts? But if he did, Keating would have told him how to get into the house, wouldn't he? Or was this guy twisted enough that he would play sick mind games on Keating's loved ones? Ollie's hasty exit made me think the latter was probably true.

"I'm not going to say anything more without my lawyer," Evan stated. He leaned back in his chair and crossed his arms in front of his chest.

The little I knew about the law, I learned from television shows. Based on that, once someone asked for an attorney, the police could no longer question them. Angie directed the Inicio's officers to take Evan to their station. She then directed Det. Deas to check in again with Keating's neighbors about Evan's presence on the property.

The patrolmen signaled Evan to stand. One moved to cuff Evan when Angie silently brushed that off. I didn't know why, but I trusted she had a reason. Before Evan moved away from the table, he returned his attention to me.

"You must be very special," he commented. When I didn't respond, Evan continued, "For Keating to keep a picture of you in his office. He never kept personal items at work. He believed that his work and personal life should never mix."

"Then, what does it say about you?" I asked.

"What do you mean, dear?" Evan asked.

I shrugged, "Keating didn't keep any pictures of you here. In fact, he never uttered your name to me. I guess if I'm special, you meant nothing."

I nodded at Angie and left the room before Evan could respond.

I exited through the back screen door and walked down the deck steps into the yard. I looked for Ollie but didn't see him. I figured he needed privacy to cool down, so I walked toward Keating's hammock, which was suspended between two large maple trees. The hammock was one of Keating's prized treasures from a trip to Peru. He had traveled there while in graduate school. While there, he hiked to Machu Picchu, volunteered with an organization that helped maintain the site and studied the Incan culture. He traveled to Peru at least twice in the time that I knew him. The farthest place I ever traveled was from New Jersey to New Hampshire. When I asked Keating what about Peru made him continually return, he shared that it was ineffable.

I carefully climbed into the hammock perfectly positioned with a view of Mt. Monadnock. I then recalled a humorous conversation Keating and I once had while talking about this hand-woven swinging chair.

*"So, you spent an entire semester in Peru without speaking Spanish?"* I questioned.

*"That's right."*

*"How is that possible?"*

*"Easy. My travel companions were fluent in the language. I stuck to them."*

The professor, who always expected his students to be prepared, hadn't followed his own rules. When I called him out on that little fact, he laughed and swore that he tried to learn the language but couldn't "hear" the words. I didn't quite understand what that meant, but knew if I used some excuse like that at work, he would have canned my ass.

I closed my eyes, inhaled the fresh air, and willed the nerves in my neck and back to settle. The tense interaction with Evan left me both physically and emotionally spent. Earlier, I confided to Ollie that I found Evan's appearance suspicious and hoped that maybe he could shed light on Keating's whereabouts. Based on the short exchange, I didn't know what to think. If Keating wanted my graduation picture and the photo of Mt. Monadnock, wouldn't he have taken it with him before he left? And if he had forgotten, would he really have asked Evan to enter his office and take them? Would he send him to his house without a means to enter? I found all of that hard to believe.

Then again, why would Evan's fingerprints be on Keating's retirement letter and his office? How did he know about me? I came after Evan had already vacated Keating's life. Would Keating really keep the decision to retire from Ollie? Or was Evan that devious and manipulative that he would purposefully toy with the loved ones of a man he once claimed to care for?

I understood that when you meet someone for the first time and fall for them, you become blind to the various facets of their personality. I only just heard part of Keating's history with Evan, but if I trusted Ollie's judgment of what happened, then I couldn't wrap my head around Keating having any further involvement with this man. Then again, I didn't understand how Keating would just vanish from his life without a word to anyone. I had to admit that anything was possible at this point.

I had no doubt that Det. Deas would continue to question Evan once his lawyer showed up. With the evidence they had against him, maybe he'd feel threatened enough that he'd tell them if and what he knew. And, if Evan was just playing mind games, then the mystery of Keating's disappearance would continue.

What felt like hours later, but was more than likely a few minutes, a gentle breeze woke me. I didn't realize that I had drifted off. When I opened my eyes, I spotted the opening to a path Keating liked to walk. It wound through the woods and ended at a small stream. He had constructed a little bench to place at the end of the path. I wondered if it was still there.

"How are you doing lass?"

I sat up and shifted over so that Ollie could sit. Once his larger frame joined me, the hammock swung lightly. He folded his hands and rested them on top of his stomach.

"I can't unwrap this. Assuming nothing happened to him, why would Keating just disappear without a word to you, to me, to anyone," I questioned.

I looked away from the path and shut down flashes of Keating and the time we spent outside. I instead focused on my and Ollie's feet. My toes just about kissed the blades of grass where his feet rested comfortably on the ground. I kicked my sneakers off. After wearing restricting heels at Top Floor night after night, I found this redis-covered freedom relaxing.

Ollie dropped his head back on the hammock and closed his eyes to the sun for a moment. I thought he was about to drift off like I did. Or maybe he needed the quiet to process his thoughts. If my mind was swimming, I could only imagine what Ollie's was doing.

After a few moments of silence, Ollie spoke. "You were right about Evan. I never liked or trusted him, but for a time, he made Keating happy, and that's all that mattered. The night we learned he was an alcoholic was at an off-campus holiday party. Keating and Evan had a row before the start of the festivities. Whatever they argued about made Keating particularly edgy. He was so miserable that I didn't want to be around him. Evan never left the bar."

"Was he drunk?"

"He was three sheets to the wind. I kept my distance from Evan. I had nothing to say to him. Angie, my beautiful lass, checked on him a few times. Keating had tucked himself into a corner and refused to socialize with anyone. From his vantage point, he witnessed Angie doing this and asked her about it. Although she downplayed what he said to her, the look on her face told me otherwise. That set me off. I confronted Keating and called him out for his boorish behavior. I told him to take it out on me if he was angry, but not on my wife."

"What did he say?"

"He mumbled that maybe we shouldn't be best mates anymore and then left."

"Ollie…"

"Later, as Angie and I were leaving, we spied Evan in the parking lot with another guy. He, ah, was rather distracted and didn't see us. I wanted to pummel him to the ground, but Angie's calmer head prevailed."

"What happened?" I asked.

"They were pulled over for a burned-out headlight. Angie had the bartender pull Evan's keys, so the other guy drove. We didn't know who he was, but neither of us thought he was in the bar with Evan."

"DUI?"

"Yes…I read about the arrest in the morning paper. Evan came to Keating's office the following week, but he wasn't there. I then confronted Evan with all that Angie and I had witnessed." Ollie explained.

"And what did the jackass say?"

"Evan mistakenly believed Angie told me what happened and threatened her badge. I shoved the newspaper article in his face and told him to tell Keating the truth. The coward refused and thought he called our bluff."

"I guess the nitwit didn't realize that the Chief doesn't do that?" I smirked.

"He's too cocky to notice. At least, then he was."

"Is that what caused the rift between you?"

"Aye. My pigheaded mate accused us, me, of interfering in his relationship. Keating believed I was jealous of his relationship with Evan. In retrospect, I knew he believed us and knew we wouldn't purposefully hurt him. I believe Evan eventually came clean; Keating told him he would give him another chance if Evan entered treatment. They stayed together for another six months or so."

"And what about you and Keating?"

"He apologized but didn't spend time with us. He refused or canceled whenever we tried to make plans with him. Eventually, I stopped asking."

"Evan eventually left him?" I asked.

Ollie nodded yes. "Keating came to the house a few days later. Angie and I were visiting her parents when it happened. We returned to a broken Keating camped out on our back deck. I've never seen him that despondent before. He loved him. So much it blinded him to who Evan was. After that, he couldn't or wouldn't open his heart to anyone else."

"That makes me sad."

Ollie wrapped one arm around me. "Me too, lass."

Ollie and I remained on the hammock for a while. We soaked in what the peace of the woods and the view of the mountains offered. Where I couldn't guess Ollie's thoughts, I'm sure, in part, they mirrored mine. Seeing Keating and Ollie together and the bond they shared, I couldn't imagine anyone stepping between them. And yet, it happened. In retrospect, some of their disagreements, the jibes Keating made towards Ollie, ones he didn't think anyone else would pick up on, now made sense.

"What do you say we head out? Stop at Pizza + for dinner?"

"Let's jet," I agreed.

Ollie planted his feet on the ground, which enabled me to stand up first. We returned to the house together to find only Angie at the kitchen table.

"I thought you were headed to the station too?" I asked.

"I am. I wanted to talk with you both first," Angie explained.

I realized Ollie left the kitchen before he heard what Angie learned. "I didn't tell him, Angie," I started.

Ollie looked between us, "Tell me what?"

Angie recapped what she shared earlier. "Evan's fingerprints were discovered on Keating's retirement letter. He was spotted around Angelo just before and after Keating disappeared. Deas just called and informed me that none of the neighbors were home. He'll come back later to question them. He believes Evan may have known nobody would be around and then was surprised when you both showed up. He panicked and ran," Angie explained.

"Do we know who actually typed the letter?" Ollie asked.

"No. Keating's home computer was packed up from our initial search. I'm working on obtaining access to his school one."

"Now what?" I asked.

"Questioning will continue at the station with Evan's attorney present. We'll sort through what he knows and doesn't know there. And then, a decision will be made on what happens next," Angie explained. She then turned to Ollie, "I'd like you to return to campus with me. I want to search his classroom and, more specifically, his lab again."

"Keating didn't keep anything personal there," Ollie started. "But we can check everything out."

I scrunched my eyes in thought. I wasn't sure if I was remembering correctly, but thought I'd toss my thoughts out there. "Didn't Keating keep a few of his personal relics in the lab? I remembered classmates talked about them."

"That's right, lass, he did. There is an itemized list of what's in the lab room in both his office and in the lab itself," Ollie stated.

I looked at Angie, "You think something more will turn up?" I asked, afraid of her response.

"I don't know, honey, but we want to be thorough," Angie answered.

"You didn't seem surprised to see Evan," Ollie asked. "Did you know he was back?"

"I knew Keating had heard from him," Angie started, only to be interrupted by Ollie.

"And you didn't tell me?"

Unphased, Angie calmly continued, "I didn't know from Keating. I was at the station when he came in and inquired about restraining orders. When he spotted me, he admitted that Evan had been in touch but he had not responded."

"So, the bit about them meeting for lunch prior to this week?" I asked.

"I believe it to be a lie, but I have officers checking. Now, are you ready to go?" Angie asked.

"Sure." Ollie agreed before he looked at me. "Love?"

"What would Keating see in a person who was capable of something like this?" I asked. I knew I only met Evan under complicated circumstances, but seriously, what did Keating see in him?

"Evan is a chameleon. He changes his colors to suit his needs. I don't think Keating ever imagined, regardless of how things ended with them, that Evan was this calculating," Angie explained, "But, yes, unfortunately, my job puts me in contact with people that are this dangerous."

My eyes drifted between Angie and Ollie. I sensed he and Angie needed some time together. I planned to tell them I'd remain at the house and, when finished, they could return and pick me up. But before I could respond, my phone buzzed. I pulled it from my pocket. The text was from Gray.

**shitstorm erupted. where r u?**
**Keating's.**
**wait there**

"Kenzie?" Angie moved closer to me. "You okay?"

I looked up from my phone and caught the concerned look that passed between Ollie and Angie. "Um…yeah. That was Gray. He's on his way here. I'll get a ride back to your house with him."

"Do you want us to wait with you until he comes?" Angie asked.

Ollie nodded in agreement. "We can, lass, if it would make you more comfortable."

As much as I wasn't comfortable being in Keating's home alone, I knew it would only be for a short time. Gray was on his way. Whatever was happening with him sounded urgent. Being alone in Keating's cabin among the trees seemed like the perfect setting for us.

# CHAPTER TWENTY

Angie hugged me tight. When she released her grip, Ollie stood beside her.

"You sure about this love?"

"Not at all," I laughed nervously, "but I must do this. I'll be okay, Ollie."

"And you'll call if you're not?"

"Promise. And Gray will be here soon."

"Okay. We'll see you home.

"You will. Now, go." I ordered as I lightly pushed them both away.

I followed them to the front door and closed it once they were both outside. I had no idea how far Gray was from here or if he even knew Keating's address. My phone was still in my hand, so I shot another text to Gray with Keating's address. He then buzzed back that he was about fifteen minutes out.

I shoved my phone back into my jeans pocket. My feet were frozen to the spot while my eyes scanned the front entryway and hall. Both were lined with bare log walls and simple light fixtures. The whole house was post and beam. It was brightened and warmed by large windows and comfortable furniture but lacked personality. Sure, there were relics from different digs Keating went on, paintings, and beautiful light fixtures, but the house was too neat. It showed the hobbies of the man who lived there, but it didn't tell the story of the man himself.

I once asked Keating why he photographed the places he visited if he never planned to print and frame them or share them with others? Keating had shrugged my question off without a response. I sketched a picture of Machu Picchu for his birthday one year and framed it in a small, wooden frame. Keating had thanked me for it and seemed touched by the gesture, but every time I visited, I casually scanned the room and never saw it. I wondered if he secretly hated it and just didn't want to hurt my feelings.

Angie and Ollie knew I was upset, and that Keating's actions reminded me of Steve and Ruth's dismissal of the gift basket I gave them. They tried to make me feel better, which I appreciated, but their words were just that. If Keating didn't like my gift, he should have said so. As an adult, wouldn't he understand that an honest rejection hurt less than a passive-aggressive one?

"What the fuck, Keating? You aren't supposed to leave people like this! You weren't…" I yelled. My voice bounced off the still walls. A burst of adrenaline shot through me and propelled my legs toward the liquor cabinet in the corner of Keating's great room. My head and heart were maxed out from today's revelations. I needed to prepare myself for whatever bomb Gray was about to drop. I knew Keating kept a cellarette stocked with Ollie and Angie's favorite whiskey.

I opened the bottle and poured the amber, smokey liquid into a crystal tumbler. With that task completed, I turned and faced the empty room. The cold, darkened fireplace made the room feel like a morgue. I felt my pulse tick and heard the blood rush in and out like the ocean tides in my ears. I raised my glass and toasted the empty room without a second thought. I drained the liquid, savored the burn as it trickled down my throat, and sighed as the waves of relaxation soothed my tightened muscles.

Relaxed, I willed my legs to move. They carried me from the great room to Keating's library. It was his private sanctuary, the space that shared more about the personal life of Dr. Keating Finn. I always wondered why, of all the space in Keating's home, this one was off-limits to everyone, even Ollie. Whenever I came to the house, the door was generally shut. It made me wonder what secrets lived in this space. Was there something in here that would offer some clue as to his whereabouts?

Seeing this door open felt odd. For a minute, I peered inside from the hall. I was afraid to enter, worried that a voice from the distance would yell at me for entering a space that was off-limits. I'd welcome that scolding if it meant that Keating had returned. It was this thought that dared me to enter the room. I paused for a moment and listened for a voice that didn't come.

With one hand, I trailed my fingers over the rugged outline of the books that filled his bookshelves and then dropped it and felt the smooth planes of his desk. I spotted the faint outline of where his laptop sat in the corner. I stood behind his high-back chair and looked around the room. I didn't know what I was looking for and yet, I naively hoped something would pop out at me. A hidden note that was overlooked or another missing photo or book. But nothing seemed out of place. All I was met with was deafening unanswered questions.

"You selfish bastard! How could you do this to us?" I chucked the crystal glass across the room. As I watched the splintering shards of crystal scatter across his neatly woven rug, I felt a fresh sense of release followed by a huge letdown. As quickly as the burst of adrenaline came through me, it left me depleted. I crumbled to the floor and gasped for air as tears of every emotion overwhelmed me. And then, before I knew it, two long, perfectly sculpted arms pulled me into his chest. My skin warmed as the sensations of the voice I knew anywhere whispered in my ear.

"I got you, Kenzie. Shh…I got you." Gray whispered while he tightened his hold on me.

I focused on the steady beat of his heart. His presence warmed and steadied me. Slowly, my breathing synced with his. After he kissed my cheek, Gray gently asked, "Did something happen with Keating?"

But I only burrowed farther into his comfort, the familiarity of his arms, strength, smell, and tickle from his perfectly stubbled facial hair.

"Kenz? What is it?"

Slowly, I found my voice. "He's missing Gray. We don't know where he is or if he's okay." I pulled away from him, wiped the tears from my eyes, and then pushed myself up from the floor. Gray followed me to the broken-in, brown leather couch positioned directly in front of the window that overlooked the backyard. The view of the surrounding woods and the slope of the rising mountains was stunning.

I ran my hand down his worried face. "I'm okay, Gray. Really. I am just overwhelmed by it all, you know? I don't know what to do with all of my conflicting feelings."

"I'm sorry I didn't call you back. Tell me what happened," Gray prompted.

We settled farther into the couch while I filled him in on everything I knew about Keating's disappearance.

"Ollie and I came to the house to check on things. While here, we found someone on the property. We stopped him while waiting for Angie."

"And you and Ollie thought it wise to do this in the middle of the woods at the end of a dirt road?"

I rolled my eyes. "Relax drama boy."

"Relax? We're surrounded by trees. The closest neighbor is, I don't even know where. I feel like we're trapped in one of those 'Cabin in the Woods' thriller movies. Yet, you and the Scot just, I don't know, stop a potentially armed thief?"

I turned so I could completely face him. "Grayson. Angie and one of her detectives were here. And the person wasn't a robber, but…" shit, how did I explain Evan when I just learned about him? "The guy, Evan, was looking for Keating, or so he said."

I then relayed the story about Evan. When I finished, I patiently waited for his response. I expected him to look surprised at this news, but instead I was taken aback by the look on his face. He was concentrating, like he was trying to remember something. "What?"

Gray slid back onto the couch and rested his head on the back cushion. "Nothing, it's just. I saw Keating at a restaurant in Atlanta with some guy."

I straightened up. "What?"

With his head on the back of the couch, Gray focused on something outside the window as if it would help him. "I don't know the dude's name, but I saw what he looked like. Keating seemed pretty upset that he was there and asked him more than once to stay away."

I then remembered the picture. I shifted my legs and pulled it from my pocket. "Was this picture taken at that restaurant in Atlanta?"

Gray took the picture from me and studied it. "Yeah. I was there for a meeting when Sam decided to take some publicity shots. They weren't for sale, though. Where did you get this?"

I took it back from him. "I found it framed in the room Keating had set up for me here. I didn't know you saw him."

"We didn't talk. There was nothing to tell you."

"Did you see or hear anything more?"

"Nothing other than, when Keating returned from the men's room, at least, I think that's where he went, the guy followed him back to the table. I then…"

"What?"

"I asked one of my security guards to remove the guy from the restaurant."

"You, what?" I asked, surprised.

"The dude was loud and distracting. And he was not only upsetting Keating, but other patrons. The management at the place did nothing about it, so I did." Gray stared at me. "Why do you look surprised?"

"I just, you helped Keating after all that he said to you. You didn't owe him that."

Gray leaned towards me. "It was the right thing to do. I guess Keating never mentioned he saw me?"

"No," I said. "Do you remember what the guy with Keating looked like?"

"Not offhand. If you had a picture, I probably could."

"You should tell Angie. Evan, he creeped me out. I don't think Angie believes he had anything to do with Keating's disappearance, but it's worth checking into."

"You think he is lying?" Gray asked.

"The fuck if I know. But I didn't trust one word from his slimy mouth."

"Where is the beautiful chief of police anyway?"

"Ollie and Angie went back to campus. She wanted to look around Keating's classroom and lab space again. I received your text just as they left and opted to stay here."

Gray nodded in the direction of the great room. "Should I lock up the tumblers?"

"It was only one. And I drained the liquid first."

"Good thing. Are you up for another?"

"Why?" I studied Gray. Although not as disheveled as the last time I saw him, he still looked like he was in rough shape. Heavy bags under his eyes told me he hadn't slept. His mussed-up hair, rumpled clothes, and tattered sneakers he never wore outside his apartment spoke volumes. "Gray?"

"Let's get that drink." Gray attempted to stand, but I pulled him back down.

He fell back onto the couch, legs sprawled out in front of him. Gray pressed the backs of his hands into his eyes as if to ward off an oncoming headache. So caught up in my pain, I momentarily forgot why I remained at the house. Gray asked me to wait for him – a shitstorm erupted. Admittedly, in the week I'd been in Kettle Cove, other than my conversation with Martin, I stayed away from the news. I didn't want to hear Gray's name tied into the Grafton mess or see any of his detractors trying to smear his reputation.

When he was ready, Gray sat up and faced me. "Sam tracked me down in Connecticut. I hadn't told her I took a meeting there because I knew she'd hate it."

"Go on."

"It was for a stage role. One of the writers from *Justice* wrote a play. She asked if I was interested in participating in the reading because she knew I wanted to return to theatre."

"And?"

"I liked the script, but we both agreed that I wasn't right for the role. Anyway, I am not sure how Sam found me, but she wanted to talk about what happened to Grafton. His arrest, all that I knew."

"What did you say?"

"I told her I walked out of Top Floor the moment I spotted Grafton. I flat out asked her why she went against my explicit wishes."

"What do you mean?"

"When I agreed to keep my mouth shut about Grafton, I did so on the condition that I would never be part of a film he was involved with. I didn't care what it was. She promised me. Even put it in writing. And then, she fucking blindsided me. She knew what she was doing, Kenzie. I needed space from her to rein my rage in. The moment I saw Grafton, I wanted to drop-kick her on her overinflated, greedy ass."

I squeezed his shoulder. "What did you tell her?"

"After a tense and impolite exchange of words, I fired her."

Shocked, "You? Wait, you canned her?" I asked.

"I sure as shit did."

"And she went without a fight? Just like that?" It was difficult for me to believe that Sam would just walk away.

"She didn't have a fucking leg to stand on. Christ, you've had Sam pegged from the start. I truly thought she cared about me and, ah...." He screamed and threw his glass across the room. "You were right, and I didn't, couldn't hear it. I'm sorry, Kenzie, for all the bullshit from me and her you've put up with over the years."

While I appreciated Gray's apology, I felt it wasn't warranted. "Regardless of her motives, Sam saw your talent in high school. She encouraged and supported you. Personal feelings aside, I am thankful for that." I stopped when I spotted the look on Grayson's face. He didn't believe me.

I crossed my arms loosely. "I mean it." I paused as his face softened. "And I'm sorry. I know it feels like you had the wind knocked out of you when you realize how wrong you are about a person. The feeling, it sucks."

If Gray caught on to the fact that while we were talking about Sam, the statement also applied to my doubts about Keating, he didn't say. "I don't understand how she thought she'd get away with this," I wondered out loud.

"I've let her get away with a lot, Kenzie, things I never told you about. She assumed that I'd let this transgression go too. She was wrong."

"Have you talked to the cops yet?" I asked as I thought about the conversation I had with Martin. "I know they're trying to reach you."

"How do you know that?"

"Do you remember Martin, the head waiter I worked with at Top Floor? I don't think you ever met, but I've talked about him." Gray nodded yes. "Well, he's an undercover P.I."

Gray sprung up. "Wait, he's, what? He's not a real waiter?"

"He showed up here and outed himself to me. I don't know all the details, but I'm guessing that whatever evidence he gathered while working at Top Floor was enough to take down Marjorie, Todd, and Grafton."

Gray crinkled his brow, confused, "And he just came here to tell you that? Does this guy think you are part of this mess?"

"No, Martin assured me that I'm cleared."

"Then what did he want?"

"Unofficially, he had more questions." I started.

"What does that mean? He's not a cop. Why's he talking to you?"

I shrugged. "Martin knows the detective in charge of the Grafton case." I tightened my arms across my chest. "He told me you still hadn't talked to the detective." I answered Gray's question before he asked it. "Yes, Martin knows about us. I guess to prep for his role at Top Floor, he ran background checks on all of the employees."

"What else?" Gray asked.

"He had questions about what I knew about your meeting with Grafton and the girls I saw Grafton with." I shared.

"He asked about the women?"

"Yeah, why? Did something else happen?"

Gray stood and walked one lap around the room. He then stopped in the doorway. "The story that's currently trending is that Grafton is being charged with trafficking girls."

"He...so the girls were not just actresses?"

"Well, he may have told them they were auditioning for a movie role, but, no, they weren't the ones he planned to cast," Gray explained.

"Todd and Marjorie?" All of this was hard to swallow when I first heard about Grafton, but now? I wondered just what Jed's suspicions were regarding his wife and manager. What motivated him to hire a private investigator?

"I don't know about them," Gray answered. "Other than being arrested and the news of Top Floor shutting its doors, the focus is all on Grafton."

"Sam?" I knew I couldn't sugarcoat what I said next about Martin's visit. "Martin had questions about Sam, too. I didn't say much, and he respected that. Martin knows you walked out on the Grafton meeting, Gray. It's time to stop hiding and talk to the police. I realize if Sam is tangled in this mess, it places you in a difficult position, but now, you need to protect yourself."

Whatever light was left in Gray's eyes faded. "I think Grafton had something over her. I don't know what, but whatever it was, it's why she set up this meeting. She thought she could use me as a bargaining chip to save herself," he paused, "Ready for another drink now? Because I sure as shit am," Gray asked.

"Make it a double," I uttered at the disappearing form of Grey's body.

Gray and I finished our drinks in silence. I suspected Gray was focused on Sam, Grafton, and his career. As for me, hell, my mind was so scrambled, I didn't know what thoughts to focus on, place on pause, or toss. Whatever we were thinking, neither of us revealed it. Instead, I took our dirty glasses to the kitchen while Gray swept the shards from the floor. Once everything was cleaned, Gray helped me loop around the house to ensure that all windows were shut and secured. I remembered Ollie had already locked the back door when we returned to the house. When I realized I didn't have house keys, I turned the deadbolt on the front door, so Gray and I exited through the garage. I directed Gray to go out. I hit the button on the wall and then ducked under the door as it closed.

Once outside, we walked towards Gray's rental car. "What happens with his house? The cars?" Gray asked.

"From what Angie told me, nothing. Everything just sits until he's found, or a legal decision is made to declare him dead."

"I'm sorry you're going through this. I know how much Keating means to you. Is there anything that I can do?"

"Just be here," I said.

"Always," Gray assured.

We climbed into the car. It was an old Subaru. He turned around to avoid backing out of the driveway. Once we were on the dirt road, I asked, "Are you able to stay the night?"

"Yeah, I have to leave early tomorrow, though."

I turned the radio on low to fill the car with something other than our breathing. I also needed Gray to relax. I worried that the death grip he had on the wheel would make him pass out. Some snarky comments came to mind, but given the day both of us had, I let them pass. Instead, when we talked, our conversation stayed light and casual.

When we arrived at the Cooper's, I directed Gray to park off to the side, so if Ollie and Angie were not yet back, they could pull their cars into the garage. I walked towards the front door and thought Gray was right behind me. When I unlocked the door and stepped in, I spotted half of Gray's body tucked into the back seat. When he emerged, he had a bouquet of flowers in one hand and a familiar bag in the other.

"Is that?"

"If you think it is all the best goodies from Fiore's, then yes."

I cheered like a giddy schoolgirl. I grabbed the food from him when he was within my reach and then moved inside.

"How do you know the food is for you and not the flowers?" he asked me.

"That's a serious question?" I loved every bit of food from this family-owned gem. Leaving Fiore's behind is undoubtedly one of the downsides if I moved to Kettle Cove. The thought caught me by surprise. I've only been here a week and have already decided to stay. I suppose when I said I'd work at Comfort, I had already decided to move here. I just hadn't voiced it out loud to anyone.

"I don't know where there's a vase," I told Gray. "Do they need water?"

"They should be okay for a bit longer."

"Angie will love them."

"And the hippie?"

"He'll huff and roll his eyes at his wife's obvious crush on you."

Gray laughed as he placed the bag of food on the table. He then stood in front of the back sliding door. "It's so quiet here."

"It's peaceful."

I felt Gray's eyes on me as I pulled out dinner plates. Usually, this didn't bother me, but this time, it felt different.

"What?" I finally asked. I returned the intensity of his stare.

But all he did was shrug.

"Don't shrug at me. Spit it out."

"Or you will keep asking?"

"And staring." I declared. I crossed my arms and settled in for what could be a frustratingly drawn-out battle.

"Relax, Kenzie, it's nothing serious. It's just, this air, being with the Coopers, you just seem lighter…" An arch of my eyebrow suggested he clarify his last statement. "I mean, you're not weighed down by living in a place I know you're not crazy about."

"You say that like I hate living in Hoboken. I don't…" I trailed off when I saw his bullshit detector flash across his handsome features.

"You forget I've seen you with these people in this area before. I mean, look at you, your hair, face, all look, relaxed. You're wearing jeans, a loose t-shirt, and no shoes."

"I know it's not your style," I commented.

"No, but it's yours. I know that while at one time, you enjoyed working at Top Floor, it was never your style," he paused, "I know I flubbed this, but what I'm trying to say is you look happy. Beautiful."

"And I never looked beautiful before?" I sassed.

"Now you're just being a smart-ass."

I smiled at him while I carried the plates to the kitchen table. I pointed to the cabinet where Angie kept the glasses for Gray to grab. Together, we set the table.

"So, what's next for you?" I asked.

"I'm going to take care of things and then lay low. News of my split with Sam is out. I have managers and agents calling. I'll check them out, see what my friend comes back with on other plays. I may look into a casting service and audition for some shows."

"Good."

"What about you?"

"I'm working at Comfort…" But before I could finish, we were interrupted by Ollie and Angie.

"Grayson!" Ollie exclaimed. He discarded his shoes and then crossed to Gray and hugged him. "It's good to see you, lad."

"You too." Grayson smiled as he returned his hug warmly. Gray is not an openly affectionate person with most people. When he became a character for a role, you would never think it. But, with Ollie, Gray has always been comfortable. Ollie sensed when a hug was needed and then offered it freely. When they first met, Ollie welcomed and accepted Gray without hesitation. He always pulled Gray aside and talked to him about, I don't even know what. But, whatever the topic, Gray was always relaxed. Happy. I even saw them play soccer, footie, as Ollie called it, in their backyard one day.

Gray came to Kettle Cove to see me, but when I saw how fiercely he hugged Ollie, I believed he also needed to see them. I knew Gray wouldn't open up to them in the same way I did, but it made me happy to see him accept their support. Gray commented that I looked happy here; I'd argue that, at this moment, he did, too.

As a kid, I wanted the adults in my life to appreciate and accept me. At work, I never missed a shift unless illness forced me to stay home. I was always on time and filled in for my co-workers. In high school, although I was not the best student, I always followed the rules. I thought if I behaved and did everything asked of me, one of the adults in my life would've recognized it. I believe the adults who were in my life before Ollie, Angie, and Keating cared about me, but they never took the time to listen and teach me. They never told me I was beautiful or that I had done a decent job. As an adult, I realized that I actively sought attention, and that led to disappointment. I maintained my work ethic because I realized that it made me feel good about myself.

Gray was different. He was more closed off, disenchanted with the need for human connection. One of the reasons he loved acting was because, as a character, he stepped into their life and world. His characters experienced human connections and the heartbreak that sometimes went with it. Once the role ended, Gray shed the role and walked away without any of the baggage.

"Hey, where's my hug? I know he's more handsome than me… but?" Angie teased.

Gray pulled away from Ollie and picked up the flowers from the counter. He bent down on one knee in front of Angie and handed the bouquet to her. "My beautiful lady. When are you leaving this guy for me?"

Angie giggled as she took the flowers from Gray. After he straightened up, Gray scooped Angie into a hug and playfully spun her around.

I looked at Ollie and laughed at the previously predicted huff and eye roll. After Grayson put Angie down, she looked him over. "You are staying the night."

He saluted Angie. "Yes, ma'am."

"Good."

Angie pulled a vase out from a closet, filled it with water, and placed the flowers inside. She saw the platter of mozzarella, both smoked and regular, pepperoni, salami, prosciutto, and olives on the table. "You brought dinner, too?"

"Of course. Anything for my best girl," Gray teased.

Angie turned to me and smiled, "Is he always this charming?"

"When around you, yes. He is a pain in my ass the rest of the time." I answered.

Grayson came over to me and wrapped his arm around my shoulders. "You love every bit of me."

"That's debatable," I sassed. "Now, let's eat."

Ollie and I poured vanilla seltzer water for everyone. After we dug in, Ollie and Angie shared that they found nothing out of the ordinary in Keating's class or the lab.

"What happened with Evan?" I asked.

"His lawyer met us at the station. Ultimately, we let him go."

I looked at Ollie. The frown on his face reflected his opinion on the decision.

"I'm not happy either," Angie continued. "The feeling was we didn't have enough to hold him. But Evan knows not to leave town."

"What about the letter?" I asked. I filled Gray in on the retirement letter.

"Still under investigation," Angie answered. "Look, I'm sorry that I can't share more. As of now, Evan and his activities are under investigation."

"Was he drunk?" I asked.

"No, but he knows that if he steps on Keating's property, near the campus, or any of us, his ass will be in jail."

"This Evan sounds like he's a bit of a stalker," Grayson commented. "Do you have a picture of him?"

"Why?" Ollie asked.

Grayson told them what he shared with me earlier. He saw Keating in an argument with a man at a restaurant in Atlanta some time back. The man was eventually removed from the establishment. Gray left out the part that he was the one who had the stranger removed.

"I'm sure we have a picture of him and Keating somewhere. I will check after dinner." Angie stated.

"Wait, I don't know why we didn't think of this before," I exclaimed. I pulled my phone out and conducted a quick search for Evan Kemp. An article came up about a business deal he was involved in.

"Kenzie, I'm impressed." Gray kidded.

"Shut up." I lamely responded. "Is this the guy you saw?" Grayson took my phone and examined the picture.

"Yeah, I think that's him. The guy at the restaurant didn't have glasses on, but it looks like the same dude. I may have some candid pics the photographer took with me and some fans. I can see if Keating is anywhere in the background."

"That would be great, thanks, Grayson," Angie said.

I thought about Evan. Was he obsessed with Keating? To the point that he would harm him, or was he just playing a game to mess with Keating's loved ones? But why? Why would someone do that? And why now, after all of these years of no contact?

"What is it, Kenzie?" Angie asked.

"I just, I don't understand Evan's role here. From what you," I pointed to Ollie, "shared with me, Keating hadn't been in touch with Evan for years. Now, he's just back?

I mean, did he know Keating was missing, and now, he's just playing a game? But for what reason? Or is he involved because Keating wanted him to be?" Of all my thoughts, I hated the last one the most.

Ollie, Gray, and I all turned our attention to Angie. I felt bad voicing my questions, but none of this made sense. I needed to find something to help put it all into perspective so I could then figure out how to begin dealing with it.

"You should be a detective," Angie smiled at me. "I'm sorry, honey. I know this is difficult and that you, us, we want and need answers. Just, please trust me when I say that just because Evan was released doesn't mean he's free and clear."

I didn't quite know what Angie meant by that, but gauging the look on her face, I trusted Angie. I believed that she and her detectives would not rest until they figured Evan's game out. I wished there was something more that I could do. But there was nothing. I didn't know Evan. All I could do was wait and hope.

Our conversation then steered away from Keating and Evan. We also avoided any talk that involved Gray and Grafton. Instead, Ollie suggested we sit outside around the firepit. When he learned that Gray had never sat around a fire, he decided that needed to change. Despite Gray's pleas that he was tired and had an early morning, he easily followed Ollie outside to gather wood. Angie and I cleaned up dinner and prepared four mugs of hot chocolate.

By the time we joined them outside, the weariness that was in Gray's eyes was replaced with childlike wonder as he watched the fire sparks dance in the air. The cool spring air, coupled with our sugary drinks, relaxed us. We shared embarrassing stories with each other and permitted ourselves to have fun. And we did. We laughed until our stomachs hurt, grateful for the much needed levity.

We all turned in sometime after eleven p.m. I knew I slept soundly, and I believed Gray did, too. He stayed on the pull-out sofa in the loft. He left before I woke up but tucked a note under my house keys. His message assured me he'd be back after he took care of some important matters and that everything would work out.

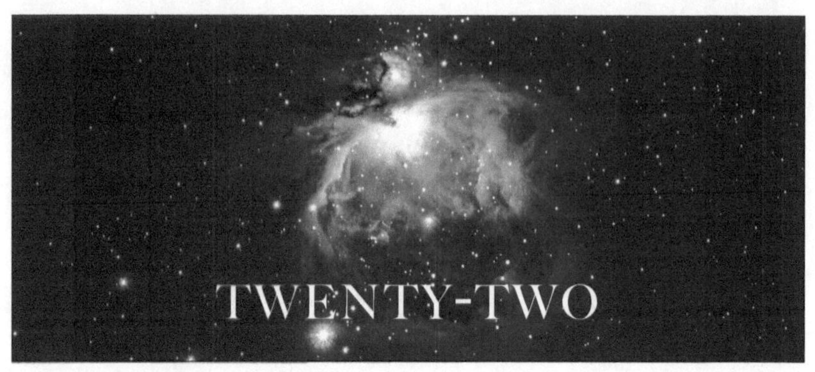



Foggy skies, wind, and the threat of thunderstorms loomed in the area two days after Gray left. It seemed strange that we had all just sat around and laughed around the light of the firepit on a night when the stars could be seen for miles. For those few hours, all the ugliness that currently surrounded our lives faded into the background. Now, the lighter sky was replaced with a dull stillness that chilled your flesh. It's like all mighty Zeus was tired of the stars and sparks, so he hit a reset button that left us with cold and empty air. It made me feel like something wicked was headed our way.

The moments of laughter we shared that night only muted the reality of our lives. Keating was still missing. The mess surrounding Gray was active. Two men that I loved were in situations that I didn't understand. Ollie and Angie stressed that I shouldn't torture myself by replaying my past conversations with Keating in the hopes that I'd find an explanation. Logically and rationally, I knew that. And yet, who just up and leaves their life without a word? There had to be a reason. A reason that none of us, including Ollie, the man closest to Keating, could place their finger on. And that made me wonder, did any of us really know Keating at all? He showed us what we needed to see, and when he didn't need that anymore, he left.

I don't know. I wanted to help Ollie and Angie unravel this mystery and yet, there was nothing I could really do other than work at Comfort. And Gray, other than showing him my unconditional love and support, there wasn't much more that I could do for him.

I knew he was optimistic about the next part of his life, that he had a plan, but I couldn't help but worry. I hoped that the business he referenced in his goodbye note meant he planned to speak with the detective. I felt like if that was out of the way, his path forward would be free to pursue the avenue he wanted to travel.

I was relieved when Gray shared that he fired Sam. I sensed that he did not share everything with me regarding Sam and her involvement with Grafton. I knew, in part, he wanted to protect me, and legally, the less I knew, the better. I hoped that whatever mess Sam was in wouldn't taint Gray and that, with time, he'd be free to pursue the projects he wanted. That he'd find a manager or agent who truly listened to him and represented his best interests.

I made my bed and pulled out clothes for the day. My planned attire, a pair of worn jeans, a t-shirt, and flannel, reminded me of Gray's compliment. He told me I was beautiful. He's told me that before, but this time, it felt different. Although we didn't know it as children, our lives were on a collision course built from situations out of our control. Now, I have this odd sense that we're on the precipice of our friendship changing direction. This isn't like when I went away to college, when our lives were still connected, and the miles between us didn't matter.

This time, when I packed my bags and left Hoboken, I sensed I wouldn't return. Although Gray didn't say the specific words, he knew it too. Maybe that was why he left without a verbal goodbye. Gray didn't flinch when I told him about working at Comfort, and although we didn't have the chance to finish that conversation, I wondered if he purposefully avoided it. There would come a time when we'd need to have an honest, heart-to-heart about where our lives were headed, but we weren't there yet.

So, instead of dwelling on a future conversation Gray and I needed to have, I showered, changed, and headed over to the main house. There, I found a lazy Ollie curled up in the corner of the couch. A green patched flannel blanket covered his legs, and his hands were curled around an oversized green mug of something steamy.

"Morning love." Ollie smiled.

"Morning. Angie already gone?"

"She left with Gray."

"No classes today?" I asked.

"Canceled them. The kids need time to prep for their exams. I'll head in later for some office hours. What are your plans for the day?"

"We have a food delivery today. I want to organize that so we're ready to open for the students." I paused, "Is there more of that?" I asked as I pointed to Ollie's mug.

"Yes, I made a fresh pot of coffee earlier."

I left Ollie on the couch and headed to the kitchen. After I fixed my own cup of java, I rejoined him in the family room. He now sat up, his tattered ash-gray sweatpants from Crestview in full view. The blanket was neatly draped over the back cushion. I snuggled into the opposite corner of the couch, pulled my legs up, and sat with them crisscrossed.

"You and Gray had a good chat yesterday while at Keating's?"

"He fired Sam.

Ollie arched an eyebrow in surprise. "Wow. Did you expect that?"

"I hoped he would, but no, I didn't think it would happen. Gray said Sam went without a fight. Gray believed Sam genuinely cared for him and his success. I believe she did, but somewhere along the way, greed overpowered her role as his mentor and, in many ways, a parent. Gray doesn't trust many people, and although he'll not admit it to me, he is heartbroken."

"You think Sam will try to take advantage of that?"

"I don't know. Remember when Martin was here? He asked me about Sam." I recalled. Ollie nodded and acknowledged that he remembered. "If she is somehow tied into this mess with Grafton, then I'd think she has more important issues to manage than worrying about getting Gray back as a client."

"She also, by some extension, involved you in this mess," Ollie pointed out. "And if she tries to make a play to return, I believe Gray will shut that right down because of his love for you."

Truthfully, I didn't think about that. Sam never approved of my friendship with Gray. Not while we were in high school and certainly not after. I'm not sure why. I always supported Gray's interest in acting. I worked with him, sometimes at the detriment of my own grades, to make sure he could always participate in theatre. Yet, she had this irrational hatred for me. I know I picked up on it and shoved it back at her.

"I hope so." I looked around the room, focused on the dark skies outside. After a sip of my coffee, I looked back at Ollie. "You've always liked Gray, haven't you?"

"I have. He reminds me of my younger self. I don't know what it is to grow up without parents, but for a lot of my childhood, I felt like I was on my own. I had an okay relationship with my mom and a not so great one with my dad. I have an older brother who was in college when I entered high school. We weren't close as kids, and now, other than exchanging the occasional phone call and greeting card, I haven't seen him in years."

"Until you met Angie?"

"I loved her from the moment I saw her and knew she would be my wife one day. She, of course, thought I was a nutter. We became good friends first and that taught me to open up and to trust in other people."

"I guess that's why..."

"Why what, love?"

"Why, as much as I love and trust in Keating, there were times when I felt more at ease with you and Angie. You accepted Gray as part of my life, understood his importance to me." I paused to gather my thoughts and forced myself to look Ollie in the eye when I finally voiced what I knew to be true. "You said before that Keating may not have liked why I returned to Hoboken after graduation, but he understood it."

"I believe he did."

"When I told Keating I was not staying, he had assured me that he understood. Even after he showed me how he decorated the room at his house. And then, when I wasn't looking, he let loose on Gray."

"What do you mean?"

"At my graduation party, I overheard them talking. Gray thanked Keating for everything he did for me," I explained.

"What did the professor say?"

"He told Grayson that if that were true, he should have insisted that I remain here. Move to a place I was happy." I wiped away the tears that quietly rolled down my face, "Instead of showing Gray the compassion he'd always shown me, he made him feel like a controlling, self-serving ass."

"Kenzie…"

"He was out of line, Ollie. I know it's hard to understand the bond that Gray and I have. When were kids, nobody understood how lost and alone we felt. They didn't understand that Gray was first abandoned by his mom and then by his dad. He lived with grand-parents, who sure, raised him, but seemed to hate him for reasons he didn't understand," I continued.

I drank more of my coffee. I looked out the window and at the darkened skies. The sight mirrored the pain that built in my chest. "In some ways, it was worse for Gray than me. My parents didn't leave me intentionally. I didn't and will never understand why my parents were taken from me, but Gray had to live with the fact that his parents just didn't want him. Yet, even with that, he's a good person and made something of his life."

I placed my mug on the table and pulled my legs up to my chest. I wrapped my arms around them. "We were two kids who found each other. Our friendship has always been equal. And for Keating to disregard all of that? In that moment, he wasn't any better than the assholes who raised us."

"Oh, darling. I am so sorry. I didn't know. That's why, when you visited, you distanced yourself from Keating."

"I didn't want to see him. His accusations really cut Gray and that in turn, hurt me. Gray tried to play it off, but I saw right through it."

Ollie's face broke into a half smile. "I believe I'm married to someone who can see through a lie before the words exit your mouth. Did you confront the professor?"

"I sure as hell did. Gray left my graduation party uncomfortable and unwelcome. If Keating really knew me, then he knew that I made my own decisions about my life, but he didn't budge. I didn't speak to him for over a year after I graduated. It wasn't until Keating contacted Gray and apologized that the wall between us crumbled. Slowly, we began speaking again and I let him back into my life. We weren't the same, but, I believed, where he never fully understood or approved of what Gray and I had, he accepted it."

Ollie sat back. "I'm sorry, love. I wish I understood why Keating did that, but, I don't."

"It's not on you, Ollie. I just thought Keating had more respect for me. Maybe I was wrong about that. I feel like I've been wrong about a lot when it comes to him. Hell, I don't even know anymore."

"Kenzie …"

"No, it's alright. I need to finish getting ready and get to Comfort."

"Do you need a ride? I can drop you," Ollie offered.

"No, I'm good. Doug is picking me up on his way in. Are you and Angie still coming for dinner? I'm making my special mac 'n' cheese."

"Of course. I'll come right after work. Angie will be there closer to six."

"I'll see you both later then."

"Later."

I brought my empty coffee mug to the kitchen and added it to the dishwasher. I felt bad leaving with my last comments about

Keating lingering in the air, but I needed time and space to let churn over my feelings. I understood Ollie's perspective. What's difficult is I never heard it from the man himself, and I more than likely never would. It's just one more situation that I needed to put to rest.

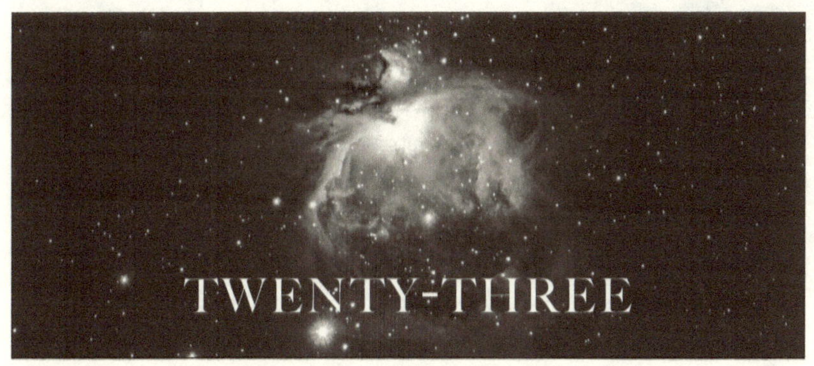


By mid-afternoon, the skies were black, but not one raindrop had fallen to the ground. For that, I was grateful. I knew thunderstorms were part of nature. I understood that rain was critical to the well-being of the earth. But today, I just needed the weather to remain calm so all our pre-opening tasks at Comfort proceeded without complication.

The food delivery came around eleven thirty. Along with Doug, Robin, and Kelly, two of the waitresses, and Tia came to work. After Doug and I checked the food order, he assisted Tia with putting away the perishables. Tia then shooed him away and banned the rest of us from entering the kitchen for about three hours. She was armed with new recipes and didn't want to be distracted.

I designed new menus comprised of different comfort foods. These items included beef and veggie chili, fried pickles, mozzarella sticks, mac'n'cheese, grilled cheese with additional add-ons, healthy yet comforting salads, and the burrito of the week. We also offered different baked goods, that included cookies, scones, muffins, brownies, and breads. The drink menu included both hot and iced tea, coffee, lattes, natural juices, flavored water, lemonade, Arnold Palmers, and, of course, blueberry lemonade. We also planned to offer different seasonal drinks and food items.

The menus were placed on each table. Doug and Kelly hung up an old chalkboard I discovered in the storage room just off the side of the entrance. We used warm colored chalk to write the week's specials for everyone to see. Playlists were created to mix music from different decades, all designed to set a calm, warm, and welcoming atmosphere.

Usually, the tables were bare, but for the week of finals, we used white butcher paper as tablecloths. We then placed a mixture of crayons and colored pencils in mason jars on the table for students to use. Comfort would be open for lunch and dinner starting tomorrow and through the five days of finals. We would open at 10 a.m. and close at 9:00 p.m.

By early evening, the energy in Comfort was electric. The bar sparkled. The glasses were clean and crisp, and the silverware was rolled into cotton napkins, ready to go. All kinds of sweet goodies were baked; their delicious smells wafted through the crevices of the swinging kitchen doors as they cooled. Tia then prepped food items for opening. For this, she enlisted my help, which was good because it enabled me to both help her and prepare for my dinner for Ollie and Angie.

I knew Doug and Tia, as they were at Comfort when I was a student. Robin and Kelly came after I graduated, but I met them when I visited the area. While we finished preparations for Comfort's reopening, it struck me how we all clicked as a team. It was like we'd worked together for years. This feeling boosted my confidence and believed that I could do this. That my years of working at restaurants paid off.

The group left around five. I had enough time to put my mac n cheese in the oven and set a table not covered in butcher paper. While I pulled glasses from the bar, I heard the door open. I didn't look up, until I heard a voice.

"The place looks great."

My eyes met familiar brown ones. "Martin? You're back?"

Martin moved closer to the bar. "Are you working here?" He asked, and completely ignored my question.

Unwilling to respond until he did, I remained silent. I hoped my stare-down would do the trick. It always worked on Ollie and Gray, and sometimes on Angie, but Martin? I didn't know. I never needed to try it.

Martin seemed to get it. He put his hands up and said, "I'm not here to question you, I promise. I'm officially on vacation and am helping my mom out at her house."

"I worked here as a college student. It is owned by someone close to me, and right now, he's not around to take care of it. And I am unemployed, so…."

Martin looked around and soaked everything in. "This place, you feel at home here?"

"Why do you ask?"

Martin shoved his hands in his pockets and shrugged his shoulders. "In all the time we worked together, you rocked at your job, but you never seemed relaxed. Here, you just, I don't know, it seems like you feel at ease, happy."

"I used to feel that way about Top Floor before Jed and Marjorie hired Todd. But, here, there is something magical about this place that, well, it's hard to describe."

"Are you going to stay?"

"Thinking about it." It came out before I could stop it. I suppose it was easier to admit my plan to Martin because it didn't impact him the way it would Gray, Angie and Ollie.

"My mom would love it here. I should take her here before heading back."

"Is she in Kettle Cove?"

"Casper. She retired from the post office and moved there. Now, she works part-time in a bookstore."

"Sounds like a good job."

"She enjoys it," Martin answered.

I watched Martin continue to take in the atmosphere. It made me wonder about something else. "How did you know I was here?"

Martin finally stopped his tour of Comfort and took a seat at the bar. "I was driving by and took a chance."

"Okay." Again, it's plausible, but something still caused me to pause. Martin's job is over. He has no reason to talk to me or see me. So, why is he here? "And you wanted to see me."

"I hoped to."

"Why?"

Martin folded his hands in front of him and rested them on the bar, "I told you the last time I was here, I wanted us to be friends. I stopped by in the hopes that you'd be here so we could talk about that."

I didn't know what to say. Truthfully, between Keating, Gray, and working here, I hadn't thought about Martin or considered his admission that he hoped we could be friends.

"Look, Kenzie, I know you are apprehensive about talking to me. I understand that you are unsure if you can trust me. I get it."

"I've been around Angie enough to know that you were on a job. I cannot hold that against you." I plainly stated.

"But…"

"But your assignment is over. I don't know if our friendship was part of your job or something real. And right now, I have a lot on my plate that takes a ton of energy."

Martin nodded, as if he understood. "In my job, I see the ugliest and cruelest parts of humanity. It makes it hard to trust. I know we only worked together and didn't hang out, but I liked you from the start. I just want you to know that. I'll get out of your hair as I see you have company coming, but please text or call me when you're ready to talk."

Without thinking, I yelled, "Wait." Martin stopped and turned towards me.

"Can I ask you something?"

He closed the distance between us. "Sure."

I took a breath. "The man who co-owns this place, he, he's missing. The cops are investigating, but I don't know, there's not much to go on. I don't know if this is the kind of work you do, but, if it is, what are the chances of finding someone?"

"The little experience I have with missing people, the outcomes have never been positive. I'm sorry."

Martin didn't say anything I hadn't already figured out on my own. I just thought maybe...

"Do you want me to look into it?" Martin offered. "It wouldn't be a problem. When my mom moved here, I obtained my PI license. I started my work as PI here before going to New York City. I've maintained my license."

The offer surprised me. "What? No, I just, it's hard, dealing with the disappearance of a loved one with no clue as to why."

"I can only imagine," Martin affirmed. "You are close with this man?"

"Keating was my advisor in college, and I worked for him here. He, well, yes, means a lot to me."

Martin nodded. "My offer stands Kenzie, I have the time and can do a little digging."

I moved away from Martin. "I, thank you for the offer, but there's no way I could pay for it. Besides, Angie and her detectives are still investigating. I hope something will come up."

"I hope so too. But, if you change your mind, you know where to reach me."

Without another word, Martin turned and left as quietly as he entered. I remained rooted to the spot. His offer to investigate Keating's disappearance surprised me. I wanted to believe the offer was made in good faith, but I didn't know if I could trust his motives.

"That was your undercover investigator? Martin Benson, right?"

I looked up and saw Ollie enter from the back. "Yeah."

"Everything all right?"

"Fine. He's visiting his mom. She lives in Casper. He was driving by and stopped to see if I was in. He again told me he hoped we could be friends."

"Is that all?" Ollie asked with a smile.

"Ollie."

"What? He's a good-looking chap, you're a beautiful person. He came here looking for you."

"Are you a matchmaker now?" I asked.

"I'm just saying maybe he's not a bad guy."

"It's strange."

Ollie rubbed his beard as if he was thinking up a plan. "We can have the chief check him out."

"Wouldn't that be an abuse of power?" I asked.

"Not if you feel like he's creepy."

"I don't know how I feel about him. I thought he was one person for months, only to learn he wasn't. I know he didn't do anything purposefully, but it's still, I don't know. I just cannot deal with Martin right now." I meant it. I didn't have the energy to figure out Martin's motives.

We walked to the office. I entered and walked to the desk to file some paperwork, while Ollie stopped just inside the door and leaned against the door frame.

"How were your office hours?"

"Fine. A few students passed through with questions about, you know, the whole exam."

"The ones who thought you'd reveal the specifics?"

"I'm done, Kenzie. I spoke with my supervisor today. She received my resignation letter, and although it did not come as a surprise, she's upset."

"Does Angie know?"

Ollie closed his eyes in response.

"You can't put off telling the chief," I reminded him.

"I'm not..." he started, only to stop in his tracks with one look from me.

"No?"

My question was met with silence. I filed a couple of items before I turned back to him. "Ollie, she's going to understand your reasons for leaving."

Ollie left his space in the door and slowly walked around Keating's office. He ran his hand along the woodwork, across the aging photographs, and finally stopped in front of his vintage oak desk. "You know, I helped him design this office. We built these shelves and that desk together."

"I didn't know that," I said. I admired their handy work. "I thought Keating was a bit of a klutz when using any kind of work tools?"

"He was. So, it was mostly me doing the work. Keating handed me the tools when I asked for them," Ollie recalled fondly. He then looked at me, "I thought I'd join you here. If you'll have me."

"Your part owner, Ollie. You don't need my permission to be here."

"When Keating and I won this place, I never thought about running it. Keating was more into that role than me. Plus, I had a wife and kid, he didn't. I worked when I needed to, but it never felt like a full-time gig for me. Now, I feel like this is right. Not in my office on the hill, but here with you, keeping the spirit alive for all those seeking comfort," Ollie explained.

"Are you sure?"

"You're not the only one who feels stuck, love. Angie heard Keating and me discussing retirement a year ago or so. We were both burnt out. She supported me, but I also think she believed Keating's decision influenced mine."

"That's why you haven't told her," I confirmed.

Ollie nodded. "Maybe she was partially right then, but now, I know it's time for me to move on. And it's not because of my best mate."

"So, tell her that. And Ollie, I'd love to help you run Comfort. 'Cause honestly? being here alone? scares the shit out of me."

"We can't have that," Ollie stated.

"Nope."

Our hands clasped each other's in a firm handshake to formalize the deal. Ollie then grabbed my free hand to pull me around the desk. Once we met on the side, he pulled me in for a hug. The moment my face connected with the warmth of his shoulder, the tears pooling in the corners of my eyes released a steady stream down my face.

It wasn't until Ollie tightened his grip on me that I realized he was crying, too. After a moment, we mutually pulled out of our embrace, as we wiped our tears away.

Once composed, I looked at Ollie. "But let's get one thing straight."

"What's that?"

"Just because we're partners doesn't mean I'll go fishing you."

"We'll see about that," Ollie winked.

"Honestly, how does Angie put up with you?"

Ollie pointed to himself with his prized smile. "Look at me. I'm hot and adorable."

We left the office with our arms wrapped around each other. As we walked towards our table, I asked Ollie a question that had been battering around in my mind.

"How long do you think we keep looking, hoping we'll figure out what happened to Keating?"

Ollie stopped and withdrew his arm from my shoulders. He turned to me but didn't say anything.

"I know Angie cannot officially close the case without confirmation of something, but we can decide what we should do on a personal level. Something that will allow us to have as much closure as possible," I continued.

"What do you have in mind?"

"We hike Mt. Monadnock and say, I'll see you when I see you," I told him.

"Are you ready to let go?"

"I don't think we are ever ready to let go of those we love, but what is the alternative? If we're both looking to start fresh here, I think we need to set his spirit free," I explained.

I thought about what Martin said when I asked if any of his missing person cases ended with the person being found. I opted not to tell Ollie about Martin's offer to investigate. I didn't see the point. What more could he find that Angie and Detective Deas couldn't?

Keating's been missing for over a week now. It's possible that more details will come together with the retirement letter and missing items from Keating's office and if Evan had anything to do with it. But would that put us any closer to finding Keating? You cannot find a man who doesn't want to be found. As much as I hated that thought, we could only ignore it for so long.

After enjoying a dinner of my special mac'n'cheese, Angie and Ollie helped me clean and lock up Comfort before we headed back to their house for an evening cocktail. Ollie encouraged me to give the recipe to Tia, but I didn't know if I wanted to share this with the public. I stumbled upon the recipe years ago while I surfed the net. However, it doesn't resemble the original. I customized the ingredients to my tastes by changing the blends of cheese, the shape of the noodles, and the spices. Whenever I made this dish, I used a different add-in according to my mood. Tonight, I used leeks.

As usual, our conversation ranged in topics. We avoided discussion of Evan and Keating. Angie asked if Gray spoke with the detectives about Grafton. I told her I didn't know but hoped so based on Gray's note. Ollie and Angie commented on the changes made to Comfort and loved the doodle paper on the tables.

I shared with Angie that Martin returned for a visit but also kept quiet about his offer to look into Keating's disappearance. I didn't know how she would feel if I even considered asking someone on the outside to investigate. I was, however, curious about Angie's take on him.

"Do you find it odd that he's now visited me twice?" I asked Angie. "I want to trust him, and yet, I'm not sure that I can. How do I know he's not just digging for dirt on Gray? Or something else?"

"When he visited, did he ask about Grayson?" Angie asked.

"No. He told me that his part of the investigation was over," I answered. "I don't know what to believe. I don't like that he looked into my past without my permission. I understand it's part of the job, but, that doesn't make it feel any less of an invasion of privacy."

Ollie and Angie exchanged a suspicious look. "What?" I asked.

"I haven't worked with too many private undercover investigators in the years I've been a cop, but the ones I have never revealed their identity to people they've worked with on a job. It's a risk they couldn't afford to take," Angie explained.

"So, Martin coming clean to me is a good sign?" I asked.

"Based on the high-profile case he just conducted, he risked a bit by being honest with you," Angie commented. "And…"

"I did a little checking," Ollie interjected.

"You what?" I questioned. Ollie joked with me about having Angie check him out, but I thought it was just that. A joke. "Ollie, please tell me you didn't."

He gestured with his hands for me to relax. "It's okay, love. I did a little research and verified that Martin's mother does live in Jasper and she did work for the post office. From what I was told, she's a lovely lady."

I dropped my head into my hands. I felt both exasperated and humiliated. I knew Ollie only had my best interests in mind, but still.

"I'm sorry that I overstepped, but I wanted to make sure that the reason he stated he was in the area was true. It is. What you decide to do from here is your call," Ollie shared.

"I, thank you. I know you're just looking out for me, and I appreciate it. I just…" I trailed off. "Martin is not on my radar right now. I want to focus on where I'm at in my life right now, my next steps in terms of living, Keating, and being there for Gray. That's about all I can handle."

"We hear you loud and clear, sweetheart," Angie affirmed. "So, let's talk cookies. I want to know what Tia has in store for us!"

From that point forward, our conversation remained light. When we finally turned in for the night, it was pouring. Angie offered to make up Jack's room for me. I almost declined. I didn't want them to think I couldn't handle the storm, but when the thunder rumbled with the lightning outside, and the windowpanes clattered in their frames, I accepted. I appreciated that Ollie and Angie played it as if it were more about me not stepping foot in the rain and less about my fear. Angie gave me a pair of Kettle Cove PD issued sweats and a t-shirt to change into.

Once I was comfortably on my side, I pulled the covers over my ear and hoped it would block out the sound of the relentless rain outside. The water rushed to the earth in a hurry, only to be caught by the howling wind. The shades were pulled, but they only diffused the lightning. Although I knew I was safe, warm, and dry inside the little blanket cocoon I created, I felt like I was trapped in the elements. To distract myself, I started to sing while the second round of hot toddies settled my nerves and helped me sleep.

When I dreamed, I sometimes heard sounds. Sometimes, I knew where the noises or voices came from; other times, I didn't. But I always pictured where I was, even when the skit was silent. Now, my picture was blank, but I heard voices. They whispered somewhere in the distance. The voices were familiar, though. Both soft and secure. I trusted them. I didn't want to leave this place, wherever it was. And then, just as quickly as I heard the voices, I was met with silence. Something happened…

"Kenzie…wake up, sweetheart."

It was Angie. She felt close enough to touch me. I then felt my body shake slightly.

"Kenz…"

My eyes slowly fluttered open. I rubbed the sleepy haze out of them to focus. I then pushed myself up and flicked on the bedside light. I then saw Angie's entire appearance. She was dressed as if she…

"What's wrong?" I asked.

"The storm's wreaked havoc out there. There are downed trees, flooded roads, fires, accidents. I need to go."

Fear settled inside of me. "Fatalities?" I softly asked while I silently prayed the fight of the Gods didn't make another child parentless.

"From what I've been told, no. Honey, I know this is hard, but I need you…"

I knew what she was asking. I had a fear of thunderstorms; Ollie had a fear of losing his wife. He accepted that her job placed her in potentially dangerous situations. One night, while I was a student, he came close to losing her. Only then, it was a blizzard that required her attention. She was in a car accident that left her with a broken wrist, rib, and a concussion. I worked with Ollie at Comfort that night and stayed with him until he knew she was okay. That was the first time I ever saw Ollie emotionally on edge. He was distracted, quiet, and scattered. When we heard she was in the hospital, I drove his jeep behind the squad car and sat with him until he was permitted to see Angie. An officer then drove me back to campus.

"I'll keep him calm, Angie. We'll open Comfort for all the responders, just like we did when I was a student."

Keating always teased Ollie for being too sensitive. I'd call Keating out on it when Ollie wasn't around. Ollie didn't possess a cruel bone in his body and never wished harm to anyone. To me, that's a rare and genuine quality. Until I met him, it had been my experience that most people, even if they genuinely cared about the welfare of others, often hid that part of themselves behind a bunch of bravado. This wasn't Ollie. When it came to Angie being in danger or in pain, he was a little nutty and wasn't afraid to show it.

I quickly climbed out of bed and changed. Angie flashed me the briefest of smiles.

"What?" I asked.

She shook her head and said, "Nothing. It's just, Ollie had the same idea about Comfort as you. He has already contacted members of the staff about coming in. The two of you make one helluva a team."

"We want to do our part to help those who help us," I said honestly.

"Thank you, Kenzie. I need to run. I'll be in touch as soon as I'm able."

I hugged her and pressed my personalized penny into her hand. When I unpacked it, I placed it on the table next to the bed. At one point last night, I must have picked it up and held it in my palm. After I fell asleep, it slipped out and onto my pillow.

"What's this?" Angie looked at me.

"Something to keep you safe. You can return it when we see you later."

Angie smiled as she tucked the coin in her front pocket and left. I pulled on sneakers and headed downstairs. It was then that I noticed the time- 2:30 a.m. Mentally, I thought we'd start with a hot drink and use the baked goods that Tia had already prepared. I remembered Keating stored large coffee urns in the basement of Comfort. We'd need to pull them out to clean and then start brewing.

My phone burned a hole in my back pocket. I desperately wanted to message Gray but pushed the thought away. I didn't know what events would occur over the day, but I knew I needed to be brave. For Angie, for Ollie, and for myself. So, I left my phone tucked away and headed to the kitchen.

I spotted Ollie staring out the window. He was dressed and ready to go. Quietly, I joined him. I took a breath at the sight outside. Their driveway was littered with broken tree branches. I could only imagine what the rest of Kettle Cove and the surrounding towns looked like. Without looking at him, I gently spoke.

"She'll be okay, Ollie."

I saw him nod out of the corner of my eye. When I thought he wouldn't respond, he surprised me.

"You'd think that after all this time, I'd be used to it. And I guess, to an extent, I am. It's just - You think I can convince her to retire?"

"Not any more than she can convince you to wear shoes. "Now, come on, partner, we have coffee to make and food to prep," I said. As we pulled out of the driveway, I prayed that this Tuesday would give way to sunshine and not more heartache.

When Ollie and I entered the back door of Comfort twenty minutes later, my heart warmed at the sight before us. Not only were the employees that Ollie contacted directly there, but the ones they reached out to via the modern-day grapevine. Tables that I did not believe were ours were already set up in the front of the dining area. The coffee pots were already up and running. We had four –regular and decaffeinated coffee, hot water for tea, and hot chocolate. Platters of the treats Tia baked yesterday were out, along with other goodies I knew were not ours. When I spotted Doug, I asked where they came from.

"My wife is the manager of the bakery at Market Basket. She donated what was made this morning, with more on the way to help us," he explained.

"That's great, Doug. Please thank her for us," I asked.

I didn't need to look at Ollie to know his thoughts matched mine. Before we could voice anything to each other, we turned at the sound of two people who entered through the front doors.

"Can we help you?" Ollie started.

"We're friends with Tia. She mentioned you were opening up today."

"Yes… We're in the process of prepping as much as we can right now," I answered.

"We'd like to help. I'm Jen, this is Sally. We own Aunt Betty's Sweets. We closed today and want to donate all our treats to you. One of our bakers is in and is making more."

"Thank you! We appreciate all the help we can get," I stated. "I'm Kenzie, and this is Ollie.  He is one of the owners of Comfort."

"We heard about Keating-he was one of our favorite customers," Sally explained. And then, she looked pointedly at Ollie, "And we know your wife. She's done so much for our community and for the children in our schools. The least we could do is repay the favor."

I gently squeezed Ollie's forearm. I called over Grace, one of our waitresses, and introduced her to Jen and Sally. I then asked

Grace to show them around. With this group set, Ollie double-checked the generator and ensured it was ready to kick on if we lost power. Although Angie mentioned there were downed lines, neither Comfort nor the campus were yet impacted. I worked with some of the waitresses to set up more tables and chairs. After that, I retreated to the kitchen to plan with Tia about additional food. While the storm raged on outside, Comfort was in full swing between volunteers and responders cycling in and out.

Regardless of how busy I was, I kept an eye on Ollie. For the moment, he was fully engaged in organizing our work staff and ensured that all responders had a warm drink, a seat, and something to eat when they entered. Although all of this kept his mind occupied, I'm sure he asked about Angie whenever one of her officers arrived.

Through the combination of firefighters, EMTs, and police officers from Kettle Cove and surrounding towns, we learned there was a fire at Wal-Mart, but it was contained with no injuries or fatalities. Unofficially, they believed a wire was struck by lightning, but it was too early to tell. The students all appeared safe on campus. We heard there were several car accidents, blocked roads due to fallen trees, and a couple of houses were damaged due to fallen branches. I mentally noted we'd need to check Keating's place out once everything was cleared.

Amazingly, everyone who showed up in the early morning hours was still here. I exited the kitchen to check in with Ollie when I spotted a stranger by a window in the back part of the restaurant. Dressed in worn jeans, hiking boots, and a flannel shirt, the man wore an army green baseball cap and although his face was shaded by the short bill of his cap, he resembled someone I knew. The man turned and faced me. I spotted a bright pair of sparkling brown eyes. Eyes that I'd know anywhere. The closer I moved towards the man, the keener my focus became. In an instant, my body warmed. Tall, solid stature, desperate curls fighting to break free of…

"What the hell is that on your head?" The individual in question shyly looked at me so I could fully see his face. "And you shaved," I added.

Gray rolled his eyes when he turned to face me completely. In a hushed voice, he said "I believe they call these baseball hats. And, contrary to popular belief, I do own a razor. I just choose not to use it."

"I know what it is; I'm asking why the hell it's on your head. No, wait, scratch that. What in the fuck are you doing here?" I asked.

"The mouth on you…"

I wasn't in the mood for his playful games. "Follow me," I directed and led him to Keating's office. The conversation we needed to have could not be conducted in front of an audience. To Gray's credit, he followed me in silence until the office door was firmly closed behind us.

"I saw the news about the storms. I was worried, so I came over. I went to the Coopers' first. When I saw you weren't home, I figured this is where you would be."

"The storms, they've wrecked fucking havoc everywhere. Angie's out there, somewhere and…"

Gray wrapped me up in his arms. "Angie is tough, smart, and will come back, honey. It's not her time."

I allowed myself to take from his solace and strength before I let him go. "How did you get here?"

Gray casually shoved his hands in his pockets. "I've been traveling through Maine and Vermont —here —checking out different local theatres."

While I was happy and grateful that he was with me, I was also pissed. I punched him in the shoulder. "You asshole. You drove in this? Something could have happened to you!"

"Ouch!" he said. Gray placed his hands on my shoulders. "It's not my time either. Now, what can I do to help?"

"Help?"

"Yes, Kenzie, help you, Ollie, everyone here. Put me to work."

Although I shouldn't be surprised at what I knew to be a sincere offer, I honestly didn't know how to respond.

"I haven't forgotten who I am, Kenzie," he whispered. His voice's soft yet low bass sent shivers down my spine. "This place, these people are important to you. That makes them important to me. I honestly want to help. And I don't want you to be alone."

"Grayson…" I started, as I shook my head. "Okay."

We exited the office as quietly as we entered it. "Why don't you start with emptying the garbage pales, replacing the full bags with empty ones, and taking the trash out to the dumpster."

"Got it, boss," Gray smiled.

"Gray…"

"Kenzie, we'll talk later. Right now, I promise, I'm here to help you, and if need be, your hot hippie over there." Gray nodded in Ollie's direction. I noted that Ollie stood firm in front of one of the windows. He held a broom loosely in his hands, but it hadn't moved across the floor.

"He's worried about Angie. We haven't heard anything about her. I need to check on him. You're sure about this?"

"I've got it. I'll still be around when all this dies down," Gray assured me.

Before I turned away, I studied him. "Did you come up with this disguise all on your own?"

"Why are you so surprised? I really am that good," he said with a wink.

"Cocky shit," I teased. "How does it feel?"

Gray leaned down and whispered in my ear. "Refreshing."

I leaned forward, placed a gentle peck on his cheek, and then frowned at the feel of smooth skin under my lips.

Gray shot me a worried look. "That bad?"

"Just different. The chief won't like it."

"What's to say she'll recognize me?" Gray asked.

"She will."

Grayson rewarded me with a smile that I knew came from his whole heart.

"You are really sure about this?"

He stared at me like he was about to let me in on an enormous secret. The look on his face, in his eyes, I didn't know what to make of it. "Yes. Now, go rescue the hippie over there before he becomes the next Superman."

And with that, Gray walked away from me. He seamlessly blended in with everyone. He chatted with people while working, carefree and comfortable. I wondered, not for the first time in our lives, why he believed he could not form genuine relationships with others. Gray had so much love in his heart. Maybe, being here among these ordinary people, he would finally see it.

I fully turned my attention to Ollie, who, as Gray correctly stated, was about to go Clark Kent on me and burn a hole through the glass. Gently, I placed my hand on his shoulder. I pulled it away when my touch made him jump.

"Sorry, I didn't mean to startle you," I said.

"No, it's fine," he started as he ran a hand over the side of his face.

"Still no word?" I asked, even though I already knew the answer.

"Some of the firemen said they last saw her leaving the fire at Wal-Mart for an accident scene. But that was two hours ago."

"Do you want to go to the station?"

Ollie turned to me. He seemed surprised at the question.

"What?" I asked him. "It's either you stay here and keep doing what you're doing, or you take some coffee and snacks to those who haven't been able to catch a break. And you see if Angie is there."

"You understand what you're suggesting, right?" he asked.

"I do."

"You know what kind of wrath I'd face later if I made that play?"

I shrugged my shoulders. "Then I guess you're just gonna have to trust that the chief is safe and that she will be here with you before you know it." I clasped his hands between mine. "I know you're worried, and I know that it's more than Angie being wrapped up in a dangerous situation."

"My best mate is missing Kenzie; I can't lose my soulmate, too."

I squeezed his hands. "I know. I have faith that she'll be back here before you know it, ragging on you about still having your shoes on."

Ollie then cracked a smile as he glanced at his booted feet. He let go of my hands and then surprised me with his own keen observational skills.

"When did your lad sneak in?"

"You noticed him?" I questioned.

"You think I wouldn't recognize the man my wife has a crush on? She has a collection of his movies and keeps a secret stash of all his pictures from when he was on that soap, particularly the bare-chested ones."

I laughed. "She may have a secret infatuation for the sexy Mr. Kent, but her heart and soul belong to you." Ollie rewarded me with an even bigger smile. "Now, Tia is transitioning to platters of her plain mac'n'cheese with some hot dogs and burgers. What do you think?"

"I think…."

Whatever Ollie was about to say was lost when the front door to Comfort blew open.

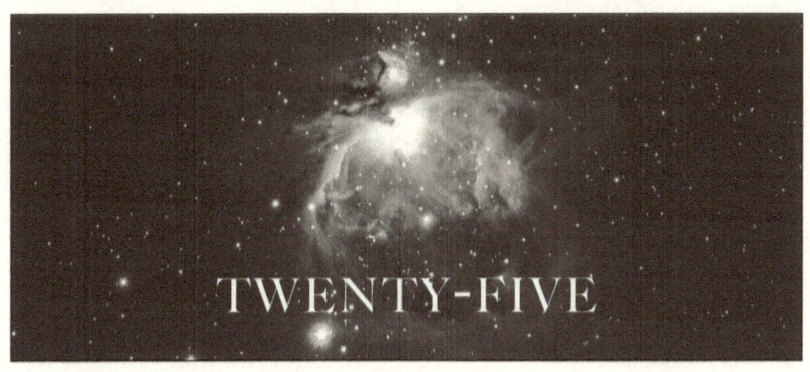

# TWENTY-FIVE

Forget Clark Kent, The Flash now had some competition. One minute, Ollie was beside me, and the next, he had Angie wrapped up so tight in his arms that I wondered if we'd need the jaws of life to separate them. Although it appeared, Angie held him back with just as much force.

"I understand now," I heard someone whisper in my ear.

"What?" I asked. I turned to face Gray.

"Why you've always put them on a pedestal. People watch soap operas and romantic movies for the fantastical relationships they covet. The angst, yearning, chemistry, sex, passion, overcoming all odds to be together. Two beautiful people the fans believe are just right for each other, and if the actors have chemistry – their moniker is created. But that's not reality. It's a nice way to spend an hour or two of your time getting lost in characters' stories, but it doesn't fill the void that may live inside of you. Watching them, seeing how much they respect, trust, like, and love one another, and knowing none of that is scripted, I understand why you want that for yourself. You deserve it, and I hope that you find it."

I grabbed his hand. "You deserve it too. You just need to be willing to put yourself out there to find it."

"How do we share our hearts, Kenzie? How do we make a relationship work with someone else when we love each other so much?"

"There's a difference between loving someone and being in love with them," I stated. I nodded to Ollie and Angie. "They are in love with each other. You and I love each other."

Grayson nodded in agreement. "Did you ever tell any of the guys you dated about me?"

"No. But, if I ever meet that person that I can tell, I'll need to know that he can accept who you are to me and that you own a piece of my heart."

"What about your undercover investigator?"

I turned to him. "Martin? What about him?"

"He's here." Gray nodded.

I turned to the space Gray indicated with his head and saw Martin. "He told me his mom lives in the area. He's here visiting. How do you know what he looks like?"

Gray went silent.

"I asked you a question. Please answer it." I waited. I then wondered if Martin lied to me about Gray being cleared of any involvement with Grafton. Maybe Martin's last trip here and his being here again was to find information on Gray. "Are you still in trouble? Is that why you know Martin? He questioned you?"

"No, Kenzie, it's not like that," Gray started.

"Then tell me what it is like," I demanded.

Then, without warning, a toxic, burning sensation formed in my stomach. It stretched my throat and remained lodged there with no way out. Gray had a secret. I decided not to wait for his response and excused myself. Behind me, I heard Grayson whisper, "Fuck." But it didn't make me turn around.

After I checked with Tia on the shift from breakfast to lunch, I retreated into Keating's office. Since I'd been back at Comfort, I only entered this office a handful of times. I came in, picked up or filed what I needed, and then left. This space felt too much like Keating's. I felt like if I worked in here, behind his desk, it was a violation of

Keating's privacy. Even when I worked here as a student, I never entered the office unless Keating invited me in. When I cleaned Comfort, I scrubbed, dusted, and vacuumed every area but this room.

It's weird, but it felt like if I cleaned his room in Comfort, then he would be erased from here. When I suggested to Ollie that we hike Mt. Monadnock to help us move forward, I did so with the knowledge that I wasn't completely ready to take that step. But I felt like if we could do that, then I could face the ghost of Keating that lived here. And then, maybe I would feel that my plan to make Kettle Cove my home was right.

*This will always be your home, Kenzie. Whether you return to Hoboken or not, you have a place here with all of us.*

You didn't want me to go, I whispered to the books that silently sat on his shelf. *A father never wants to let go of their child, but we know that we must at one point. That's part of life. I was wrong to blame Grayson for your choice.*

"I don't know if I can let you go. If I can make my own place here," I told the room as I leaned against the wall.

"You can, sweetheart." I turned to see Angie enter the office without Ollie or Gray. "Tell me, how does Grayson make taking out the garbage look sexy?"

I couldn't help but chuckle. "Please don't tell him that. His ego is stroked enough."

"I give him props for the disguise. I don't think anybody has recognized him," Angie commented.

"Ollie did."

I shifted my attention back to the books in front of me. These inanimate objects seemed easier to focus on than Angie's more than likely compassionate expression.

"Thank you for being there for Ollie. I know he is unsettled and distracted when he worries about me," Angie shared.

"I love you both and would do anything for you."

"Back at you, sweetheart," Angie paused, "I know today was harder for Ollie because of Keating."

"He's afraid of losing you, too," I shared.

"My hippie Scot is a big softie, isn't he?"

"He is," I agreed.

"Your coming to Kettle Cove now, working here, helps him. It helps both of us."

Finally, I looked at Angie. "Does it? I feel like all I've done is lean on both of you because of the stuff with Gray, and then when you told me Keating was missing, I thought if I stayed, then maybe he would return. That he wouldn't leave me like my parents did."

Angie gathered me into her arms just as I started to cry. "Let it go, sweetheart. Let it all go now." She rubbed my back.

After I settled down, Angie took my hand and walked us to the sofa that sat to the left of the desk. Once seated, Angie pulled me to her, held me against her chest, and continued to rub circles on my back. Being held like this was something I dreamed of. I watched mothers do this with their kids on TV and in movies. I was jealous of what fictional characters had that I didn't. It struck me that I had no memory of how that felt until now. Angie's physical strength, the steady beat of her heart, and the kindness in her voice soothed the ache that strangled my chest.

Scripted and not real, Grayson just told me. This, right now with Angie, was real.

"I'm relieved that you are okay," I started, "I don't know what…"

"Shhh…I wasn't ever in any danger, Kenzie. I'm sorry that I was unable to communicate with you and Ollie."

"How is everything out there?" I asked.

"A natural war zone, but thankfully, so far, no loss of life."

"So, all kids still have their parents."

She ran her hand through my hair and said, "Yes, sweetheart. And thank you for what you and Ollie did here," Angie stated.  She released her hold on me and encouraged me to look at her. "The two of you jumped right in without a second thought and provided warmth and comfort to all of us. You have no idea what that meant to everyone out there fighting fires, working accident scenes, rescuing people from damaged homes, knowing that we had a safe place to come at the end of it."

"It was nothing, Angie...I mean, other places would do the same."

"But they didn't, Kenzie."

"Well, that's what Comfort is about. A place for people to gather with strangers or friends and feel welcome, loved, and appreciated. Keating would have done it, too."

"I love Keating, you know that, but he at times, was a difficult man to read. He willingly gave the shirt off his back to anyone who needed it but could also shut down for periods without explanation. I saw him hurt my husband and you with his words and actions."

"Angie..."

"I'm saying this because I need you to understand just how much you offer all of us. You did the same when you were just a student who worked here. Remember?" Angie asked.

I nodded yes.

"That was a wicked snowstorm. You and Ollie rallied the staff and provided shelter for all of us. And that night, the power did go out. But the two of you kept the fire going and ensured we all had something warm in our systems," Angie continued. "And when you heard of my accident, it was you who came with Ollie to the hospital and stayed with him. I never forgot that Kenzie. And neither has my husband."

I didn't know what to say. That night, like tonight, I knew people needed help, even if it was just a cup of warm tea or a chocolate chip cookie. I didn't plan all this because I wanted anything from it other than to show that people weren't alone.

"The staff's willingness, both then and now, to come out in this weather to cook, bake, and provide a safe space for the community shows how much you are respected. You are a kind, amazing, and loveable person. And brave. You are so brave to have gone through all you did and not only survive but also grow from it. You teach us every day, Kenzie. I love you, and know my sweet, bare-footed husband thinks the world of you. And I know Keating loves you very much."

And then, just as I was helpless to hold in my tears, the one question that's been stuck in my mind since I learned of Keating's disappearance exited my mouth. "Then why did he leave? What did I do that is so wrong that makes me lose people that I love? I want to hope that he is returning, yet in my heart, I know he's not. And I don't know if that's because he can't, like my parents, or if he just doesn't want to."

"Oh, honey…" Angie soothed.

She once again pulled me into her. "You've lost so much in your life. And none of it is fair or your fault. I wish your parents were here to see the woman you've become. I am sure that they would be proud of you. As for Keating, he made his own choices, and he alone."

Angie's comment regarding Keating surprised me. This time, it was me who pulled out of her embrace. I then waited for her to continue.

"Deas doesn't believe Keating was abducted. It infuriates me that he did something this selfish and cruel to you, my husband, the people here, his students, and co-workers. I don't care what his reasons were. You don't purposefully do that to the people you love," Angie stated. The anger in her voice was clear.

"How do you know he wasn't taken? Or that something happened to him?"

Angie pushed strands of hair behind my ear. "Keating was spotted, alone, leaving a convenience store just over the Maine border."

"He was spotted? How do you know that?"

"Grayson," Angie stated.

I didn't know how to respond. What did Gray have to do with any of this?

"He hired your friend Martin to look into it and to tail Evan."

"He…"

"Don't be angry with him, Kenzie. He knows how much you love Keating. Gray wants all of us to have answers. He didn't like how much Evan spooked you and thought, if we kept eyes on him, maybe we'd learn something."

"Why didn't he tell me?"

"I encouraged him, to, but he didn't want to get your hopes up," Angie explained.

"That's why he recognized Martin earlier. Martin offered to investigate Keating's disappearance, but I turned him down." I straightened up. "I didn't want to upset you or make you think I didn't believe in your abilities as a cop or in the officers under your watch."

"Oh, sweetheart, I would never think that," Angie assured me.

"When Gray recognized Martin, I thought it was because Gray was in more trouble than he let on and that was why Martin was hanging around. I never thought…" I started and then stopped. I was too angry with myself for jumping to the wrong conclusion.

"I'm sure Gray understands," Angie affirmed.

"What about Detective Deas? Did Gray talk to him, too? Does he know my connection with him?"

"No. Gray only spoke to me about Martin. And then Martin contacted Det. Deas directly."

"Wouldn't your detective be suspicious of Martin? An out-of-town investigator looking into the disappearance of a local college professor?" I asked.

"I assured Hunter that Martin's interests were true after I ran my own background check on him. He seems like a good guy, Kenzie," Angie shared.

"Does Ollie know?"

"No. Grayson offered to tell Ollie, but I asked him not to. My love is many things, but a liar is not one of them. I would not put him in the position of needing to keep that from you, so we decided to keep it a police matter."

I understood and appreciated that. "Why are you telling me now?"

"I saw the look on Gray's face when you retreated to the kitchen. I connected the dots after seeing Martin watch you from across the room. I realized you figured out they knew each other."

"He asked about Martin and wondered why he was here today. I questioned how he knew Martin. To my knowledge, their paths never crossed at Top Floor until the night Grafton was arrested. But I think Gray left without realizing that Martin saw him. I need to find him before he takes off."

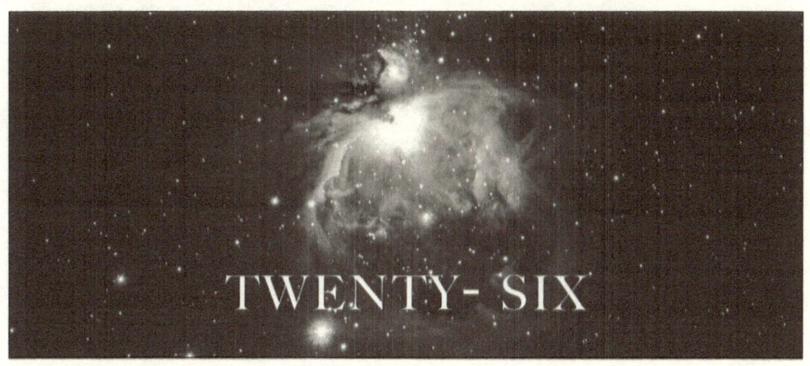


I ran out of the office, scanned the crowd, and looked for his ridiculous green baseball hat, but I didn't spot Gray. I checked the kitchen and the back parking lot. No sign of him. Gray slipped away as silently as he appeared.

I pulled my phone out of my pocket and quickly unlocked it.

**Sorry I walked away.**

After hitting the correct icons to type up my text, I saw Gray beat me to the punch.

**I'm guessing Angie filled you in. Talk tomorrow. X Fav Color**

I didn't want to leave his message without a response.

**Yes. I wish you told me. I hate secrets Gray, but, I understand.**

I tucked my phone back in my pocket and jumped at the sight of Hunter. So caught up in my thoughts of Gray and this whole fucked up situation, I didn't pay attention to who was around.

"You know, speculating motives is my territory. I was suspicious when a New York City PI appeared in Kettle Cove and told me he was hired to look into Keating's disappearance."

I squared my shoulders and looked Hunter square in the eye. "And?

"And nothing. I checked his credentials and found that he was clean."

"You sound disappointed," I commented.

"Not at all," Hunter stated.

But I spotted something in his demeanor that said otherwise. "Are you jealous that Martin discovered something that you didn't?"

Hunter remained still. It looked like I hit a nerve.

"A man's gone missing, and you're upset that an out-of-state investigator discovered his last whereabouts?" I admitted to Angie that I didn't accept Martin's help because I didn't want her to think I didn't trust her abilities. I guess I was wrong to think someone who worked for her would be insulted.

"It's interesting to me that, while you and Martin seem to know each other, you seemed to be out of the loop in his involvement with Keating Finn's case. Then I saw him chat it up with Grayson Kent and made the connection. You and Kent are close. I spotted you leave Finn's place together the other day."

I wanted to wipe the smug look off Hunter's face.

Just as my emotions got the best of me when I broke down with Angie, they were about to blow again. Only this time, it wouldn't be tears that I shed. An irrational rage blossomed inside of me. I admit I have lost my temper before. I am direct, but I have never resorted to physical violence. But, at this moment, so help me, I was about to lose my shit.

"Angie told you to trust Martin. If you did that instead of running a background check, maybe you would have something more important to share now."

"Hey, I'm damn good at my job," Hunter defended. "I call them as I see them. Your hotshot actor friend hired a top-notch PI to investigate Keating's whereabouts and kept you out of the loop. If he kept that from you, what else is Kent hiding?"

I balled my hands into fists and squeezed them as tight as I could. I hoped the action would stuff the anger that threatened to tip over.

I stepped closer to him to make sure he heard me. "As a hostess in a top restaurant, my ability to characterize the behavior of our guests was paramount to anticipating their needs and allowed us to provide excellent service. This includes identifying the obnoxious pricks from the non."

"You're calling me an obnoxious prick?"

"I believe I did. What would your boss say if she knew you disobeyed her orders?"

My threat was not an empty one. Hunter figured that out quickly by the look on his face. His mind wheels started to backpedal as he tried to figure out how to salvage this conversation. Yet, nothing came out of his mouth.

"Piece of advice detective? If you disagree with how Angie runs the department, leave." Without another word, I walked away. How dare Hunter insinuate anything about Gray. He didn't know me, him, or us. Our lives were turned upside down and that landed us in a ditch that we needed to climb out of. But I knew we would because we were strong. Gray would move past the Grafton mess. When I tell him about my decision to move to Kettle Cove, we'll make it work because that's what family does. It will be hard, but I knew it was the healthiest move for both of us. To hell with Hunter Deas and his unwanted opinions.

I decided I'd given Angie's asshole detective enough of my time. Instead, I focused on the life within the walls of Comfort. As I looked around, I observed people drinking, eating, and warming up from the biting cold of the storms. Comfort was crowded. Hushed conversations could be heard throughout the room. Everyone talked with each other as if they'd known each other forever.

Martin sat at a table with an older woman. Someone I didn't recognize, but I could see the resemblance between her and Martin. I wondered if she was his mom. When Martin caught my stare, he waved me over to the table. I started in their direction, only to be stopped by Angie.

"Hey, sweetheart, everything okay with you and Det. Deas?" She asked the question with an arched eyebrow that left zero room for bullshit.

"I'm sorry, Angie, your detective may be great at his job, but his social skills suck. I just let him in on that little fact." I paused. "Do you know who that is with Martin?"

Angie turned to look, only to be waved off by Ollie. "That's his mom. He dropped her off to help us while he fielded calls for Angie at the station."

I looked at Angie. "He did?"

"Yeah, he was a great help. I learned he was a cop prior to becoming a PI," Angie told us.

I glanced in Martin's direction again. This time, he didn't turn toward me, as he kept his attention on whatever his mother shared with him.

"I'm going to say hello," I told Ollie and Angie.

I left them and walked straight to Martin's table.

"Hi," I stated once at their table.

Martin turned to me with a smile. "Hey, yourself. What you and Ollie did here, it's amazing Kenzie."

"Thanks. We, uh, had a lot of help. Angie told me you helped at the station?"

I turned to the older woman seated next to Martin. When I looked at her, I saw that Martin inherited the olive shape of his mom's eyes and the slope of her nose. "You must be Mrs. Benson. I'm…"

"Kenzie Mulroney! My goodness! Your Cathy and Jamie's daughter! You are a perfect mix of them."

Frozen, my eyes darted to Martin's. He turned to his mom. "Mom?"

Mrs. Martin stopped, as she realized how her remark came across. I saw the regret darken her features. "I'm sorry, dear; I didn't mean to make you uncomfortable. It's just when I saw you, I saw your parents. Your dad's eyes and hair color, mom's waves and heart-shaped face."

"You knew them?" I asked as I dropped into the chair, stunned.

"I grew up with them. Your mom was one of my best friends."

I then remembered Martin telling me his mom spent time near Moose Creek. It didn't cross my mind that she could have known my parents. "How do you know them?"

"Your mom lived down the road from my grandparents. I spent my summers with them. I befriended your mom and eventually your dad. It's a terrible shame what happened to them. I am so sorry."

Still shocked, I looked at Martin. "I didn't know Kenzie, I swear."

"He didn't dear. I know my son is in a challenging profession, but he's a good and honest man. He told me all about this place and had mentioned your name. But I never put the connection together until I saw you just now."

"I don't know what to say," I said softly. And I didn't. Of all the people I served and greeted over the years, I never came across someone who knew my parents. A zillion questions came to mind and yet, I couldn't get one of them out.

"This place, your parents would have loved it," Mrs. Benson shared.

"A rainy day is perfect for Comfort," I whispered.

"And I imagine a hard day for you." Mrs. Benson placed her hand over mine. "I met you when you were born and saw you until they passed. I moved away from the area for a time after that. I tried keeping track of where you were, but you know, I wasn't privy to anything. I wanted to take you in and raise you as my own. But, at the time, I didn't have the means to do so."

"You wanted to raise me?" I asked, shocked.

"Of course, dear. Your mom was my best friend. It's what best friends do. Your parents loved you so much. Your arrival only added to their happiness."

I felt the familiar sting of tears cloud my eyes. I blinked them away. "Can you tell me a little about them?"

"Of course. You can ask me anything."

"Did I have any grandparents? Aunts? Uncles?" I asked.

"Both of your parents were only children. Your dad's parents passed away before he and your mom married. Your mom's mother, Mammie, was at the wedding and met you when you were born but died shortly thereafter. Your mom's dad, Popa Pete, died when you were three."

"They never spoke of other family?"

"No. But your grandparents, from what I remember, were good people," Mrs. Martin shared. "The Thomases were too."

At the mention of my foster parents, my head shot up. "You knew them too?"

"I didn't know them well, but my aunt was friendly with them. From what I remember, they often kept to themselves, especially after their son died."

This statement surprised me. I figured out they had a son, but they never talked about him. I thought, given how they treated me, they did the same to him. That's why he never visited. Mrs. Benson read the surprise in my face and spoke before I could.

"You didn't know?" she asked.

"I figured out they had a son. I saw pictures of him and saw the box of toys they wouldn't let me play with. I always thought he didn't live close enough to visit," I paused, "How did he die?"

"He was eight or nine. I believe he became ill, but I'm not certain. Travis was, from what I heard of him, a quiet, good boy. He liked baseball, played with his cars, and played with his friends. It was a devastating loss."

"Are they still alive?"

"As far as I know, yes. They live in the same house."

I tucked that information away. I didn't know why. Why would I try and contact them after all this time? Would they even want to hear from me? These are questions for another day. I pushed these thoughts aside. Then an image of my parents' kitchen popped into my head. Light green countertops and that box tucked into the corner.

"Who liked the Ring Dings? Mom or Dad?" I asked.

The strength of Mrs. Benson's laugh had her leaning back in her chair. "Oh dear, now that is a story to tell. Your father had the biggest sweet tooth that I have ever seen! And your mother, she hated anything sweet. Cathy could not understand how Jamie could eat them. So, for your mom's twenty-first birthday, Jamie wrapped up twenty-one boxes of Ring Dings! He decorated the packages so she would never guess what was inside…"

"And what did mom do?"

"By the twenty-first box, she was ready to pound him! But….in that box was an engagement ring."

"My dad proposed through a box of Ring Dings?"

"He did. And your mom melted at the sight. The box that was on the counter in your home? That was the box the ring was in."

When I arrived at Comfort this morning, I was worried about Angie returning to Ollie and me safe. I worried that the storms would take another child's parents from them. I never imagined that these storms would introduce me to a person who not only knew my parents but would share personal stories with me. Now, I know about the Ring Dings. I had context to the box that sat on my counter. The box that I no longer had, but the story behind it filled that void.

little over a week after the storms rattled through the area, the sun, blue skies, and cooler temperatures returned. Thankfully, even though the storm was wicked and left a trail of debris, Mother Nature did not claim any lives.

It was a collective effort to provide the first responders with food and drink as they sought refuge from the weather on that stormy day. It took another effort for Comfort to re-open to Crestview students the following day. But we did it. Tia basically lived in the kitchen. Other staff members chipped in to help clean Comfort and re-set the tables. Like the first responders, the college students were grateful for the reprieve. They gathered in singles, doubles, and multiples throughout the week of finals. Soft music wafted through the speakers and filled the air with ease. And the butcher paper was a hit! When we cleaned up each night, we discovered doodles that ranged from math equations to literary quotes, to mindless dabbles. We planned to keep the paper on tables for the foreseeable future.

Angie, Ollie, and I set a date to hike Mount Monadnock. Ollie needed time to finalize his student's exams, and I needed time to mentally prepare myself for this hike. Both Ollie and Angie assured me it could wait and that we could hike the mountain anytime, but I felt like it was something we, well me, needed to do so we could take the appropriate steps forward.

It's now the night before our planned hike. We decided to spend the night at Keating's place, given its proximity to the mountain. Ollie and I spent the day at Comfort and left for Keating's just shy of 5 p.m. The drive to Keating's house this time felt easier than last time. Although last time, I didn't plan to spend the night.

Ollie stopped just outside the garage. He turned off the engine and we exited his jeep at the same time.

"I'll grab your bag," Ollie told me.

"Thanks." I turned towards the stone-lined path. I noticed the soft lights on the porch were turned on and cast a warm glow over the weathered wood. Although the sun had yet to sink into the sky, the lights, I suspected, were on a timer. We should probably change it, but none of us seemed inclined to do so. It was like an unspoken agreement between the three of us, that we'd keep the lights as is. They would show Keating the way home. Or maybe that was just the way I thought of it.

I paused and remembered the last time I stood before these steps. Ollie was with me then, too. I hesitated to enter Keating's home. I knew I would be met with the spiritual memory of the man who lived here, not the physical man himself. Now, I'm going to eat and sleep in this space. It was only for one night, but still, it was difficult to face that silence again.

I had not been back to Keating's since Ollie and I were here, since I met Evan, and learned about the role he once played in Keating's life. Ollie and Angie, however, had been back to check on the house and picked up his mail. They also checked to make sure the house didn't suffer any damage from the thunderstorms. Other than broken tree branches that we saw everywhere, Keating's house was untouched. Ollie had also been in touch with Keating's attorney and made sure she was apprised of everything.

To my surprise, Keating did not have any debt. The one credit card he had in his name was closed. He owned his house and vehicles outright. Until Keating was found, or we could legally declare him dead, his phone, cable, Wi-Fi, electricity, everything remained active. His cell phone was at the station, in the evidence box, sans charge. Although, it didn't matter. I tried to call him after the interaction with Evan, only to learn the line was no longer in service.

"Are you ready to go in?"

I didn't need to turn to know Ollie was next to me at the base of the steps. "I hate that this house is empty. What will happen to all of Keating's things if he's never found?"

"I don't know, but we'll figure it out. For now, we'll just keep an eye on it." Together, we climbed the steps and walked through the front door. We were greeted with the sweet smells of pasta ala Angie.

Ollie placed my bag just inside the entryway and then removed his shoes. I couldn't help but laugh at him.

"What? Why are you laughing at me?"

"You should work as a lifeguard. This way, you never have to wear shoes."

"I'll give you three minutes before yours are off," Ollie teased.

Just as we turned, Angie greeted us, as she wiped her hands on a towel. "There you two are."

Ollie greeted his wife with a kiss. "Sorry darling, we got caught up at Comfort. Can we help with anything?"

"Dinner will be ready in ten minutes. You and Kenzie have dish duty."

I laughed. I knew how much Ollie hated cleaning up. But he smiled and kissed her again. "Deal. Is the table set?"

"Not completely," Angie answered.

Ollie looked at me. "I'll take care of setting the table. You go and get settled," Ollie told me.

"Okay."

Without a word, Ollie gently squeezed my shoulder and then took Angie's hand. They returned to the kitchen. In the time I've known Ollie, I wished I had a cloning machine. Whenever I said that to Angie, she laughed and teased that Ollie saved his charming behaviors for me. "I once told you your Orion is out there. You'll find him, sweetheart," she'd say.

I shook away these thoughts, grabbed my bag, and moved to the room Keating had set up for me. After I flipped on the lights, I noted that everything was still in the same place as the last time I entered the room. The only item that was missing was the photo of Gray. I kept that.

I placed my overnight bag on top of the dresser. I then sat on the bed and looked around. Although I knew the closets and drawers were empty, I wondered about Keating's clothes and other belongings. Do we pack them away and store them? Or do we donate? Could we even do that since we were not family and legally didn't have any rights? I learned that Keating didn't have any living family. Ollie was the executor of his will should Keating be found dead or if he was eventually legally declared deceased. In the meantime, we were left with nothing but unanswered questions. As these thoughts passed through my mind, I imagined his whispered responses. *Stop kiddo. This is not on you. On any of you.*

"Then what happened? Where are you? Why did you leave?" I asked the room.

I lifted my leg and pulled my phone out of my back pocket. I had placed ringer on silent and hadn't checked it in a while. I hoped there would be a message from Gray, but my inbox was empty.

When Keating found me by the pond, upset about Gray, it was because Gray shut me out. Only then I didn't know why. Now, he's kept his distance again. Only this time, I knew it was for my protection. Although his full statement to the police was not released, some bits found their way to the press. He was cleared of any involvement with Grafton, but the press was all over him, and some of his fans waffled on their support of his work. It was an ugly time for him. Sam's involvement with Grafton still wasn't clear, but, it seemed that she had nothing to do with his activities.

For the first time since Gray became a recognized actor, I wished our friendship was not kept in the shadows. If it weren't, I would stand next to him without hesitation. Maybe there was a way, once the smoke cleared, for us to not hide anymore. Maybe it was silly to keep our friendship private to begin with.

Before dinner, I washed up in the bathroom. I then went to the bedroom and picked up my discarded phone. I re-entered my password and then dialed the one number I knew by heart. Gray laughed at me every time I did this. He couldn't understand why I didn't just hit his name in contacts.

*You've reached Grayson Kent. Please leave a message, and I'll be in touch. Thank You.*

I wondered if all actor's personal voicemails were so formal. Did directors and producers contact him directly? I always thought that was what agents and managers were for.

"Hey, Gray, just checking in. Tomorrow, we're hiking Monadnock, and then we will eat a wholesome lunch full of carbs and all the things you would frown upon at Comfort. I'm heading back to Hoboken soon. We need to talk. If you can't call, please text and let me know you are alright. Love and miss you."

After I disconnected the call, I tossed my phone onto the bed. I stared at the silent object and imagined the snit bits of conversation Gray and I would have the next time we connected.

*How are things at Comfort?*

*Great.*

*Are you staying at Keating's place in the haunted forest?*

*It's not haunted.*

*Right. Have you watched The X-Files? Twin Peaks? The Twilight Zone?*

*You're so dramatic.*

The silliness of this conversation was absolutely the way we'd start. When we talked, I needed to ensure he knew I supported him. And that I'd make more of an effort to understand the world he made his living in. Gray never indicated that he wanted me to show a greater interest in his work life, but I didn't know if that was because it was out of respect for me or if it was because he honestly didn't want to talk about it. I never asked and Gray never brought it up.

If we're not living in the same place, it would be an adjustment for both of us. I believed Gray suspected I planned to stay in Kettle Cove, but I needed to know he understood why. As I sat in this room decorated by Keating for me, I almost felt like he was with me. If I focused hard enough, I heard his voice.

*Maybe it's you who's changed. You've made your mind up about your life and what you want out of it. As a result, your interactions are different, not because you don't want to share things or feel you can't, but because you finally decided to do something just for you. And that, that's a foreign feeling.*

"Kenzie, dinner's ready!"

I woke from my reverie. "Be right there!"

Angie and Ollie were seated at the table with a mound of pasta on their plates. I took my seat across from Angie, with Ollie to her right.

"Hungry?" Angie asked.

"Starving!" I responded. My eyes watered at the yumminess in front of us.

"Before we eat, I wanted to fill you both in on Evan," Angie started. Ollie and I turned our attention away from the food and focused on her. "My officers arrested him for theft, forgery, and attempted breaking in and entering."

"Here?" Ollie asked.

Angie shook her head no. "The office. He entered the building when a student exited, but we found evidence that he stole a key to Keating's office. He accessed a retirement letter Keating typed some time ago, updated it, and then forged his signature. He took your photo, Kenzie, and the picture of Mt. Monadnock from his office to make us think he had reconnected with him."

"So, he didn't have anything to do with Keating's disappearance?" I asked.

"No, I'm sorry sweetheart. Martin tailed him for a while in the hopes that he would slip up, but no. We believe he tried to reconnect with Keating, but Keating rebuffed him. Evan learned of his disappearance and thought he'd try to make it look like he knew something we didn't."

Angie's update silenced all of us. We knew it was a long shot that Evan was somehow connected to Keating. It was sick to think that someone could find amusement in playing mind games with people. Then again, my recent string of bad Tuesdays placed a spotlight on the uglier parts of humanity.

"I'm sorry guys. I wished we learned something different," Angie admitted.

"It's okay," I said without thinking. I felt Ollie and Angie's eyes on me. "I don't have the history with Evan like you do, but my introduction to him made me sick. I'm relieved that wherever Keating is, it's not connected to Evan." I meant it. If Keating left us on his own accord, it's easier knowing that it is not because of Evan.

The silence that settled over the table made me think I said the wrong thing. I scrambled to think of a way to make up for it until Ollie spoke.

"Shall we toast?" Ollie asked as he raised his wine glass full of sparkling cider.

Relieved, I exhaled and picked up my glass. Angie and I raised ours with Ollie.

"His equal will never be among us again," Ollie whispered.

Instead of clinking to one another's glasses, we tilted them towards Keating's empty chair. We each took a sip and then placed our glasses down. Angie passed around the bread and then we all dug into the meal while casual conversation filled the air.

"Are you sure you don't want to stay upstairs?" Angie asked me.

Ollie smirked. That earned him a swift smack on the arm, which caused him to choke on his drink.

"What gives Chief? Are you trying to kill me? They are just stairs."

"Open stairs are unnatural. Everyone knows this," Angie defended.

"I don't think the construction company members received the memo," I dryly commented.

Ollie busted out in laughter as I calmly chewed my food.

"I need to limit the amount of time you two spend together," Angie said with a smile. She then winked at me. This told me, that unless Ollie told Angie he retired while I was out of the room, she figured it out.

And that's how the rest of our dinner conversation went - playful bantering mixed with calm discussion. I knew we were all mindful that Keating was not physically with us, but I couldn't help but inwardly smile at the knowledge that he was in spirit. Maybe, wherever he was, he was not, nor would he have ever be fully lost to us.

*Now you're getting it, kid.*

Summer mornings in New Hampshire can be cool. Today was one of those days. That meant our trek to the summit should be comfortable. We arrived at the mountain at 7:30 a.m. and began our two-and-a-half-hour trek at 7:45. I last climbed the mountain about six years before. Although I preferred being surrounded by woods than buildings, I never fully caught the hiking bug. The times I've visited, Ollie and Keating always planned a hike. They believed I needed nature to rid myself of the city.

I didn't think it worked that way, but it didn't matter. Even if I am not fond of hiking, I always enjoyed myself because I was with them. When Angie's schedule allowed, she came with us. I cannot remember a time that it was just Ollie, Angie, and me who hit the trails. It felt strange and yet, I realized it would be our new normal from today forward. When I pulled on my hiking attire this morning, I realized that dressing the part has been my profession for years. I perfected my persona as a hostess at Top Floor right down to the neatly manicured nails and sleek heels. I convinced the Top Floor patrons that knew that I was in charge. Today, even though I was dressed for a part, I wasn't playing a role. When I looked in the mirror, I just saw me in the reflection.

I've been awake since 4:30 a.m. My mind raced. I couldn't shut off what Angie shared at dinner about Evan. I meant what I said, I was relieved to know that Evan wasn't involved with Keating. At the same time, it also meant we were still at a standstill in regard to Keating. The hike today wasn't just a stroll through the woods on a nice summer day, but a way to honor Keating and let him go. Personally, I knew that if I made my peace with Keating being gone, I could also admit that the next chapter of my life would begin here. That I was ready to move away from Hoboken and from Gray.

Gray had yet to return my call or message from last night. I shared with Angie and Ollie what I learned about my parents from Martin's mom at dinner. I also wanted to tell Gray. And I wanted to talk to him about hiring Martin. I wasn't happy that he left me out of the loop. I felt better knowing that Gray was clear of any involvement with Grafton. That lessened my suspicion that Martin was hanging around to investigate Gray.

Regardless of Martin's motives, from what Angie shared, Detective Deas and Martin were at an impasse. Angie relayed that Martin traveled to the store where Keating was spotted but, other than confirmation that he was there, nobody saw where he went once he left. We learned that Keating used cash and purchased coffee and a breakfast sandwich. Martin apparently hung around a bit to see if Keating returned, but after a few days, when he didn't see him, Martin returned to Kettle Cove.

I asked Ollie and Angie if they thought it was worth keeping Martin on the case. I knew Detective Deas needed to push Keating's disappearance to the side for other immediate cases. They both shared that they would support whatever decision I made.

These thoughts weighed on my mind as we continued along the White Cross trail's bends, twists, and inclines. The subtle ache in my legs reminded me that where I may have walked miles pounding the cement of the city, it was different than the rigor and traps of natural terrain.

*Mind over matter, Kenzie, Keating used to tell me.*

So, I kept going. I used the natural surroundings as my strength. Change was as familiar to me as my favorite multicolored flannel. Yet, change wasn't easy. Other than the four years that I attended Crestview, I've always lived in New Jersey near Gray. I knew in my heart this was the right move for me, yet, I was terrified.

"Penny for your thoughts?" Ollie asked.

"Why just a penny? Aren't our thoughts worth more than a cent?" I mused.

"Do you really want a lecture on where the phrase originated?"

I laughed. "Pass. Tell me again why you and Keating enjoyed hiking so much?"

"The professor introduced me to the sport just after we met. I hated our first couple of outings but came to love and appreciate the beauty of nature and the peace and calm that lives here. That is if you are willing to look," Ollie explained.

"Calm is not the word I'd use to describe my muscles right now."

"You're doing fine, lass."

"Keep telling me that!" I begged.

Silence settled between us as we continued. I thought about the bizarre and twisted path my life has followed to this point. My cursed Tuesdays not only connected me to Gray, but led me to these people, to Kettle Cove, and to Comfort. If I'm honest and examined the broader picture, like Gray, once Ollie and Angie entered my life, they remained a constant presence. If I left Hoboken, I wouldn't have Gray, but I would have them.

As much as I loved Keating and am grateful for all he did for me, my desire to have a father blinded me to some truths about him. This time without him forced me to see him objectively. I realized that he was reclusive and secretive. That didn't take away all that he did for me. Whatever happened with Keating, whether by calculated moves or tragedy, he was still there for me when I was lost and alone.

I was so caught up in my thoughts that it was not until I heard Angie's voice that I realized we had reached the summit.

"It took you long enough! Did you stop for groceries along the way?" Angie teased.

"Listen to this one," Ollie pointed out. "Not all of us are gifted at running up a mountain, Chief. Besides, there is such a thing as taking your time, soaking it all in."

"You mean taking oxygen breaks," Angie snarked.

"Hey!"

I smiled. Whenever Ollie and Keating hiked, Keating liked to rib him about something. Ollie wandered and soaked in everything he smelled, observed, and felt into his soul. Keating, where he may have enjoyed the moment, never became philosophical about them. While Ollie and Angie continued to tease each other, I looked around.

The rolling granite rocks, clear of trees and other plant life, was deceiving. You believed you were above the tree line, but you were not. A fire struck the top of the mountain and killed the trees. The vegetation never grew back. I climbed onto a higher cluster of boulders for a higher view. From the top, I spotted the campus, the Green Mountain Range of Vermont, and the dominant presence of Mount Washington in the White Mountains.

I inhaled the crisp, clean air and allowed it to filter through my lungs; I found solace in the peace. It filled me like water filled a canteen. It refreshed my mind and soul. All the pain in my back, thighs, calves, and feet died away as the meaning of it all claimed ownership in my mind.

"It is breathtaking, isn't it?" Angie asked.

"It is," I answered.

"Ollie and I are going to have a snack. We found a quiet cluster of rocks to rest by."

"Okay," I said. I turned and followed Angie.

"Oliver!"

I looked around Angie and spied Ollie's fingers on his laces. "I'm just tightening them!"

I chuckled at the look on Ollie's face, only to stop when I saw another familiar presence next to him.

"Gray?" I whispered.

"I wanted to return your messages in person," he shrugged.

With another ball cap on his head, face still clean shaven, Gray wore sweats, a heavy sweatshirt, and hiking shoes. The magnitude of his presence had me launch myself into his arms. I didn't care about anything other than him. Once my head was comfortably settled against his chest, I closed my eyes and soaked in his strength.

"Nothing was going to stop me from being here with you today. I'm so sorry you are going through this. But I'm here, Kenzie, for whatever you need. I want you to have your Orion, and if that means being here, then that is what you need to do," Gray whispered.

I pulled out of our hug. "I…"

"It's okay. I figured it out when I saw you with the Cooper's around that firepit. This place is your home more than Hoboken ever was or could be."

"Grayson…"

"We will be okay."

I looked at him. "Why didn't you tell me about Martin?"

He shrugged and crossed his arms in front of him. "I didn't want to get your hopes up. But I wanted to do something to help."

"I don't think Keating wants us to find him," I told Gray honestly.

Gray's silence confirmed he agreed with me.

"Do you want to tell me more about the acting industry? How it works?" My question took Gray off guard. It probably was not the ideal time to ask the question, but it was on my mind, and I couldn't let it go.

"Where did that come from?"

Now, it was my turn to cross my arms in front of me. "I was just thinking…it's wrong that you're my best friend, and there is so much I don't know because I never asked. I made you think I didn't care to know."

Gray placed his hands on my shoulders. "Stop. We both decided it was best that there were things about my job that we wouldn't discuss. It's always been okay with me that we don't talk about it. But let's put all of that to rest. We're not up here for that."

I agreed to put the conversation on hold. We sat under the shade of the rocks with Ollie and Angie. When I pulled water and snacks from my bag, I noticed Gray did not have anything with him. In fact, he didn't have even a sparkle of sweat on his perfect face.

Gray smiled at me. "Don't ask."

"What?"

"How I got up here."

"I wasn't..." I started. I looked around and wondered how he pulled this one off. I was not crazy about hiking, but I sure as hell knew Grayson Kent would never purposefully take one step on a dirt path.

"You're overthinking," Gray mused.

"You bought hiking boots, yet you didn't climb up one rock?"

"I pulled myself up and over a couple," he answered.

"Part of the journey is hiking up, the sense of accomplishment you feel when you reach the summit. Taking in the view, finding the meaning." I lectured.

"And you believe that?" Gray asked skeptically.

"Shut up."

After some quiet small talk, I caught Ollie's eye. "Is there anything you want to say?" Ollie whispered to me while casually munching on his granola bar. "You don't have to; I just thought if you wanted to, we are here."

My eyes misted over. Only this time, I didn't let a tear fall. This moment wasn't just about my pain. I knew how much Ollie was hurting. I leaned into him and placed a gentle kiss on his cheek.

"What was that for?" Ollie smiled.

I shrugged. "Just because."

Ollie leaned back against the rock and stretched his long legs out in front of him. With a satisfied look, he turned to Angie, "See, someone finds me loveable."

Angie tossed a water bottle at him. "Good, you can move in with her, and she can deal with tripping over your discarded shoes!"

Ollie grabbed Angie's arms and pulled her towards him. "After all these years together, why is it so hard to admit you find my naked feet endearing?"

"Maybe if they weren't funny looking…."

"Funny looking?"

Gray and I laughed as Ollie and Angie tickled and teased each other. Eventually, Angie moved so she could sit comfortably between his legs. Ollie wrapped his arms around her waist. I smiled at them and the joy they gave each other. I looked at Gray and thought about all that I had in my life. I spent so much time upset about what I was missing in my life that I didn't fully appreciate all I had and could have.

Emboldened by Gray's hand in mine, I spoke without hesitation. "I returned to Kettle Cove when Top Floor closed. I thought being here with you, and Keating would help me figure out my next steps. When you told me Keating was missing, I couldn't think or feel anything other than pain, loss, and despair. I wanted to believe there was an accident or that his stubborn arrogance finally bit him in the ass. To think he did this by choice is, I don't think I can ever unwrap that, but we need to move forward without him here. As hard as it is."

I stopped and looked around. Gray squeezed my hand and gave me the courage to continue. "The truth is, we may never know the truth. I know the investigation will remain open, but, for us, or maybe for me, hiking up here today is a way to wish Keating good luck."

"Are you sure, love?" Ollie asked.

I nodded. "Letting Keating go doesn't make us love him any less, but we need to try and move forward together."

Angie reached over Ollie's leg to grab my hand. She squeezed it until I looked at her. "We will. And we'll be okay. All of us."

I wiped the tears that escaped my eyes with my free hand. "I love you all so much."

"We love you, sweetheart," Angie smiled. She then looked at Gray, "Ollie and I love you too."

Although Angie and Ollie didn't know it, Gray tightened his grip on my hand when he heard Angie's declaration. I've always told Gray how much they cared for him, but I didn't think he truly felt it until that moment. The emotion that clouded his face was enough to make me thank whatever means he used to drop him at the top of the mountain.

We talked more while we sipped our water and ate our snacks. Gray and I snapped a selfie together, a picture I planned to print and frame for both of us. It was the first photo I had of us since I graduated from college. In a way, I felt like I just earned another diploma.

As afternoon approached, we all stood. Ollie, Angie, and I pulled our packs back on.

"We'll wait for you by the path," Ollie told me.

Gray and I were alone. When my focus returned to him, I saw Gray look around and take it all in.

"It's true, you know," he said.

"What?" I asked.

"What the view teaches you."

I smiled. "Yeah, it is."

I secured an early morning flight from Manchester to Newark. With only a carry-on, I exited the plane and terminal without delay. Jesse picked me up outside of arrivals. It was a one-way flight, and I didn't have any luggage. I knew from Gray that Jesse had offered to drive me back, but flying was easier and faster. When I originally booked my flight, I thought I would purchase a car in Hoboken to drive back, but, after talking to Ollie and Angie, I realized it would be easier to buy a car in New Hampshire. I started car shopping and planned to test drive some SUV's while in Hoboken. I reserved a rental car to drive back to Kettle Cove with more of my clothes and smaller items.

Jesse dropped me in front of my building just after 9 a.m. Thursday morning. I thanked him and then headed inside. The sky was thick with clouds, which made it feel later than it was. When I entered my apartment, I stopped at the sight. It was sparkling. I left it neat before I left for Kettle Cove, but not like this. The place had been thoroughly vacuumed, straightened, dusted, and cleaned. Which meant one person had been here...

Grayson.

My little too neat friend. I giggled and wondered what his fans would think if they knew the sexy Grayson Kent found cleaning relaxing. Give him cleaning materials and Gray was set. Dusting, vacuuming, and scrubbing bathrooms were three chores his grandparents assigned him that he never complained about. In fact, when home, he took it upon himself to do more cleaning then they asked him to do. And when he was at the Thomases, he always helped me clean up.

I texted Gray and let him know I was back. I then checked in with Ollie and Angie. I laughed at the number of texts Ollie sent me throughout the course of my travel. I kicked my checkered Vans off and crashed on the couch, phone in hand, and dialed.

Ollie answered on the second ring.

"Do I need to take away your phone privileges at work?" I told him.

Ollie's warm laugh tickled my ears. He shared that he just wanted to make sure I was okay.

"I walked into my apartment about five minutes ago," I shared.

Ollie then asked about my flight.

"Nope, no problems. Angie still at the campus?" I asked.

When Ollie and I left for the airport, Angie received a call from the station. Apparently, fire alarms were set off in the president's office. The office is in a building originally built in the early 1900s as a manor. Although the dwelling has undergone several renovations, a walk inside the doors revealed its character and history. You couldn't tell from the walls, but the old wooden, creaky, and uneven floors and wide staircase that led to a second and third story, revealed its age.

During the day, the manor served as an office space for different college administrators. In the evenings, the large living room was open to students to study. This room had a fireplace and large, dark brown leather couches. One sat in front of a picture window overlooking the courtyard and library. That was the couch I claimed as my own. When Maddie and I were friends, sometimes she'd come and study with me. I continued to, even after she and I stopped hanging out. I loved the history of the place. Like Comfort, I felt like I belonged there. At night, I often wondered if the walls could really talk, what intriguing stories we would hear.

"I hope everything is okay…" I said. I prayed it was a false alarm and that nothing happened to the building.

When I left, I told Ollie and Angie I planned to stay in Hoboken for at least two weeks. They both assured me to take as much time as I needed. I told Ollie I'd be in touch, and we said our goodbyes. I tossed my phone onto the coffee table and then dropped my head onto the back of the couch. Without warning, exhaustion took over and I fell asleep.

My body shook as a violent shiver coursed from my head to my toes. Still hazy, I lifted a blanket higher while I nestled my head into the pillow below my ear. Once warmed and comfortable, my conscious mind kicked in. Where did this blanket come from? And how was my head on a pillow? The last thing I remembered; my head rested against the back of the couch.

Still, I willed myself to sleep more. Yet, my senses had other thoughts. My nose detected the unmistakable scent of fresh and familiar food. My eyes fluttered open to the glorious sight of my favorite sandwich in front of me: fresh Italian bread filled with thinly sliced prosciutto blanketed with several pieces of heavenly mozzarella. I knew this sacred meal did not materialize out of thin air, so I looked around for the culprit. I spotted Gray, seated in the chair opposite mine, mid-bite of his own sandwich.

"Welcome back, sunshine," he stated.

I pushed myself up to a seated position. "Did anyone ever tell you it's rude to talk with your mouth full?"

Gray rolled his eyes at me and then placed his sandwich on the dish before him. After a drink of what was likely his favorite mango-flavored club soda, Gray wiped his hands and mouth with his napkin before he settled back into the cushions.

"Seriously? You're lecturing me on eating manners?" Gray questioned.

"At this moment, yes."

He rolled his eyes. "I'm assuming that sass means you had a good nap?"

I rolled my head, neck, and shoulders in slow circles to work the kinks out.  "I did until my senses were assaulted. When did you get here?"

"About twenty minutes ago. I texted to let you know I was on my way over. When you didn't respond, I figured you passed out. So, I let myself in." He pointed to my food, "Eat."

I grabbed half of my sandwich, took a bite, and savored the wonderful mixture of salty and savory textures that aroused my taste buds. "God, I love this bundle of pleasure," I moaned.

"Most females I know love chocolate, yet the secret to your heart is muzzie and prosciutto. The men in Kettle Cove will have a tough time sweeping you off your feet…" Gray teased.

When Gray surprised me at the top of Mt. Monadnock, he told me he knew I wanted to move to Kettle Cove. We didn't have much time to talk about it then. Now, I'm uncertain about how to take his comment. Was he teasing me? Was he angry? Both? Or did he understand my need to be there?

"I'm neither Kenzie. I just know you." Gray pulled his legs up and tucked them under him. "God, it seems so long ago now, but I know I pushed you to go. All the shit went down with Grafton, Top Floor closed, and we were, I don't know, in a weird place because of it. I know you were disenchanted with me. And I'm sorry about that. I'm sorry that I made you feel like I was pushing you away."

"You're right, it did hurt. But I understand and know it wasn't because you didn't want my support, but wanted to protect me." I assured him.

"And then you learned Keating was missing. Even with the shitstorm that threatened to eat us whole, seeing you back in Kettle Cove? Running Comfort? With the Coopers? Shoeless in jeans and flannels? I just knew. You were at ease."

Gray was right. Even with all that went on the last few weeks, I felt more at peace than I had in a long time. I felt useful at Comfort and gratified when I saw how our customers responded to the ideas I implemented.

"When I left, I honestly believed that the change of scenery and air would help me decide what happened next. Staying there permanently was not my plan when I left here, but, once there and back at Comfort…"

"It felt right," Gray finished.

"Yes."

"I get it, Kenzie. I know it's not the same, but it's how I felt when I returned to Hoboken. When I'm here, I feel like me. It's that way for you in Kettle Cove."

"What does it mean for us?"

"What? Are you breaking up with me?" Gray playfully asked.

I threw a pillow at him. "It's not funny! As much as I know in my heart, living in Kettle Cove and running Comfort with Ollie is right, I'm worried about you, about us. This is different than when I was in college, Gray."

Gray moved off his chair and settled next to me. With his arm wrapped around me, he pulled me close. "You will always have me. As much as I will miss you, this is the right move for both of us. We'll make it work. What we have, it's too important to lose."

"You're my family, Gray, and I love you. I always will," I confided.

"I love you too."

We finished our food and reviewed my "To Do" list. Once I was satisfied that we had everything covered for my move, I brought up the other conversation we started on the mountain and didn't finish.

"Why didn't you tell me you asked Martin to investigate Keating?"

"I hated seeing the devastation all over your face when you told me he was missing. I couldn't sit by and not do everything in my power to help. I didn't tell you because I didn't want to get your hopes up if nothing panned out."

"How did you even connect with Martin?" I asked nervously. Grayson had to know that when Angie told me about Martin, I'd worry about Martin's true intentions. "Grayson, the guy worked undercover and came to Kettle Cove twice to talk to me. One of those times was about you. You didn't think it strange that he wanted to just help me knowing that?"

"Oh wow, I didn't think that. Shit," Gray admitted. He honestly looked shocked that my mind went there and his didn't. "Kenzie, Martin never talked to me about Grafton. I spoke with the detectives and gave them everything I knew."

"Okay, then, how did you connect with him?" I asked.

"We ran into each other at a coffee shop. When I saw him, I recognized who he was from Top Floor. I saw him a couple of times when I was there. He told me he had offered to investigate things for you but that you declined. He told me he planned to spend time with his mom in the area, so I asked if I could hire him on the down-low. I told him a little about Evan, and we contacted Angie. You're sure you want to call him off?"

"Yes. I know it's selfish and naive, but I thought that maybe if somehow Keating knew I was back, that if Evan was connected to him, that maybe he'd come back. But he's not coming back. Not now, maybe not ever."

Gray wiped the tears from my face. "You're not stupid or selfish. I think we always want more time with the people we love. To have one more chance to talk to them and get their advice on something. I wish I had that with my dad. During this Grafton mess, I wished he was here for me to talk to."

"It's why you let Ollie in, isn't it? You can trust them like you trust me," I promised.

"I.."

"You can, Grayson. There are people in this world that you can trust that won't let you down. You just need to be willing to let them in."

"They accept me because of you."

"They accept you because of you," I countered. "Sure, they met you because of me, but they don't see you as just my friend Grayson, but as someone they love and care about separate from me."

Grayson nodded as he wiped away his own tears.

"Did you ever think about looking for your mom?" Of all the things we discussed, his mom was never one of them.

"No."

"But you never wanted to know why?" I pressed.

Gray shook his head. "No. I'm not interested in learning about a person who abandoned her husband and child."

"What if something or someone took her away?"

"If that happened, where has she been all this time? From what I remember, she left for work one day and never came back. I accepted that a long time ago and grew up just fine."

Gray's perspective on his mom struck me. He didn't want to know why she left him and his dad and never tried to locate her. And obviously, his mom never tried to connect with him once he became famous. Could I apply the same thought to Keating? From what we knew, Keating left us by his own choice. As hard as it was to swallow, maybe that was the better way to view it. I didn't want anger in my life and at the same time, Keating, like Gray's mom, made a choice. They had to live with that too. But Gray's dad also left him behind and yet, he didn't seem to view his mom's and dad's actions the same.

"You know, I always thought my dad killed himself, but I learned he didn't."

"What? How do you know?" I asked surprised.

"When you told me that Martin ran a background check on you, I figured he probably ran one on me too. And if he didn't, he had the means to. I asked him if he could find out for me how my dad died. My grandparents never spoke of him. I wanted to know."

"So, how did he die?"

"He was sick Kenzie. My dad had cancer. My mom left him just after he was diagnosed. He couldn't take care of me, so he left me with his parents. He didn't want me to see him weak, so, he let me go and died alone. Do you know how much I hate that? Hate my grandparents for not caring for him? He was their son."

I gathered him in my arms and held him tight. I wondered if maybe Gray's dad didn't want their help. That whatever was broken between them couldn't be repaired and that all his dad wanted was for Gray to be taken care of. His grandparents did that, even if they didn't show they loved him.

Gray pulled out of our embrace. "He's buried not far from here. I went to see him a couple of times just to talk." Gray turned to me, "Do you think he'd be proud of me, Kenz?"

"I do, Gray. I do."

I clasped Gray's hand in mine and let him feel my strength. He then lifted our joined hands and kissed mine before he let it go. "Will you really be, okay?" I asked.

He kissed my hand again. "I will, I promise."

We sat for a few moments in silence. I knew there was one more bit that I needed to say. "I'm sorry."

Gray turned and looked at me. "For what?"

"For how I handled everything with Grafton. I'm sorry that I doubted who you were. That I even questioned it," I explained. The night Gray told me what he knew about Grafton, I was furious that he hadn't reported it. I accused him of not caring about doing the right thing.

"You have nothing to apologize for. You were right. I lost myself after I left the soap. I got caught up in the movie world, in the fame, and how it made me feel. I lost sight of what was right and took a lot for granted," Gray admitted.

"You should be proud of yourself, Gray. I'm proud of you, I always have been."

"This Grafton mess served as a wake-up call. When I came to Comfort the night of the storms, you let me help, blend in, and find me again. As much as I wanted you to hold me like you did when we first met, I needed to handle all of this on my own. I needed to know that I could."

"And did you?"

"Getting there," Gray admitted.

"This stuff with Grafton? The press, will it hurt your career?"

"It will blow over. I learned the girl I saw my former co-star with was another actress and not one of Grafton's trafficked girls. She and my co-worker were willing participants."

"Is that good or bad?"

"It doesn't matter. I'm clear of it and of movies for a while. Which means I'm yours. Put me to work."

It turned out that in addition to food, Gray packed a suitcase. He stayed the week as my quiet roommate. If we needed anything, I went. Gray remained indoors and, amazingly enough, offline. I couldn't remember the last time I saw him disconnected from the web. The only form of technology he used that week was his phone. I heard bits of his conversations that he had some theatre projects in the works, but when I asked, he told me nothing was confirmed, and he didn't want to jinx anything.

So, in between his phone calls, we sorted my clothes and separated Top Floor apparel from the rest. I planned to donate all my dresses, skirts, tops, heels, and other items I hadn't worn in a while. I then packed the rest of my casual and comfortable wear.

Gray arranged for a moving company to come and pick up the few pieces of furniture – my comfy couch, bedroom set, photographs, books, sheets, towels, and some of my kitchen items.

I didn't need to contact an agent about my listing the place. I met up with Karen and Amy one night for drinks. They both landed hostess jobs in the city that paid more and had better management. They offered to buy my apartment when I told them I was moving to New Hampshire. It turned out Amy's sister was a realtor who agreed to help us with the sale. I canceled my phone, cable, and internet service and filled out the necessary paperwork to have my mail forwarded to the Coopers.

Before I knew it, two weeks had passed. Gray and I sat on my couch and looked around at my mostly empty apartment. In my thirty-five years, I've prided myself on being honest with others and, most importantly, myself. I can't lie now and say that leaving this place, the first home I owned, was easy.

These past two weeks, I desperately pushed my emotions down to maintain focus. Now, they all bubbled to the surface in one shot. I broke down in Gray's arms and used his black slub t-shirt as my tissue. Initially, no words were spoken. Gray's gentle, steady breath calmed me. Without letting go, he stated the one thing I needed to hear: "I think you've always known where your Orion was. The difference is, now, you are ready to claim it. Even though this is the end of our time together here, it's not the end of us."

He loosened his grip on me so he could look at me. "We're starting a new chapter of our lives. You in Kettle Cove, New Hampshire, and me returning to the theatre."

"Sounds like we both found our Orion," I mused.

"We did."

When I've returned to Moose Creek, I never drove myself. As a result, my visits to the cemetery where my parents were buried were limited. I always came in the spring and planted flower's and brought wreaths for Christmas. Now, as I walked to their shared site with a bouquet of flowers in my hand, it felt strange. For the first time in my life, I owned a car. I now had the independence to go wherever and whenever I wanted.

Last week, Gray surprised me. He presented me with a wrapped plastic key.

"I know you planned to buy your own car…but I wanted to do this for you," Gray had started. "Don't be mad! I just want you to use the money you have saved to secure your own place."

Gray thought I'd be upset with him, but I wasn't. Gray has never pressed his money on me. He's always respected my desire to be independent and to pay my own way. As excited as I am about this new chapter in my life, I'm worried about finances. I have money saved, but if I spent that on a car, even a used one, I wouldn't be able to get a place of my own. At least, not right away. This gift from Gray, enabled me to find a place of my own sooner.

Jesse brought me to the car dealership to pick up my new car. the day before I left. Thankfully, I secured a space in front of my building. Karen and Amy came by first thing in the morning to help me pack my stuff and saw me off. In exchange, I gave them the keys to the apartment. Hoboken disappeared in my rearview window as I headed north. Before I made my way to New Hampshire, I planned to visit Moose Creek and my parents. Gray offered to meet me at the cemetery, but I assured him that I wanted and needed to do this on my own. So, we said our "see you soon" last night.

* * *

My parents were buried towards the back of the graveyard under a tree. Whenever I visited, it seemed like I was the only one there. I didn't mind though. It offered me the privacy to say whatever I wanted to. When I reached their site, I gently placed the flowers on the ground and then kneeled on the grass. With the small gardening shovel, I dug a hole and then placed the flowers in it. Once satisfied that they would hold, I pushed the dirt back around and then smoothed it out.

Once finished, I sat back on my knees and stared at their names carved in the grey granite: Cathy and Jamie Mulroney.

"Hi Mom, Hi Dad, it's me. I'm sorry I haven't been by to visit in a while. I have so much to tell you..."

And I did. I told them all about Gray, Top Floor closing, Keating, and my decision to move to Kettle Cove.

"I know that's far from here and that I won't be able to visit often, but I promise I will be back when I can. But, mom? I love it there. It's a lot like around here, with all the trees and mountains. Ollie and Angie are still there. I'll miss Gray, so much, but, I know this is the right choice. For both of us."

After I had spent more time with Keating and the Cooper's, I had told my parents about them. I talked about my job at Comfort and wondered if they would be disappointed that I graduated with a degree that I never used.

"Keating, he's missing. We don't know what happened, but, it looks like he just disappeared into the night. He was last spotted just over the Maine border. And then, he just vanished. It's been hard, you know? When you died, I eventually understood that you weren't coming back. But with Keating, I'm struggling with how to feel. But I'm trying. Being with Ollie and Angie helps. Ollie and I are running Comfort together."

While I talked about Comfort, I remembered meeting mom's childhood friend, Martin's Mom and the story of the Ring Dings.

"I met your friend mom! Mrs. Benson. Of course, that wasn't her name when you knew her, but she told me that she spent her summers here with her grandparents. And that you lived down the street from them. She told me how you proposed Dad! Twenty-one boxes of Ring Dings!"

Tired of sitting on my knees, I dropped to my bum with my legs crossed. I pulled my shirt around me and crossed my arms over my stomach. I looked up when I heard some voices in the distance and then returned my attention to my parents.

"I wish I knew that story, that the box you kept on the kitchen counter was empty. I would've insisted on taking it with me. But I have the story now and I guess that means more than the box. Mrs. Martin, she seems cool. She lives near Kettle Cove too! So, I can, I don't know, maybe spend more time with her and learn more about you both."

I felt the warmth of the grass through my leggings. Although I was in the shade of a tree, the sun was overhead. My face was flushed from the heat. A single band of sweat trickled down my cheek. It tickled my skin. I wiped the sweat away with the back of my hand.

"I promise I'll always try my best and to be a good person. I hope that wherever you are, that you can see me and know that I'm okay. I wasn't for a while, but I am now. And I miss you both so much and I love you."

I sat a little longer in silence and enjoyed the chatter of the birds overhead. When I was ready, I placed the shovel in the bag and stood. I kissed my hand and placed it over their names.

"Bye for now."

With a final look, I turned away and walked back towards my car. It was then that I caught sight of a face I hadn't seen in seventeen years. A few rows away from my parents was Ruth Thomas. Uncertainty froze me to the spot. Do I approach or do I walk away? I just told my parents that I was trying to be a good person. I didn't want to show them otherwise.

After I dropped off the bag with the shovel in my car, I returned to the row where I saw Ruth. I slowly approached her. From a distance, I saw that she was by her son's grave. She too had just planted some flowers. They were a bright yellow. I wondered if that was Travis' favorite color.

I didn't know if there was a particular protocol for approaching someone in a cemetery, so I just went with my gut.

I closed the distance between us. I wasn't close enough to crowd her or invade her son's place of burial, yet I was near enough to talk without having to shout.

"Mrs. Thomas?" I called softly.

She turned to me. Her green eyes widened when she took me in. I momentarily wondered if she recognized me.

"It's Kenzie," I added.

But she remained still. Uncomfortable with her silence, I realized this was a bad idea. "I'm sorry, I didn't mean to disturb you, I just, well, I just wanted to say hello and that I'm, I'm sorry that you and Mr. Thomas lost your son."

I swore at myself for the last comment. Honestly, that's the best I could say? I was about to turn and walk away when her voice stopped me.

"Kenzie, please, stay," she asked.

I turned around but remained in my spot. Ruth looked at her son's tombstone and then back at me. "Travis would be a few years older than you are now."

I felt like she had more to say, so, I took a step closer, but remained quiet.

"Steve and I were devastated when we lost him. We tried to have other children but couldn't. That's when we decided to foster. Well, I decided to, Steve wasn't on board at first. And then, we met you."

She looked at me full on. "You were so young when your parents died. A terrible tragedy. You were cute as a button, scared and confused, but a gentle little girl that we fell in love with right away."

I sucked in my breath as my body tensed at her admission. I couldn't speak. They loved me?

"I know you never felt like we did. And we didn't do much to show it. We were so caught up in our grief, so afraid that if we let you in, we'd lose you too. I'm ashamed of how we made you feel Kenzie. I have been since the day you left. The gifts you made, they meant the world to us. I'm sorry that you, that we didn't tell you that."

"You opened them?" I squeaked out.

"Yes, dear."

"I saw them on the donation pile. I thought…"

"Steve placed them there because he had to move something. We never meant for you to think we were going to toss them out."

"But you didn't tell me otherwise," I added. I knew my voice was laced with anger. But when Mrs. Thomas dropped her head, I felt bad about snapping.

"No, we didn't."

I moved closer to her. "Was yellow his favorite color?" I asked.

Mrs. Thomas smiled. "Yes. Everything had to be yellow."

"I wish I knew my mom and dad's favorite colors," I whispered.

And then, Ruth did something unexpected. She wrapped her arms around me and hugged me to her. When my tears started to fall, she rocked me as I imagined she once rocked her son. I returned the hug when I felt my shirt moisten from her tears. We remained that way for a few minutes before we both pulled out of the hug. Mrs. Thomas pulled a tissue from her bag and handed it to me. I wiped my eyes and blew my nose. I then stuffed the dirty tissue in my pocket.

"How is Mr. Thomas?" I asked.

"He's as stubborn as always, but he is good."

"Is he still trying to build that birdhouse?" I asked.

Mrs. Thomas laughed. "No, thank goodness!" She wiped the last bit of her tears away. "How are you?"

"I'm really good. I'm moving to New Hampshire. I'm on my way there now."

"That's wonderful. I am happy for you. Are you still friendly with the Kent boy?"

Without hesitation, I answered, "Yes. Gray and I are still as close as we were as kids."

"I'm happy to hear that. He was such a good boy. I always told Harold and Agnes that. They were proud of him and what he accomplished."

"I don't know if they ever told Gray that," I said. I knew the Kents had passed away a few years ago. Gray handled the arrangements. I offered to go with him, but he insisted he'd go alone.

"Mrs. Thomas?" I asked.

"Hmm?" she turned to me.

"Do you think we can keep in touch? I mean, I'd like that if you would."

Mrs. Thomas smiled as she took my hand. "I'd like that very much, Kenzie."

I jogged to my car for a piece of paper. I wrote my phone number along with Ollie and Angie's address. I then returned to Mrs. Thomas.

"Here's my contact information," I shared. "I really am sorry about Dennis and that I couldn't, that I didn't know how to help you heal. But I do thank you and Mr. Thomas for raising me."

Mrs. Thomas grasped my hand that held the paper. "You did help us heal Kenzie. I'm sorry that we failed to do the same for you. I know you're all grown up now and don't need us…"

"A child always needs their parents. I miss my mom and dad very much. And I wish, with everything that I have, that I had the chance to know them." I squeezed her hand and placed my other hand on her forearm. "I think we can still help each other if we're open to it."

"I'd like that very much," Mrs. Thomas whispered. Her voice cracked with emotion.

We remained by her son's grave a bit longer. I then carried the shovel and bucket that she had filled with water back to her car. With a final hug, we parted ways.

"I am proud of you Kenzie," Mrs. Thomas had whispered in my ear. "And I do love you," she said.

Although I thought the words in my head, I couldn't voice them. I realized that I loved them all along. If I didn't, I wouldn't have thought to leave them with gifts that I knew had meaning for them. And if I didn't love them, my assumption that they rejected my token of love and gratitude wouldn't have hurt so much. If I didn't love them, I would have left the cemetery and never looked back.

It's Tuesday, just after eleven a.m. I returned to Kettle Cove on Sunday afternoon. I took Monday off from Comfort to unpack the boxes that filled the Forrester. The rest of my furniture was scheduled to arrive toward the end of the week. I planned to stay in the loft for a bit longer. Ollie and Angie said I could store my furniture in their basement until I secured a place of my own.

Ollie was officially done at Crestview, and although Angie knew, she did a good job pretending to be surprised when he finally told her. She was happy he planned to run Comfort with me. I think Ollie was energized by the thought of sinking his teeth into something different than ancient artifacts. I knew he loved his field and I'm sure part of him would miss teaching. He was offered the opportunity to stay on and teach one class, but he declined. I secretly wondered if he didn't want to teach without Keating. When I was a student, it was odd to see one without the other. Maybe at one point, he'll return. For now, although he was emotional when we cleaned out his office, Ollie appeared refreshed. He was ready for this next part of his life.

Jack was stateside. He flew in from Germany the weekend I returned. Ollie and Angie invited me to join them in Boston, but I insisted they spend this time with their son. They deserved to spend time as a family. I assured them I would be fine between unpacking and running Comfort. Jack planned to be home for the holidays, so I would spend time with him then. I baked a batch of his favorite maple scones and sent them with Ollie and Angie as a hello.

*  *  *

It's a rainy day today. Not the stormy rain, but just the steady yuck that made everything damp and uncomfortable enough that you didn't know what to do with yourself. Right now, Comfort was quiet. I expected business to pick up when people didn't want to be out any longer.

I wasn't complaining. As much as busy was good, I enjoyed the lull. It gave me the chance to sort through the notes that were left for me while I was in Hoboken. While I reviewed Tia's new recipe ideas, the addition of different teas to the menu, and a possible change in our summer hours, another idea struck me.

The area is full of artists and musicians. I wondered if we should consider having music nights on certain days over the summer. Nothing loud and crazy, but something soft and comforting that filled the air as people gathered. I knew of a particular piano covered in dust in Ollie's garage that would be a perfect addition to our little space. I made my own note to talk to Ollie about it. I was about to move on to our inventory lists when Alec, a new waiter, popped his head in the door.

"Kenzie?"

"Hey Alec, what's up?"

"Martin's here to see you."

"Okay, tell him I'll be right out," I said.

The last time I saw Martin was at Comfort the night the thunderstorms rolled through the area. The same evening, I learned that his mom knew my parents. She shared several stories with me before Martin took her home. She left her number with me with an invitation to dinner whenever I was ready. Mrs. Benson also told me she had pictures of my parents that I could have. It's strange. I always wanted to know about them, and now, I had the opportunity to, and it scared me. I didn't know if the knowledge would continue to help me heal or make it hurt even more.

Then again, when I saw Mrs. Thomas at the cemetery, I found closure. It hurt to think that all those years, they missed their son, and I missed my parents; we could have helped each other. I guess when they took me in, they weren't prepared to love and become attached to another child. But they loved me, they were just too afraid to show it. So, they kept this wall up and pushed me away. I learned that just as I questioned why they kept me all those years, they punished themselves for their treatment of me. For the first time since I was brought to their house, Mrs. Thomas and I comforted each other while we mourned our losses.

Before we parted ways, I gave her my phone number. I didn't know if she would use it, but I decided that I would contact them. After all, they were the people that raised me and despite all the other pain, I knew I had to let it go. For far too long, I allowed my hurt and anger to dictate how I lived my life. It was time for that to end.

When I returned to Kettle Cove this time, it was truly a fresh start. I was in a good place. Even though I had not seen Martin since that night, we texted a few times and talked on the phone. Martin hadn't decided if he wanted to remain with his firm and continue private investigative work or return to the police force. I knew Angie contacted him about joining the Kettle Cove PD. Apparently, while I was in Hoboken, Detective Deas submitted his notice. Disobeying Angie's direct orders was a regular thing for him. Although Ollie did not reveal exactly what Angie said, the gist of it seemed to go like this: Either pull your shit together or leave.

When I walked out front to greet Martin, I wondered if Gray told him to stop searching for Keating. The last Keating siting was at the convenience store in Maine. Since then, the trail had gone cold.

"Hey," I called to Martin. He sat at the bar with a glass of iced tea in front of him.

"I'm sorry to just drop by, but I wanted to share some news with you."

I poured my own glass of tea and then sat next to him. "It's not a problem. What's up?"

Martin spun the glass around in his hands. Whatever he had to share, seemed important.

"Did you hear that Grafton was found dead this a.m. of an apparent suicide?" Martin asked.

"I did. Both on the news and from Gray." I paused to take a drink. "What does this mean for Todd and Marjorie?" I asked.

"I don't know."

I nodded. I knew from the news that a slew of other people connected with Grafton were brought down because of Martin's initial investigation. I also knew that Sam was cleared. Whatever deal she had made with Grafton regarding Gray had nothing to do with his other business. I was happy about that. Even though I hated her for the position she put Gray in, I knew if she was more involved with Grafton's business, he would be devastated. Now, Gray, although he did not have a new manager yet, was rehearsing for a play in a small theatre in Maine. Ollie, Angie, and I planned to see him in the fall.

"I'm guessing the Grafton news is not the only reason you're here."

"You're right. It's about Keating."

"Did Gray talk to you? I told him to call off the investigation," I said.

"He did. I wanted to make sure that's what you wanted."

"I'm sure. I appreciate everything you did.

"Okay. I'll make sure Angie has copies of my notes. I'm headed back to Hoboken in a few days."

"You decided to stay then?" I asked. I tried to keep the disappointment out of my voice when I asked. A part of me hoped he would decide to leave and maybe come here.

"Yes, at least for now."

"Your mom will miss you," I stated.

"Not as much as you think," Martin teased. "I make her crazy."

I laughed. "When do you leave?"

"Couple of days."

"Would you like to have dinner before you go?" I asked.

"I'd love to," Martin smiled. "Tell me when and where. I'll be there."

Martin agreed to meet me for dinner at The Brewery in Jasper tomorrow night. With dinner details worked out, Martin excused himself. After I saw him out, I returned to the office. I decided I had my fill of paperwork for the day. In need of a paper clip, I opened one of the top drawers of Keating's desk. I planned to clean out Keating's desk but wanted Olie to go through it with me. It was a task we'd complete after he returned from Boston. When I didn't find what I needed in the first drawer I opened, I moved to another. Inside this middle drawer, I found not only a box of paper clips but also a letter addressed to me.

I sat back in the chair and kept my eyes trained on the paper. I took a deep breath, steadied my hand, and when ready, I pulled the folded paper out. On the front side, I spotted Keating's neat cursive. I ran my thumb across my name before I unfolded the paper. Once opened, I stared at the words on the page before I allowed myself to read the words.

April

Dear Kenzie,

I've always been better at planning my lectures and teaching lessons than expressing my feelings to the people I love most. It is one of my greatest flaws. We are supposed to learn from our mistakes and always do our best to do better the next time around. I'm sorry to say that it is a lesson I never learned. I've hurt my best mate and his beautiful wife. And I've upset you with my treatment of Grayson. I know how much he means to you, and I'm sorry that my words and actions hurt you both.

There will come a time when I am no longer here. I want you to know that I am very proud of you and love you as if

you were my daughter. I hope that you find your way back to
Kettle Cove when you are ready. Know that you always have
a home here and that Grayson is always welcome.

Fondly,
Your Professor

I reread the letter a few times before refolding it. I then placed it
on the desk and watched it as I let Keating's words sink in. They were
honest and true. I heard his sorrow and felt his apology. He loved me
and was proud of me. Those words meant the world to me.

I didn't know how to interpret the meaning behind "There will
be a time when I am no longer here," but, it didn't matter. This was
Keating's way of saying goodbye. I hoped that Ollie found something
similar because he deserved that too.

I decided to place the letter back in the drawer. After I pushed the
door forward, slowly, the dread and nervousness that always settled in
my bones on this second day of the week slowly began to lift. This
Tuesday may be a sign of better ones to come.

# AUTHOR'S NOTE AND ACKNOWLEDGMENTS

One of my best friends from college, Dennise (she used to say Dennis with an E), once said that "Orion was the only man she could depend on." We'd walk to the beach on campus, sit on the dock, and look at the stars. I think about her every time Orion becomes visible in the evening sky. I wish that she was still with us and that she had the chance to find her Orion.

The inspiration for the book's title came from Dennise. She possessed a wicked sense of humor, loved to dance, and made procrastination an art form. Dennise and I did work in the theatre together; we only lasted a semester. It is safe to say that power tools were not our strong suit. But we did build a bench for one of the shows. We were quite proud of ourselves! It was through this semester that Dennise and I forged our friendship that lasted over four years. She was strong, feisty, and an amazing friend whom I miss very much.

When I was in college, Dennise and our group of friends loved Mudslides (the drink). At one point, we joked that after college, we would open a restaurant together where this drink would be served. My original title for this novel was *Mudslides.* I planned to tell the story of a group of friends who went their separate ways after graduation, only for a tragedy to draw them together again. Through their mutual loss, their friendship with each other is reignited. They decide

233

to take over the restaurant left behind by their friend and build it as a place where people go to have good food, drink, and friendships. Through this place, each friend rediscovers themselves and carves a new space in this world.

One of the original characters from *Mudslides* was Kenzie. Through my rough drafts, Kenzie took on a life of her own. I decided to focus on her story and the relationships in her life. When we meet her, she's already at a crossroads in her life, stuck and ready for a change. Losing her parents at a young age created a hole in her heart and her life. Since that moment in time, she's longed to find a place of her own that she can label home. Her friendship with Grayson is the most important relationship in her life. They are each other's family. The bond they share is as unique as the love and affection they have for each other. As much as Kenzie loves Gray, she longs to find her Orion. Through her journey, she discovers other people in her life that she can trust and learn from.

Like Kenzie, I believe different people enter our lives for a reason. It is important for us as humans to never take for granted the people who mean the most to us and to know we can make it through any difficult time with these individuals in our corner. It is my hope that readers can identify with Kenzie and the different relationships she has with Gray, Keating, Angie, and Ollie. I hope they are encouraged never to stop looking for their own Orion. Whether that is a person, a place, or a state of being.

When I decided to write about Kenzie, I changed the title of the book from *Mudslides* to *Finding Orion*. Comfort became the restaurant that Kenzie worked at in college and decided to run in Keating's absence. Dennise was killed by a drunk driver shortly after we graduated. I decided to make Comfort a restaurant that didn't serve alcohol because of this and because it is important for people to know that you do not need to drink to relax, to have a good time, and to be comforted.

Over the last six years, the characters of *Finding Orion* came to life. When I first began this writing journey, the school year had ended, and I settled into my condo in Maine for the summer. With my handwritten notes, I began to write. Slowly, the characters that inhabit *Finding Orion* came to life. In the pages of the first draft, Keating died. After some thought and discussion with friends who are readers, I decided to have Keating disappear. I liked the element of mystery that this added and the different emotions a person feels when a loved one vanishes.

Kenzie is not a stranger to grief. But how do you grieve someone who has walked away from their life seemingly without a second thought? Truthfully, even as an adult, Kenzie has not let go of the pain she felt over losing her parents. She relives some of this emotion with the disappearance of Keating. Although he is different than her father, he, in many ways, is a father figure to her. As an adult, with other adults in her life that she trusts, Kenzie can come to terms with loss, channel the strength she possesses, let go of her fear, anger, and pain, and move forward.

By the end of that first summer, the first draft was not yet finished. I returned to school and continued to write when my schedule allowed. When I wasn't physically at my computer, different scenarios and conversations between Kenzie and the other characters played in my mind. I discussed the story with friends and family. Through the Spooky Ladies, my former writing group, I sought advice on narration and how much of Gray's story should be told. When I made the decision to have Keating missing, I also decided that neither Kenzie nor the reader would know what happened to him. Through conversations with retired police officers and watching different documentaries on missing persons, people can and do walk away from their lives and are never found. While all these ideas battered around in my mind, I suffered a personal loss that not only stopped the progression of this story but made me want to stop writing completely.

Before one word of *Mudslides* and then *Finding Orion* was committed to paper, I shared the idea with my mom. For all my writing projects, Mom was my sounding board, editor, public relations person, and greatest fan. Her unwavering support and guidance meant everything to me. When she unexpectedly became ill, she made me promise to keep writing. I told her I would. But when she passed away, I struggled to find my voice and continue to give life not only to this story, but to others.

I stepped away from Kenzie, Gray, Keating, Ollie, and Angie for a while. When I thought about walking away from writing completely, I realized that meant breaking my promise to my mom. I knew that if I did that, she would absolutely come back and haunt me. When I was ready to return to this world, I returned to my preferred method of writing – paper and pencil. I printed the story and began to edit. With fresh eyes, I started at the beginning. I remembered the story I wanted to tell. This is Kenzie's story: who she is, what the people in her life mean to her, and how she comes to terms with the losses she experienced. Before I knew it, I slipped right back into her world and the people that live there. I hope my mom would have enjoyed this story and would be proud of me for finishing it.

All the characters and the story are fictional. The history behind Crestview College, the buildings, and the land is based on my alma mater, Franklin Pierce College in Rindge, NH. Crestview was the name of my freshman year dorm that is no longer there. The White House and barn did exist. The history of the college that Kenzie shares is based on my own knowledge when as a student and as an admissions tour guide. I also took some information from the school website, and of course, the ghost stories are primarily based on the rumors I heard. I never saw the ghost of the boy in the White House or any of the spirits that allegedly haunted the Manor.

When I first walked onto Pierce's campus, met the people, and walked around, I felt at home. I have the same feeling now every time I visit. For Kenzie, the people and the place provided her with the comfort of what she missed growing up.

While writing and exploring Kenzie's world, besides my mom, there are other important people I need to acknowledge and thank. Unfortunately, some of these people are no longer with us.

Vince - Although he only knew bits and pieces of my ideas for Finding Orion, my dear friend served as a solid sounding board for me. We discussed writing and characters from novels and movies for hours on end. I miss him and our conversations very much.

Jerry - A few years ago, the guidance department in the school I work in hosted a career fair for our students. I contacted actor Jerry ver Dorn, who lived in the area, and asked if he'd be willing to come to the school and talk to our students about acting. He was! When I began to develop Grayson, I contacted Jerry and asked if he could explain a bit about managers, agents, etc. Through our correspondence, he showed me nothing but kindness and support. Including when my mom passed. Jerry shared with me that when he was in high school, a local actor spoke to his class about the performance industry. It was important to him to one day pay it forward. Coming to our school and helping me was his way of doing that. If I ever have the opportunity, I will do the same in honor of him.

My Spooky Ladies - Our discussions helped me form the original structure of this story, and your encouragement to continue with it means more than words can express. You are all amazing writers, and I will forever appreciate the Saturday mornings we spent together.

To Dorothy – Thank you for your kindness and support. Your retreat is what helped me get back on track with this story.

Becky, Beth, Vicki, Liana, and Kathy- My friends who read the earlier drafts of this story, thank you for your feedback and support. Always. I hope you enjoy the final product.

Mary, Kathi, and Sarah - My northern neighbors, thank you for reading the finished draft.

Jess -Thanks for helping me pick out my outfits for the photo shoot and for your excitement about this book. I appreciate it!

Mary - For all of your support and guidance. You stepped in after my mom passed, reading, editing, and, most importantly, encouraging me to continue writing. My mom valued your friendship so much. I do, too.

Stacey – You are my pal. Thank you from the bottom of my heart for being a sounding board, to letting me vent, and for helping me step outside my comfort zone.

Theresa – You are an incredible friend. I thank you so very much for always being there. Our conversations about writing and characters always inspire me.

Kelly, Carol, Marion, Ashley, and Eli –You mean the world to me. Thank you for always supporting me and for talking writing with me, and helping me (even when you didn't know it).

To Donna - Thank you so much for reading one of the later drafts. Your honest feedback on Kenzie and Gray, was invaluable. Thank you for your friendship. You are amazing, and I am lucky to have you in my life.

And to my family, Dad, Michelle, Ben, Elliot, Nathan, Marianne, Barry, Aunt Di and Uncle Ray, and Aunt Dee, Brent, Jason, Liz, Jeff, Jess and Justin - Thank you so much for everything. Dad, for reading some of the earlier drafts, Michelle, for answering my random questions as someone who enjoys reading. Elliot for our conversations about reading and writing. Nathan, for the same. I hope this story attracts non-readers. To everyone else, for always supporting me, and encouraging me to keep doing what I love.

Whether we are family or friends, I know you are all a part of my life for a reason. I am grateful for every one of you. I love you all very much.

Until next time…